Castles in the Air:

a Durant Family Saga

Sheila Myers

Cover Design
Brendan Cox Design Studio
http://www.brendancox.co.uk

Cover photo: Ella Durant courtesy of the Winterthur Museum: Joseph Downs
Collection and Printed Ephemera
Author Photo by Pippin Photography

This is a work of fiction. Although some of the characters in this story are historical figures and some events are based on facts, the story is a product of the author's imagination.

Published by:
Zähigkeit Press

ISBN: 0692600590

ISBN-13: 978-0692600597

DEDICATION

This book is dedicated to all of those people who like to take risks—those
who climb aboard and put up a sail,
not knowing which way the wind will blow.

I am longing to be with you, and by the sea, where we can talk together freely and build our castles in the air.

—Bram Stoker, *Dracula* (1897)

If you have built castles in the air, your work need not be lost; that is where they should be. Now put the foundations under them.

—Henry David Thoreau, *Walden* (1854)

List of Characters
*Fictional

U.S.
William West and Ella Durant (brother sister)
Hannah Durant (mother)
Margaret Molineaux (Hannah's companion)
Janet Stott (William's wife)
Elizabeth and Francis Stott (Janet's parents)
Julia Stott (Janet's cousin)
Louis Stott (Janet's brother)
Estelle, Howard and Frederick Durant (cousins)
John Barbour (family lawyer)
Arpad Gerster (William's friend in Adirondacks)
Alvah Dunning (guide)
Charlie Bennett (Antler Hotel owner)
Mrs. And Mr. Callahan (caretakers)
Father Kelly
*Ike Lawrence (trapper and William's guide)
*Sarah, Emaline and Louise Lawrence (Ike's sisters)
*Jake Lawrence (Ike's brother)
*Nate Lawrence (Sarah's son)
Jerome Wood (guide)
Collis P. Huntington (head of Central Pacific Railroad)
William Sutphen (Adirondack Railroad Company lawyer)

England
Aunt Sylvia (Ella's aunt)
Anne Thackerary Ritchie (Novelist)
Reverend Alfred Locock (family friend)
Poultney Bigelow (family friend and Ella's former lover)
Bill and Jack Napier (Durant family friend)
Count de la Salle (Parisian aristo)
Pierre Berton (Actor)
Charles Arkwright (Durant family friend)
Arthur Frethey (medical student)

PART ONE

1885

ONE

New York

The dead leaves crunched under their feet as they ascended Mount Marcy. William West Durant carried a pack of food, Edward Bierstadt the camera equipment. Up ahead, the guide Bierstadt had hired out of the Algonquin Hotel in Saranac bounced along the rugged trail with the sure-footedness of a mountain goat despite the full pack he carried. The air grew thinner as they climbed, and the rising sun cleared the last wisps of fog lingering in the canopy. William stopped to catch his breath and take a swig of water.

"Good day for photography," Bierstadt said, looking into the sky.

William nodded his agreement before resuming his stride up the mountain. Through his panting, he could hear the wind rustling the golden leaves clinging to the treetops. Before long, the oaks and maples, so common on the lower slopes, were replaced by stunted evergreens. These too disappeared as the soils thinned and the granite face of the mountain became the dominant feature. Only mosses survived at this altitude. Grasping rock outcrops for the final ascent, they crested a ridge and paused to collect their breath, dazzled by what they saw: the Adirondack mountain range, imbued with gold, red and deep green, blanketed the horizon. For a few moments nothing stirred and no one spoke. A familiar feeling of peace came over William.

After catching his breath, he rested his pack on the ground. "We made good time," he said, checking his pocket watch. "We should be able to get back down before dusk."

Bierstadt and his guide set up the tripod and camera while William unloaded the food. Wandering over to a rock outcrop, he sat down and bit into an apple while admiring the array of colors. It was desolate up here because it was autumn and few people took to hiking the mountains this time of year. A stiff breeze made William shiver; he took a wool hat out of his coat pocket and placed it on his head.

Out of the corner of his eye he saw a man appear over the rise on a different trail than the one they had used. The stranger cupped his hands over his eyes to avoid the glare of the sun while he searched the mountaintop, and when his view landed on William he immediately started walking toward him. When he reached William, he bent over clasped his hands on his thighs and gasped for air.

William shot up from his rock perch.

"Are you all right?" he asked the man.

"Yes, sir. I'm looking for Mr. Durant," he managed to say. His face was flush from the exertion of hiking. "Been climbing all morning trying to beat him up the trail. I'm thinking he took a different route."

"I'm Durant. What brings you here?"

"Sir, the hotel received a telegram this morning right after you left. It said urgent, and the hotel owners thought you were expecting word from someone." He handed William the crumpled telegram and settled himself on a rock while he took out a flask and drank from it.

William's heart began to race as he opened the telegram, thinking something had happened to his wife Janet, or infant son Lawrence. Why else would a guide be sent to chase him seven miles up a mountain?

Your father has taken seriously ill. I'm afraid he may die. Come to North Creek as soon as possible. Love, Mother

"Sir, is everything all right?" the messenger said.

"Yes. No." William turned to find Bierstadt standing beside him. "I have to go to North Creek. My father has taken ill."

Bierstadt's brows knit in concern. "Do you want me to continue?"

"Of course. You can't waste a day like this. I'll head back and send word to you," William said.

He left Bierstadt with his guide to finish their business and descended the mountain with the messenger from the hotel.

He tried not to be irritated by this interruption, but he had spent months lining up Bierstadt, a popular landscape photographer. William was keen to develop a new Adirondack travel brochure. The current one for the Adirondack Railroad Company was over a decade old and most of the photographs, although well done, were of people and places, not scenery. With this guide, William hoped to use Bierstadt's photographic talents to showcase the beauty of the mountains for city dwellers looking for a holiday escape.

And he wondered if his mother's urgency was partially hysteria. Previously, when his father had become seriously ill he'd miraculously recovered. Still, his pleurisy was weakening him, and it was only a matter of time before he succumbed to it. William hated to admit it, but part of him hoped this would be the last time he would be called home to attend to his ailing father.

"I gotta tell you, sir, you're one of the few men I've descended this mountain with that can keep their footing," the messenger said, waking William from his thoughts.

As if on cue, William's foot slipped on a round rock and he almost fell backward. He grabbed the trunk of a small tree to keep from falling.

"Yes," William said. "Possibly I am."

The messenger laughed. "You ok?" He didn't wait for William to answer. "This trail is much steeper than the one you took. But it shortens the time spent hiking by at least an hour if you don't trip."

"I see," William said, trying to avoid any further conversation so he could continue thinking about his father.

He was ashamed of himself for not feeling dread, remorse, or worry. In fact, he felt the opposite. His father's death would lift a weight off William's shoulders, and he would be free. If, as his mother was predicting, this was the end for Dr. Durant, for the first time in his life, William would not be living under the shadow of the giant man his father once was, and who everyone expected William to become.

He tried to recall when he last felt anything like love for his father. It was over a year ago now, when they were discussing William's arranged marriage to Janet Stott. His father was almost, but not quite, apologetic that his own misdeeds had caused such a scandal that William's prospects for alternative marriage arrangements were limited. They were smoking cigars in Dr. Durant's study after dinner.

"I know it's been hard on you, Will," he had said. "All those years I was away building the transcontinental, and then the bankruptcy. God knows it's been hard on your mother." He neglected to mention that Ella may have felt the hardship as well.

"But I've always tried to do my best by this family." He jabbed a finger toward the floor as if nailing his conviction to the carpet.

"We know that, Father." William tried to sound convincing.

"And this marriage may not be what you wanted. Or to the woman you wanted to be with," Dr. Durant continued, knowing that William was once in a doomed relationship with an Indian girl. "But she'll make you a good wife. She comes from good stock," he added, as if marrying Janet was like choosing a horse.

"With those wide hips she'll be fertile as well. Mark my words. I should know. I am a doctor." He stubbed his cigar out in the ashtray for emphasis, and let out a loud, racking cough.

William felt the blood rise to his face and remained quiet. He didn't need to be reminded about Janet's shape, nor that Dr. Durant had, in his early years, practiced medicine. As his father aged, he increasingly reminisced about the profession he gave up to become a railroad tycoon. William wondered if he regretted it.

His father was right about one thing: within months of their wedding Janet was pregnant with Lawrence. And now William was a father. Would Lawrence one day have mixed emotions about William as William did about his own father?

"We're almost at the end," the messenger called back to him.

"Yes, we are," William said.

Ella was sitting on the veranda at her cousin Frederick's hotel on Blue Mountain Lake, soaking up the rays of the afternoon sun with Frederick's sister, Estelle.

They were talking about a gala at Eliza Vanderbilt Webb's townhouse in New York City. At least Estelle was, because *she* had been invited and felt the need to recite every detail she could remember of the event.

"You should have seen her dress. It was gold and had thousands of tiny pearl beads sewed into it, and the lace, oh Ella, the lace! You should have seen it," she repeated.

Yes, Ella thought, I should have. But I wasn't invited. One would have thought Ella's newly published book of poetry, combined with the Durant family name, would have landed her an invite. But it didn't. Her only consolation was that William hadn't been invited either.

"And you wouldn't believe the guest list," Estelle said, adding salt to the wound. "They had — ".

Before she could finish, a hotel steward came up to them.

"Miss Durant. This came for you." He handed her a telegram.

Ella opened and read the urgent message from her mother.

"What is it?" Estelle asked.

Ella passed the telegram to her.

Estelle read it and said sympathetically, "I'm sure he'll be fine."

"I'm not so sure this time, Estelle."

Estelle didn't like that answer so she started in about her own father, Charles—Dr. Durant's brother—and his extended illness and eventual death the prior spring. Ella ignored her cousin's chatter and turned her attention to Blue Mountain Lake.

She remembered the time she and her mother and brother were living abroad. It was 1869; Ella was almost fifteen. Dr. Durant was in America, building the transcontinental line. It was his birthday and her mother was worried because they hadn't received a letter from him in weeks. Her mother, Ella recalled, had been melancholy that day. To cheer her up at dinner, Ella put a chair at the table across from her mother where she thought her father would sit if he were with them. She put flowers on his plate. She insisted they keep that chair empty, and would not allow anyone to sit in it because it made her believe he was really there. The next day she wrote him a letter, telling him how much she loved her dear Papa and how much he was missed. She begged him to send word to their mother.

A breeze riffled off the water and Ella shivered as she wrapped her shawl more tightly about her shoulders. Her father was dying. Cold and wary, sorry for her mother, yet excited about her own prospects, Ella felt a range of emotions. Grief, however, was not one of them.

TWO

New York

William arrived at his parents' North Creek home in the evening, bruised and exhausted after travelling for hours by coach on the rough rural roads only made worse for travel by the drenching rain. His father's valet, Mr. McFarland, greeted him at the entrance and helped him out of his coat.

"Bit of a storm this evening, isn't there, Mr. Durant?"

William handed McFarland his top hat and umbrella. "It is that, a real soaker. Where's Ella?"

"She's on her way home now."

"Let me know as soon as she arrives," William said. "And send a telegram to John Barbour. Tell him to wait until he hears from me before coming to the house. Tell him my father cannot speak to anyone. I will be making the decisions for him from now on."

William started toward the stairway and his father's bedroom thinking about what happened the last time Dr. Durant was on his deathbed. Lawyers from the Adirondack Railroad Company tried to wheedle Dr. Durant into signing off on some papers selling his remaining stock in the company. Much to everyone's surprise, his father rallied back to health and gave William hell for allowing anyone to try and take advantage of his illness. It was not going to happen again. This time, William was going to remain in control, no matter what became of his father.

He turned to Mr. McFarland, "Tell Mrs. McFarland to bring me tea in my father's study."

"Yes, sir."

William stepped into his father's room and walked over to his bedside. His father's skin was gray, his face sunken. Death was inevitable. Maybe the man would finally find peace.

It had been a trying year. The Durants had almost lost everything to the state due to the back taxes owed on their property in the Adirondacks. Dr. Durant had hounded William to take care of the matter by any means with the politicians in Albany. Unlike his father, William detested the political maneuvering that had to be done to keep the Adirondack Railroad Company solvent.

He took his father's limp hand in his and found consolation in the fact that once his father died, he'd be in control. With his father gone, William would be able to revive the family's fortune.

William turned when he heard the muffled voice of his mother's companion, Margaret, in the hallway outside the door. In moments, her voice rose a pitch as if she were arguing with someone. William frowned.

Ella had arrived.

Ella opened the front door and stepped inside. She didn't wait for a servant to help her out of her things. She tore off her coat and went straight to her father's bedroom to find Margaret guarding the door like a mother bear over her young.

"He can't be disturbed now," Margaret said sternly, putting her arm across the door.

Ella reached for the door handle without slowing and said, "You will not stop me from saying good-bye to my dying father."

She brushed past Margaret and entered the room to find William standing over their father's bed. She clicked the door shut, leaving Margaret outside sputtering about impudent behavior.

"How is he?" she asked.

"Sleeping," William said.

She came over to the bedside and sat down next to her father.

"He'll be missed," Ella said.

"Mother will miss him. As it is, they spent more time apart than together," William said.

"That was his choice," Ella said with bitterness.

"Now is not the time to revisit old wounds."

Ella could hear Dr. Durant's slight wheezing; the pleurisy had weakened his lungs and taken his strength. The mighty railroad magnate was now only a sliver of a man.

"I'm taking tea in Father's study. I suggest you visit with Mother to keep her company. I'll check in on you both later," William said, and left her.

Ella watched William leave the room and then took her father's cold hand in hers. She leaned over and whispered in his ear, "I forgive you."

When she looked up, Margaret was standing in the doorway with a disapproving grimace Ella knew all too well.

Thomas C. Durant died at three o'clock the following morning.

The next day after breakfast Ella was instructed by William to wait in the parlor to be called to her mother's bedroom chamber. They were discussing matters in private, or so Ella was informed. He told her not to interrupt, but she had been waiting for over two hours and was losing patience.

Finally, at thirty-one, Ella was free. Dr. Durant had shackled her these past eleven years — long enough. She knew what she wanted: to return to the society she had been forced to leave in London.

She glanced at the stairway. *What the devil are they talking about up there?*

Enough is enough, she thought, and was about to ascend the stairs to her mother's bedroom when Mr. McFarland appeared at the top of the stairs.

"They will see you now, Miss Durant," he said, masking his

displeasure to find her at the bottom of the stairs and not in the parlor where she had been instructed to stay put.

When Ella entered the bedroom, her mother was in bed, fully dressed in mourning, a black dress laced up to the neck with heavy black chintz wrapped over her bodice. Ella went to her and kissed her lightly on each cheek.

"Mother, I'm so sorry for your loss."

"For all our losses you mean," William said.

"Sit down, both of you," Hannah said wearily. They complied, facing each other across the bed.

"Ella, William and I have been discussing a few things. We might just as well get to the point. When John Barbour arrives, you'll be requested to sign over management of your affairs to William."

For a moment Ella stayed seated, shocked into silence. Then their conspiracy dawned on her and she sprung from her chair. She had not expected such deceit, especially from her mother.

"I will not put my future in his hands!" Ella said, looking pointedly at William. He stared back at her coolly.

"No one said you would, Ella. Now calm down and lower your voice. You'll raise the roof with your shouting," Hannah said.

"I know what he's up to. He's been waiting for this opportunity to take control. Well, I have waited too, William, and I have waited long enough. I want my freedom, and you're not going to take that away!"

William slowly lifted himself off of the wingback chair he was sitting in and walked around the end of the bed to where Ella stood and looked down at her. "You'll get what's due to you. We're only asking you — no, as man of the household now, I am *telling* you — to sign over your power of attorney to me. Mother has already agreed to it. It was Father's wish."

"I don't care whose wish it was," she said. "You'll not take charge of my wealth. You cannot handle your own finances, William. You were always better at spending money than making it. Father never trusted you. So why should I?"

William raised his hand to backhand her. Hannah intervened.

"Enough! Both of you! William, you'll not raise a hand to your sister. Ella, you're acting like a child. Now sit down both of you so we can discuss this with dignity before John Barbour arrives."

The two siblings settled back in their chairs, staring icily at each other from opposite sides of her bed.

"Now, Ella, I know you don't want to hear this, but your father left William and me with strict instructions that you would not be in charge of your own finances. You burned your bridges that fateful summer when you invited your friends to the Adirondacks against his wishes and caused such a scandal. He never forgave you for it. That summer, you caused all kinds of problems for us *and* your cousin. If it had not been for me, Alvah Dunning would have taken a gun to your cousin's head."

"Mother, really, are you going to bring up the past now? As if Alvah didn't know what the Durants were up to. Charles had what was coming to him from old Alvah," Ella said.

William rolled his eyes and smiled sarcastically. "Oh, yes, poor Alvah, the squatter. The only thing you and your friends accomplished that summer was to antagonize the natives with your sympathy for the oppressed. His rights were not being violated."

"At least I can say I have not taken advantage," she said between pursed lips.

William simmered in his chair.

Hannah rolled her eyes before leveling them back on Ella with a look that made clear her patience was wearing thin. "Again, we need to get back to the matter at hand. Ella, when John Barbour presents the papers for power of attorney, you are signing yours over to William, just as I am. You'll have to have faith that we're in good hands. I know I trust my son to take care of me."

"That's the difference between you and me, mother. I don't share your faith."

"Well get your head out of the clouds and stop your silly musings. Your drama doesn't bode well here. Save that for your writing," Hannah said. "God knows it could use it."

William watched Ella's face fall as Hannah's words speared her. For a moment, he felt sorry for Ella; he knew how much their parents' approval of her writing meant to her. And it was unlike Hannah to be so cruel. His mother was obviously tired from dealing with their father's extended illness.

"We have no choice at the moment, Ella," he said to soften the blow, "but I think you'll find that my management of the family's wealth will allow you to lead the life you wish—that of a writer. I, for one, think you have the talent to prove yourself worthy."

Surprised, Ella managed to smile at William. This was the William she used to know and trust, the one she grew up with: her friend. She paused and took a deep breath.

"All right, William," she said. "I'll consider it."

John Barbour, the family attorney, arrived the evening before the funeral and entered Dr. Durant's library to find William waiting for him. "Good to see you, though I'm sorry for the circumstances. My condolences," he said gravely as he shook William's outstretched hand.

"Thank you, John. Have a seat." William gestured to the armchair opposite his in front of the hearth.

"What are your plans for the funeral?" Barbour asked as they settled down.

"A special train is bringing father's family and friends tomorrow from New York City. We've reserved a hall."

"How many are you expecting?"

"Over two hundred."

Barbour cocked his head before nodding. "Not surprised, even in the current circumstances. Your father's death reminds people of how far our country has come since the Civil War. He was a great pioneer, may he rest in peace."

"After the funeral Mother and I will travel by train to Brooklyn to inter my father in the mausoleum he had built at Green Wood."

"And how are Janet and the baby?"

"Fine, thank you. Lawrence is too young to travel. They're staying in Saratoga. I sent word to Janet that I may not be home for a couple of weeks until I have things settled here."

Barbour nodded. He paused, then said, "I've spent the last few days unraveling your family's business affairs. Have you spoken about them with your mother and Ella?"

"Yes. I think we are all in agreement that I should, as Father wished, take over power of attorney."

Barbour knit his brow and puckered his lips as if debating with himself what to say next. He avoided William's stare and turned his gaze up at Dr. Durant's portrait on the wall.

"John, do you agree? This is what my father wanted?"

"Oh, yes, yes," Barbour said, shaking his head and turning his attention back to William. "I have two documents here; we'll review them shortly." He patted his leather satchel that sat next to him on the floor between them. "But there are one or two matters we must discuss before we see your mother and sister. I'll get right to it because I know they're waiting for us." His expression grew more serious. "There are a few things I think you should know about your father's state of affairs."

"They have got to be better than mine, John. I have one hundred dollars in my savings. My father's lack of generosity has left me a pauper. You would never know that I am President of the Adirondack Railroad Company."

McFarland knocked lightly on the door and walked into the study carrying a tray. "I have your supper, Mr. Barbour. Smoked trout and Mrs. McFarland's sauce." McFarland set the tray down and left the room.

"You must be hungry. Eat first, we can talk afterwards," William said. He went to his father's bar to pour a glass of sherry.

Visibly relieved to be eating, Barbour spread the thick sauce over a biscuit. "I've never been able to tell, is it curry in the sauce?"

A smiled formed at the corners of William's mouth as he lifted his glass at Barbour to concur.

William watched with satisfaction as Barbour sliced a thin piece of fish and placed it, along with a slice of egg and some capers, on top of a cracker and delicately placed it in his mouth.

"This is good trout!" Barbour said as he wiped his mouth with his napkin. "How I miss fishing. What I wouldn't do to get away from my work and spend a week at Pine Knot." He prepared another trout-laden biscuit and ate it, then poured a cup of steaming tea and sat back in his chair.

"There is a lot to talk about. Before your mother and sister assign power of attorney to you, I feel it is my obligation as your family lawyer to let you know what you are getting yourself into and the tremendous responsibility you are undertaking. As we suspected, your father did not leave a will. Or if he did, I have been unable to find it anywhere in his papers. I certainly didn't prepare it for him. But more daunting than trying to figure out what he wanted us to do with his assets when he died — well, quite simply, William, your father left you with close to nine million in debts."

William clenched his jaw and swallowed what was left of his sherry. He poured himself another before speaking.

"I knew he was in debt, but how could it be *that* much? I thought most of the debt was relinquished when Sutphen and I took ownership of the company." William took another long swallow and walked back to his seat by the fire.

Barbour shook his head. "Your father didn't want anyone, even me, to know the extent of his problems. I only found out how bad it all was when he last took ill. The creditors smelled blood and started pounding at my door. It seems your father never could get the refinancing he needed to pay back all he owed to the investors in the Adirondack Railroad Company, and he was still contending with creditor lawsuits from his days as head of the Union Pacific Railroad. I'll not make it sound rosier than it is. He left you a mess to clean up."

William, noticing his sherry glass was already empty, got up to get another, but instead started pacing the floor.

"Bloody hell! My mother. She won't lose the house, will she?"

"No. We took care of that remember? The house is in her name," Barbour reassured him. "William, please sit. You're making matters worse with your agitation. Now is the time to keep your head clear."

William regained his composure and sat down.

"Now, listen. I can fight most of these claims. They are, after all, being made by some of your father's closest associates, who played the same game he did for decades. Land acquisition, rail building, and speculation are a gamble they are willing to take. But that is not my greatest concern. My concern is that you follow my lead on this."

"And what are you proposing? Because if Ella finds out her inheritance is worth nothing, she will never give me power of attorney until she has hired her own lawyer to sort the whole affair out. I know her too well. She won't give up easily."

"Exactly. All the more reason to listen to my advice. I am your attorney now."

William rose and went to the bar to pour another sherry. He lifted his glass up in a gesture to see if John wanted one as well. John shook his head.

"What do you propose then?" William asked from the bar.

"Your father put most of the bonds and certificates for the Adirondack Railroad Company in your mother's name. She is the biggest stockholder."

"Why would he do that?"

"You'll have to ask Sutphen why exactly. I'd guess he was using your mother's name to leverage stocks with money he borrowed from the company. When he needed cash, he'd sell them."

William recalled the squeamish feelings he'd had during all of those agonizing meetings in Sutphen's office in New York City, that sickening smile on Sutphen's face as William signed blank stock certificates, the owners anonymous. Now he knew. He was just as much a pawn as his mother in his father's financial schemes.

"What we need to do is buy as much company stock as we can under Janet's name," Barbour continued, "No one will know what we're doing. I'll have Sutphen start the process as soon as you give the go-ahead."

"Why drag Janet into it?"

"She mustn't know. No one must know."

William eyed Barbour, took a sip of his sherry, and went to the fireside. He sat back in his chair and let Barbour's statement, and the sherry, soak in for a moment.

"With most of the stock held in your mother's name rather than your father's, these claims against your father are worthless anyway." Barbour waved his hand as if he could brush all of the Durant troubles aside.

"Your father knew what he was doing. And now that he's dead, the rest of the stockholders will assume the company will be sold and the family will claim bankruptcy."

"I won't allow that," William said.

Barbour shook his head. "Listen to me. These businessmen will be clamoring to sell their stocks in the company before that happens."

William raked his hands through his hair and sighed.

Barbour continued. "That's when we instruct Sutphen to buy the stocks from them in Janet's name. Once the transactions are complete, Janet will own all of the company's debt, which, of course, she will never claim. In name, she becomes the company's second largest creditor, after your mother."

Barbour was puffed up like a peacock as he spoke.

"But the brilliant part is," he said, as he leaned closer and lightly batted William's knee, "your debt to Janet will be a quarter the amount you would otherwise be required to pay when you finally sell the company."

William stared into the fire. He was always amazed at the inner workings of men like John Barbour and the railroad company attorney, William Sutphen. What kind of mind thinks up these transactions? This was the way his father made his fortune. By deceit.

"William, are you listening to me? Do you understand what I'm telling you?"

William watched a log fall and the coals pulse from the heat. He took his hand away from his upper lip when he realized he had been stroking his mustache. Over the past few months William had often caught himself fingering his facial hair—that, and pacing the floor. These were things he used to see his father do when nervous and it bothered William to find he was taking on the same bad habits.

"I understand it all quite clearly," he said. "The stock holders will be clamoring to sell their stocks in the Adirondack Railroad Company, deeming them to be worthless. Sutphen will buy them up at a greatly reduced rate under Janet's name, but the stock holders won't know who is buying them."

"Exactly. You've got it!"

"But where am I going to raise the capital to purchase the stock under Janet's name? I have no cash."

"Simple," Barbour said. "We mortgage your father's lumber mill here in North Creek."

"And we reveal nothing about this to any of the women? Not Ella, Janet, or my mother?"

Barbour nodded yes.

"I suspect my mother will know what we're conniving anyway." William stared back at the flames and decided to add another log to it.

"You may well be right about that," Barbour said.

William rose to fetch a log and threw it into the flames. His father should have converted this fireplace to a coal stove years ago, he thought. He turned back to Barbour.

"But what of Ella? She will demand her fair share of the inheritance."

"I think I have a way to handle her demands."

"Not many men know how to handle Ella," William said wryly.

"Well, I have the two documents in my satchel, one for her to sign, and one for your mother. You will be in complete control of your mother's affairs for as long as she is alive, which is how it should be."

"And Ella? I don't trust her capriciousness. I'm not sure she'll sign off," William said.

"You need to assure her that she will receive her fair share of the estate, once everything is settled, of course, and let her be on her way with a monthly allowance," Barbour said. He inhaled deeply and let out a gust of air.

"I think I might take that sherry after all."

William poured them both a drink and gave one to Barbour.

"The next few months will be trying; I'm sure of it," Barbour said and raised his glass to William. "Here's to your father."

William raised his as well, but said nothing.

An hour later Ella entered her mother's bedroom and was confronted with the grim faces of her brother, John Barbour, and her mother's companion, Margaret. They all stood next to her mother, who was sitting up in her bed with a wool blanket covering her legs.

Ella noticed a document sitting at the end of the bed with Hannah's signature on it. She moved closer, picked it up and read the first few lines. It was a document assigning power of attorney over to William. Her hands were trembling as she set it back down on the bed. She knew they were watching her closely, probably expecting a scene.

Turning to Barbour, Ella said, "Tell me, John, what is my father's estate worth?"

Barbour stood searching for words, unable or unwilling to answer.

"There's plenty in the estate to live the life you want in England, Ella," William replied for Barbour. "John has informed me that, once we relinquish the debts, it should be worth over one million."

Barbour cleared his throat and said, "Ella, I think it would be in your best interest to sign over power of attorney to William. Rest assured, you will receive your inheritance once we sort out your father's tangled affairs and legal obligations to the Adirondack Railroad Company."

Ella shook her head, signaling her disagreement with Barbour that William was a capable steward of her affairs.

William was tired of trying to cajole her. "Listen, Ella, it's my duty to act as trustee for the family now. Mother has granted me power of attorney and we could both, if we wanted, squeeze you out." He turned to Barbour to back him up. "This is true in American law, correct?"

John mumbled something incomprehensible.

"Squeeze me out, William? What does that mean exactly?" Ella said.

"It means that Mother and I could divide the estate and leave you with nothing."

Hannah was fiddling with the hem of her wrap. A sly smile crossed Margaret's face and Ella resisted the urge to slap it off her. She was confused and distraught. Her freedom had seemed so close. All she wanted was to return to the life she had left in England and write, but signing over her financial affairs to William without the proper counsel felt wrong.

Reading her thoughts, William said, "I think you should consider when would be the best time to leave for London."

"I'm still considering my options. I'd like to consult with a lawyer on the matter."

Her mother let out a large sigh. "Ella, I have complete confidence in William to manage the estate."

William locked eyes on Ella and dared her to retort. She would allow her mother to remain delusional about William's abilities to manage their affairs. It was not worth arguing over.

"I will not sign it. I need time to think. Father has just been laid to rest and I've barely had a chance to mourn him," she said.

Everyone stared at her, and when she gave no indication of relenting, Hannah broke into the dead air.

"I'm too tired to argue anymore. Leave me, all of you," she said, motioning to the door. "Except Margaret."

THREE

New York

Ella waited for William in the empty corridor outside Mr. Sutphen's office in New York City. She was nervous, aware that this meeting, "to discuss business" as William told her, was another attempt to get her to sign over power of attorney to him.

Knowing full well that John Barbour was not on her team, she asked the advice of Abram Hewitt, another family friend, and prominent member of Congress. She thought he would make a good ally if she needed one, and so asked for his opinion. His reply was not very helpful:

> *Without knowing the value of the estate, Ella, I'm not sure how much I can help. William, though, is a fine man. I doubt he would squander your inheritance once he and Mr. Barbour work out the Adirondack Company's affairs.*

She heard William's footsteps clicking on the hard wood and turned her head in his direction. He nodded at her, she stood, and they entered Sutphen's office together.

"Believe me, Miss Durant, this is in your best interests," Sutphen said from across his luminous desk once they had settled into their seats.

Ella glanced at William for reassurance. This man, Sutphen, made her uncomfortable. Although his outward appearance seemed on the up and up, she sensed that inside the man was sinister. Who else but a devil would agree to do her father's dirty deeds all of these years?

"We've completed the paperwork," he said, gliding a folder with a document in it across the desk. He got up, walked over to where she sat, and placed an inkwell and pen beside her hand.

"You will receive a sum of five thousand dollars, which will be placed in a bank account in your name, and a monthly allowance of two hundred thereafter."

Ella remained suspicious. "Excuse me for appearing ungrateful, but my father's estate is worth far more than you are providing."

Sutphen produced a half smile, which only made him appear more untrustworthy.

"Your father's estate, madam, is currently being assessed for its true value. There are many things that must be done. Firstly, we have the creditors to account to." At this point Sutphen waited for William to agree.

"Yes, indeed," William said. He straightened in his chair as if coming out of a trance. "It will take considerable time to sort this business out. Meanwhile, I've purchased this for you." He took out of his satchel a first-class ticket for a steamer heading for London and held it out to her.

"You can pack your trunks and start a new life in London with your old friends." He produced a wan smile.

Ella eyed the ticket longingly, then caught herself lest she seem too eager to retrieve it from his hand. "You mean, *our* old friends, William?" she said.

William flushed, but he didn't respond.

The room was quiet. Both men stared at her, waiting for an answer. What choice did she have? It was obvious they were not going to give her any more, not until they had worked out their tedious business matters.

"When can I expect another payment from the estate then?" she asked, and turned to William, purposely ignoring Sutphen. It didn't work. William opened his mouth, but before he could say a word, Sutphen spoke.

"Of course we will keep you informed of any changes in the financial situation of the Adirondack Railroad Company."

Ella's hands were trembling when she finally signed the document and left the men to talk about railroad business. She went to her hotel for tea, after which she sent a telegram to Mr. McFarland to have her trunks shipped to New York City. He had been waiting for instructions.

A week later, William met her on the docks in the New York City harbor. All around them people were sniffling into handkerchiefs and waving good-bye to family and friends. They nervously waited for Ella's turn to board.

"It has been so long since I've been on a ship," Ella remarked.

"Yes. The last time you crossed the Atlantic was 1874."

"So much has changed since then, hasn't it?" she said timidly. When he didn't respond she continued, "Well, I'm sure it won't be the same in England either. So many of our friends are married and have estates of their own to look after."

William stayed silent.

"We used to have it so good at one time, didn't we?" Ella said. She was thinking about more than just their carefree lifestyle before the financial panic of 1873 had sent their family into a tailspin.

William understood this. He relaxed his shoulders, which he had pressed forward against both the cold and anticipation of a scene. "Yes, we did," he said. "Until father made a mess of it."

Ella let out a small laugh. She took one hand out of her fur muff and placed it on his shoulder for a moment. "I'm sure you'll be able to make amends for him."

"I hope so, for Mother's sake."

"Yes, she deserves better now that he is gone from us." Ella watched the people boarding the ship.

"I wish I could join you on your voyage to England, but there is work to be done here, and I have my family now to think about," he said.

The passengers waiting on the docks were now becoming more eager to get onboard, hurriedly saying good-bye, making their rounds of last minute hugs, and picking up their bags to get in line for the stairs that would lead them into the bowels of the ship.

"I brought you a gift," William said. "It's already loaded on the ship. A keg of oysters, on ice. They should survive the journey without spoiling," he said.

"What a treat that will be for Aunt Sylvia," Ella said.

"Are you sure she knows when you'll arrive?"

Ella appreciated that he was being protective, the way he used to be toward her.

"You're shivering," William said. "You'd better board now. It will be warm in your cabin." He bent down and lightly kissed her cheek.

"Give this letter to Aunt Sylvia," he said, handing her a letter he had kept in his coat pocket. "It's from Mother. And be sure to tell her I plan to visit England as soon as I have put this Adirondack Railroad business behind me."

"Of course."

The ship's horn bellowed. Ella jumped slightly at the sound. "Oh, dear. I must go now. Good-bye, William! Give my regards to Janet and the baby! Say good-bye once more to Mother for me, and tell her to not worry!"

William watched her as she ascended the steps to the ship, waving back at him, looking so happy to be leaving America.

PART TWO

1886

FOUR

England

She was a foreigner in the place she once called home. It had changed since she had last lived here more than a decade ago. Her nerves were jangled from the long voyage, but even so, everything looked and felt different from the small town of North Creek, where she had lived with her parents. She had taken for granted the wide rural roads that led to the mountains, the grand churches and houses that lined the newly built streets, named after people like her father who had christened the mines and built the lumber mills, employing half the town. Even New York City, where she lived briefly and visited often, with its bustling streets and immigrant smells, was nowhere near as crowded as this port town in England.

As she stood on the dock waiting for her aunt and hired driver to arrive, she felt suddenly claustrophobic. Where did all these people come from? And where were they going? She questioned whether her move to England was the right one.

She had also forgotten how moisture-laden the air was in England. Every droplet of water seemed to cling to her mink coat, weighing her down so that she couldn't move. She opened her umbrella to protect her coat from the soft mizzle and shivered. Looking around despondently for signs of her aunt, she didn't notice the man coming directly at her. He bumped into her forcibly, which caused her to stagger and drop her umbrella.

He reached out to keep her from toppling over and said, "Excuse me, madam! My apologies."

"Goodness, everyone is in such a hurry!" she said.

He picked up the umbrella, brushed it off, and handed it back to her.

"Oh, dear me," she said, regaining her stance.

"Are you hurt?"

It was then that she got a good look at him. He was dashing, in a dark navy frock coat made of fine wool that Ella could tell was cut and tailored on the continent. He stood out in the crowd, like her, as a foreigner.

"Ce n 'est pas grave," she said.

He bowed slightly and then said, "You speak French, madam? I'm sorry, then, that I thought you American. Not many from that country have mastered our language as well as you obviously have."

Ella blushed at the compliment. Her self-doubt about the move to England evaporated. How charming he was. "Oh, dear," she said, "but I *am* American." She gave a small tinkling laugh that surprised her for its coquettishness.

"Ah, from America! I suspected, as this steamer has just arrived from New York City." His laugh revealed straight white teeth and twinkling gray eyes. His English was perfect. He was obviously well educated, and from the looks of his top hat and coat, wealthy.

"And why then are you standing here looking so lost? Waiting on your husband perhaps, while he hires a cab?"

Ella was taken aback by the boldness of his question, but his earnest look made her feel at ease.

"No, I'm not married," she assured him. "I'm waiting for my aunt with her driver." She glanced nervously around her, noticing for the first time that she and this gallant man were the object of more than one passerby's attention. "I'm staying with her in London for a long-overdue visit."

He let out another small laugh. "London is a big place. You will find, as I have, that to say you are staying in London can mean many things. Where in London?"

With this question, Ella thought his curiosity into her affairs had gone too far. She became slightly annoyed by it. Of course, she knew how large London was, and that there were numerous parishes, even if she was a bit muddled from her travel and the crowds pressing in on her. As she was about to say something that would appease him—so she could continue to look into his engaging eyes—while warning him not to ask too many more personal questions, Aunt Sylvia approached with the driver.

"Ella!" Her aunt embraced her and kissed both cheeks. "I found you at last. We were so worried." She pulled away from her and noticed the stranger standing beside Ella. Her raised brows caused the stranger to tip his hat and introduce himself.

"Comte de la Salle, madam. Unfortunately, I was very rude and bumped into your niece by accident in my haste to get to my next destination."

Ella wondered for the first time where this man, this count, was going when he bumped into her.

"Well, then. No harm done, my Lord." Aunt Sylvia turned back to Ella. "Let's be on our way, shall we? I've been quite anxious to see that you have arrived safely, and we need to catch the train back to Chelsea."

The driver lifted her luggage off the ground and headed for the cab. There was no more reason to linger, although she desperately wanted to. She put her hand out to the count. "It was a pleasure to meet you."

"The pleasure was mine," he said. He flashed his brilliant smile, took her hand in his, bowed again, and was on his way.

"My," Aunt Sylvia said. "Quite the dandy, that one."

Ella took her free elbow as they walked to the cab, glancing backwards to see in which direction the count was headed.

At first Ella welcomed the daily visits to and from the many tea parlors of Aunt Sylvia's friends and relatives scattered about London. Her aunt's calling card tray was always full, and the cards she had printed up in anticipation of Ella's arrival were almost all gone. But within a couple of months, Ella began to grow weary of the conversational fare.

She shouldn't have been surprised to find that her station had changed since she last lived in London; she was no longer a debutante. Rather, she was what most considered a spinster. And the homes she visited belonged to ladies who had married well and were managing a country manor along with a house that they either let or occupied in London for the season. Ella had nothing in common with them anymore. The conversations revolved around their children, or troublesome estate matters and servants who were let go for insubordination or, worse, thievery, though sometimes she could steer the conversation toward her own interests, such as literature and theater.

One particular social visit brought home the truth of Ella's situation. Aunt Sylvia was feeling unwell, so Ella called alone on a distant cousin.

Her cousin, Lillian, poured the tea and said, "You must be such a comfort to Aunt Sylvia now that Uncle Peter has died."

Ella hadn't thought much about it but then realized Lillian was right.

"And to think, she has a companion now to help her pass the time. We were all so worried about her, you know." Lillian continued to prattle on, evidently not waiting for Ella to contribute to the conversation. Ella did, however, wonder whom she meant by companion. It didn't take long to find out.

"Of course, when we heard you wanted to return to London, the first thing *my* mother thought was to request of *your* mother that you stay with Aunt Sylvia. She needs you, you know." Lillian rested one of her hands lightly on Ella's for emphasis.

"She has been ever so lonely. Come to think of it, so was your mother when she lived in London without your father. My mother talks all the time about how trying those years were for poor Aunt Hannah! Raising you and William without the guidance and direction of your father. If it hadn't been for Miss Molineaux, it would have been terribly difficult for her, I'm sure."

Ella almost choked on her tea. Her mouth went dry. The truth hit her like a blast of cold air. She had been invited to live with her aunt so that she could become what Margaret was for her mother. Of all the people in the world Ella would want to compare herself to, Margaret Molineaux was the last on the list. That woman was her nemesis, a constant, painful presence in her life, like a blister that wouldn't heal.

"Yes, I'm so glad I could be of some service to the family," Ella managed to say. *It was time to take control of her calling cards.*

When Anny Ritchie invited Ella to a dinner party, she felt a wave of relief. Anny's recently published book, *Mrs. Dymond*, was receiving good reviews, and she invited friends to her London home to celebrate. It was for Ella a chance to find acceptance amongst the types of people with whom she wanted to consort: other writers and intellectuals. And Anny was in the center of that crowd.

Ella had already visited a seamstress in the West End to make her new gowns, anticipating that the frocks she had brought from America would not live up to expectations in London. The evening of the party, she pulled out a forest-green sleeveless velvet gown that accentuated her small waistline and set off her dark eyes and hair.

She was admiring herself in the mirror when Aunt Sylvia came in.

"You look absolutely lovely! But don't you think it's too early, dear, to be wearing that?"

Ella suppressed the urge to scream and went to her wardrobe to find the drab black silk gown her mother had given her as a gift before she left America. Ella knew that Aunt Sylvia was communicating regularly with her mother and could just imagine Hannah's displeasure if she heard that Ella wasn't wearing black to publically announce the Durants' sorrow at the loss of their patriarch. *Leave it to the British to prolong the mourning season.*

"Here, I brought you some of my jewels," said Sylvia. She handed Ella a string of pearls as if trying to placate her.

Ella put it around her neck and admired her reflection.

When the coach arrived at the designated house she lost some of her nerve. With her father's illness, and the economy he insisted they keep these past few years, it had been a long time since she had attended such a function as this. What if she didn't fit in?

She forgot her fears as soon as she entered the room and was presented to the other guests. From the stares she attracted, and the small but polite nods of the other ladies as they whispered about her behind their fans, she knew she had finally arrived.

Anny was introducing her to a small circle of ladies when Ella saw him out of the corner of her eye: Count de la Salle was talking with another woman in a corner of the room. He lifted his gaze and leveled it on Ella. She quickly turned away and brought her attention back to Anny. After the introductions, Anny excused herself to welcome other friends. The ladies were discussing recent reviews of Ellen Terry's performance as *Olivia* at the Lyceum Theatre. Ella was thinking how she would like to see it herself when suddenly he was standing beside her.

"How grand to find you once again," Count de la Salle said gallantly as he bowed in front of her. The ladies around her went hush. "Ladies," he nodded to them. Ella's blood rose to her cheeks.

"Count de la Salle," she stammered, aware of the stares they were attracting.

His eyes concentrated on Ella's.

"I see your glass is empty. May I find a waiter for you? It is the least I can do to make up for my previous clumsiness."

"That would be very kind," Ella said. She tried to relax under the scrutiny. She told herself she didn't care what people thought. It had been so long since she was the object of anyone's attention, much less that of such a handsome man. He bowed to the group and left to find a waiter. The women looked at her for an explanation. She remained silent.

"Spending a night with him would be the top of my bent," said one of Anny's friends, while she fingered a tear-drop emerald dangling from her earlobe.

The woman with the large heron feather attached to her headdress said, "I agree."

"He stumbled into me at the port. Let's hope he's not as clumsy with the waiter," Ella said.

The ladies laughed.

"Here you are." Within minutes he was back with a flute of champagne.

The ladies gave Ella a look of respect mixed with envy, and realizing that it was *she* not them that had landed the attention of the most desirable man in the room, dismissed themselves to find other conversations.

He was wearing a coat and tails. His tie was a royal blue and his jet-black hair, which he wore longer than was the usual fashion for men in London, skimmed the top of his collar, creating a striking contrast with his starched white shirt. His steely gray eyes were penetrating. It was hard for Ella to remain looking at them for too long. She opened her fan and waved it gently over her face.

"Thank you," she said. She was nervous and sounded too shrill. She lowered her voice and said, "I do not know your first name."

"Gabriel. And now, I must admit I already know your name, as I heard your aunt calling to you at the port. What I didn't know then was that you are the famous writer Heloise Durant."

Ella was pleased he knew her as a writer. "Yes, but you may call me Ella."

"A lovely name."

"Thank you." She felt her face glowing.

"I have to confess, I have never *read* your poetry, but I have heard from our hostess how wonderful it is."

"She is a dear friend, but I'm sure she exaggerates the extent of my talent."

"No, no, she doesn't appear to be one to tell—how do they say it in America?—tall tales?"

Ella laughed. *This man could charm a snake out of a pot.* She was so consumed by Gabriel's aura, she almost forgot where she was, until she saw Poultney Bigelow across the room. He caught her looking at him and gave her a rakish grin. She turned away, disgusted.

"So tell me, what else do you write?"

"I'm working on a novel," Ella said.

"A novel! So, a major undertaking."

"Yes, well I have a short story that I am basing it on. It's about a family whose son dies in a horrible riding accident, and they find out that he has a mistress and children. A saga," Ella said.

"I see. So you are not like Zola, or your own country's esteemed writer Twain. They enjoy writing about the downtrodden. And doing so makes them very rich."

"I would hardly call Tom Sawyer downtrodden," Ella said.

"Yes, but he did not grow up as well off as you or I, did he?"

"Where I come from, there are many people like Tom Sawyer," she said.

Gabriel appeared interested.

"They survive off the bounty of the Adirondack forests and sell that skill to wealthy businessmen who want to pretend they are just like them, if only for a short while."

"I've never heard of the Addrondax," Gabriel said, mispronouncing the word.

She thought the conversation had focused too much on herself and was about to ask him where he was from when Poultney Bigelow appeared in front of them.

"Ella Durant!' he said.

"Poultney Bigelow," Ella said, shocked. Dreadful timing, she thought, although she knew it was inevitable that she'd have to confront him again. He had moved to London a year ago to work as a correspondent for the *Times*.

"Poultney, this is Count de la Salle," Ella said, trying to sound polite.

"So I've heard," Poultney said with a hint of disdain.

Gabriel's eyes narrowed on Poultney's. "A pleasure to meet you," he said.

"Sorry to interrupt, old chap," Poultney said. He ignored Gabriel's outstretched hand and gripped Ella's elbow. "Ella, I'm so glad to see you here. This saves me from calling on you at your aunt's house. I received a telegram from your brother today and must talk to you at once about some urgent business." He started to drag her away.

Ella's eyes widened and she put her drink in the Count's outstretched hand to avoid spilling it on the floor. She wrested her arm away from Poultney as delicately as possible so as not to cause a scene. "Surely this can wait?" she said in a low tone.

"No, no it can't." Poultney took her elbow once again, more firmly this time, and led her away before she could protest again. They bumped into Anny on the way into the drawing room.

"Please excuse us, Anny, but I have urgent family news for Ella, and if you don't mind I need to whisk her away briefly into the guest room."

"Don't tarry; dinner will be served shortly," she said. Her eyes followed them until Poultney shut the drawing room door behind them.

"The impertinence!" Ella snapped as she finally was able to pull her arm away from Poultney's.

Poultney ignored her and walked over to the small bar to pour a tumbler of whiskey for himself. He downed it in two swigs and poured another. Then he turned to face Ella.

"Do you even know what you're doing?"

"What are you talking about?" Ella sputtered.

"That man," Poultney nodded his head in the direction of the ballroom, "the *count*. Or so he says."

"Poultney, I am in no mood for your jealous antics."

"Hah. Ella, my dear, this is not about me being jealous. It's about you making a fool of yourself with that scoundrel."

"He's a gentleman."

"And how would you know that?"

Ella puffed herself up and went over to the looking glass that was hanging on the wall to adjust her hair and aigrette.

"He's only here because that idiot Lord Thompson invited him." Poultney gestured with the drink in his hand toward the door. "They met yesterday at the racetrack. Thompson was besotted with the count's ability to beat the odds and in the process lost a small fortune, which the count graciously covered," he added sarcastically.

"Well, there you have it then. Only a gentleman would cover the debts of an acquaintance," Ella said as she fussed with her hair piece.

"Hah," Poultney laughed at her as if she were an imbecile. "Only a scoundrel looks for easy prey to lure in, and Thompson, poor drunk, is an easy mark. Now he owes the count not only money, but a favor. How else do you think he ended up here at Mrs. Ritchie's dinner party where he could scope out ladies dripping in jewels looking for a respite from their tiresome marriages?"

Ella reflexively reached for the pearls at her throat. She rounded on Poultney.

"Speaking of marriages. How is yours to what's-her-name?"

"Edith, you mean? Convenient. For both of us." He peered into his glass.

Ella turned back to the mirror and straightened her collar. "She's not here in London with you then?" She tried to sound as if she didn't care.

"She's in confinement again. I left her at our home at Malden-on-Hudson," he said casually.

"Another child for the happily married couple? And your wife in the states while you travel abroad," she said, her lips curling. "Hmm, I'd say that is convenient. For you, anyway. But having children does not make one an expert on the state of other people's marriages, does it?"

"Take a look around you, Ella. Your esteemed friend Mrs. Ritchie is trying to hold on to the reins herself. Her 'boy-husband' as he's called behind his back, has another lover."

Ella stayed quiet for a moment. Poor Anny, she thought. It was a mistake for her to marry someone seventeen years her junior, especially one so sulky as Richmond. She deserved better.

"Who?" She was ashamed to even ask but couldn't help herself, realizing the tea parlor chatter she had been exposed to over the past couple of months was not as delicious as this.

"Tennyson's daughter-in-law, Eleanor."

"Idle gossip, I'm sure," Ella scoffed. "Anny told me that Richmond is helping Eleanor sort out her affairs." Eleanor was recently widowed. Her own deceased husband, the poet Lord Tennyson's son Lionel, was unfaithful as well, from what she heard. It appeared to be an epidemic in London society.

Poultney replied with an annoying smirk.

"Now, you must excuse me. This ruse of bringing me here under the pretense of a pressing family matter has gone on long enough. Since you have nothing to tell me of William, I shall take my leave and return to the party." She picked up her skirts to leave.

"So you didn't know, then, that William is finalizing the sale of the Adirondack Railroad Company any day now and will be quite rich from it?"

Ella stopped in her tracks. "How do you know this? Has William been in contact with you?"

"My dear, you forget I'm a reporter. I don't need to hear it from your brother. Not that he would tell me anyway."

He left his spot near the bar and walked over to stand in front of her. She turned around again to face the mirror, pretending to ignore him. As he stepped closer, she smelled the familiar scent of his cologne, mixed with whiskey. She stared at his reflection as he stood behind her, breathing on her neck.

Ella bit her lower lip to stop it from trembling. How humiliating it was to be confronted by the man who had thrown her off, telling her they were just 'friends' and then to have him inform her that her brother was withholding information. It took all of her effort to maintain her composure in front of Poultney. She said, "I'm sure William will be sending word to me soon about these developments."

"I doubt that," Poultney said bluntly.

Ella swirled around and glared at him. "How dare you! First you tell me that I'm making a fool of myself in front of friends, and then you tell me I'm a fool for trusting my dear brother."

Poultney let out a hearty laugh. "Why, Ella. You're angry. There was a time, if you remember, when I could soothe that passion of yours." He put his palm on her chest, above her left breast. She could feel her heart beating under its warmth.

"Take your hand off me," she said. Her voice was thick.

"You're blushing. I always found that attractive. He leaned closer and whispered in her ear, "I also remember a time when you moaned under my touch." He started to move his hand lower on her chest toward her breast, but she raised her left arm to slap him. He grabbed her wrist before she could strike. She then raised her right arm and he gripped that wrist as well. He pinned her arms against the mirror behind her head.

"You'll break the glass, you fool!" she cried.

She could see the small wrinkles that had started to form at the corner of his brown eyes. Frown lines framed the edges of his mouth. He had matured since his college days when they canoed and swam together at Raquette Lake in the Adirondacks.

"And you're drunk," she hissed.

"Your temper becomes you. But I have lost all patience for it," he said. "You forget I was a champion boxer at Yale. I know how to defend myself."

She lifted her foot in the air and was about to bring her heel down on his shoe when he planted his lips on hers and kissed her hard. At first she resisted, but it was useless. She went limp, her legs feeling as if they would give out from under her if he weren't holding her up. Memories of their summer days together at Camp Pine Knot came flooding back to her. She couldn't help but respond to his need; she felt it as well.

When the kiss was over, they both paused in disbelief that their desire for each other was still so strong. Poultney's lips were wet with whiskey and his sandy hair was tousled. She sighed. He let go of her arms and stepped back from her, combing his hair back with his hand.

They were snapped out of their reverie by the sound of Anny clearing her throat. She was standing at the doorway. How long, Ella wondered, had she been there? Ella moved away from Poultney.

"Anny, I was just about to return," Ella said, straightening her gown with as much dignity as she could muster.

"I just came to inform you both that dinner will be served." Anny eyed Poultney with suspicion.

Ella half walked and half wobbled toward Anny and let her lead her out of the room, leaving Poultney standing by the mirror, looking both disheveled and forlorn.

"I should tell you that Count de la Salle has requested to be seated near you at the dinner table. I have not given him an answer yet," Anny whispered to Ella as they left the drawing room to enter the ballroom.

"That would be my pleasure," Ella smiled.

Count de la Salle may have a questionable reputation, but he was what she needed: a distraction from Poultney Bigelow.

FIVE

New York

William picked himself up off the ground where he had been kneeling, watching as one of his workmen finished nailing the frame of the bay window on the nursery wing. He stood back and admired the almost-complete building. He provided the vision, the forest provided the supplies, and his workmen the tools, turning Camp Pine Knot into a piece of architectural art.

The bay window was held up by two bent tree limbs that protruded from the building as if they were an outgrowth of the siding. There were nine panels of leaded glass, each with four panes, all framed by large spruce limbs.

It was a calm, spring day. The lake ice had broken up and pieces of it floated by, like large blocks of marble, glistening in the sun. He only had a few days here before heading back home to Saratoga, and then on to his office on Broadway in New York City. He took advantage of every minute he could, mentoring his workers and hiking into the woods to look for more prime lumber. He hoped that when he did return to the city, Sutphen would have good news for him about the sale of the railroad company.

The buyer in the recent deal had backed off. Still, thanks to

Sutphen's brilliant caveat in their original offer, William had pocketed most of the thirty-thousand-dollar deposit when it fell through.

The money was more than enough to pay for the materials and labor for the nursery and an addition on his own cabin at Pine Knot. He straightened and slapped at his trousers to knock off the duff and sawdust that had been accumulating all day. He went to the kitchen to see if the new cook had arrived.

On the way, he checked the colored kerosene lanterns lining the pathways to make sure they were full and in working condition. He noted where he needed to place planters along the trail, and thought about where to find new stone for the fireplace in the guest quarters. As he passed the trapper's cabin, he heard sounds coming from inside. Ike was delivering furs from his winter harvest.

"Hello, Mr. Doo'Rant," Ike said and came out of the cabin to see William.

"Ike, good to see you again. How is the bounty this year?"

"Good as can be expected."

"What do you have for me?"

"Marten, mink, and a bear skin," Ike said proudly.

William stepped into the cabin with Ike to view the furs. As they both reached for a mink pelt, William's pale hand brushed against Ike's bronzed forearm, which created a flashback: Ike's sister, Louise, entangled with William, as they lie in their bed after making love, in the hunting cabin set back in the woods.

"These should fetch a good price," William said, trying to shake the image from his mind. "How are your wife and child?"

"Well as can be, sir. Thanks for asking," Ike said. He looked so much like Louise. And how he had aged since her death. Not so long ago he was just a lad living in the loft of the hunting cabin that Louise shared with William.

William congratulated Ike on his take, assured him it would fetch a good price in New York City, and left to find the new cook.

She was in the kitchen already, a small round woman with ruddy cheeks.

"Oh, hello, sir, you startled me!"

"I'm Mr. Durant."

"Yes, sir, Mr. Doo-Rant, sir. I recognized you right away."

"You did?" William was surprised. When he worked at Pine Knot he tried his best to fit in with his workmen.

"Yes, sir, you're so tall!" She inclined her head upward.

"What's your name?" he asked.

"Mrs. Callahan, sir."

"You're married then?"

"Yes, sir. Mr. Callahan, John, my husband, works for Charlie Bennett at the Antlers as a caretaker."

William nodded. He knew Charlie Bennett well and felt sorry for anyone who worked for him.

"I have a recipe here for you to follow. We will be celebrating the final construction on the nursery in two days and I want to reward my workers. This will be a test, to see if you know what you're doing." William reached into his pocket and handed her a folded recipe from the *New York Times*.

She eyed it skeptically. "Tsk, tsk," she said, and shook her head.

"What is it? You can't read?"

"No, sir, it's not that. This recipe for terrapin soup? I don't agree with the spices they've added. My papa used to make this. He'd catch a snapper from the ditch and boil it up with the leeks and onions from the garden, and let me tell you, you've never—"

"Yes, well, I'm sure your father's recipe for stew was perfect for your family. But the type of people we entertain here may be expecting more—how should I say it?—*flavor*, in their prepared dishes," William said.

"I tell you what, Mr. Doo'Rant. I'll try it *my* way, a trial you might say, and if you don't like it, I'll follow this." She waved the paper in the air as if it was contaminated.

William was shocked at her impertinence. But what harm would it cause for her to cook it the way she liked as a test for the workmen? He could always tell her he disliked it and make her do it his way. He didn't want to lose her just yet. It had taken months to find a woman living within miles of Pine Knot who could read.

"Alright then."

"And sir? Do you need me to send one of the boys out to the pond to catch a snapper?"

William knit his brow and sighed, then almost chuckled, imagining one of the boys that worked in the kitchen dangling a dead frog from a stick over the pond in the woods in order to lure in their dinner.

"No need," he said and gestured toward the window. Outside in a wooden box were diamondback turtles he'd had shipped from Massachusetts, waiting to be slaughtered.

Her jaw dropped. "Blimey, I didn't know you could order turtles!" she exclaimed. "Oh, dear, excuse me, sir." She upbraided herself. "But one other thing."

"Yes?" William said impatiently.

"I see we have plenty of ice and sugar, but how are we going to make this roman punch without lemons?"

William rolled his eyes, gently took hold of her shoulders, and turned her stout little body around to point at the crate of lemons sitting on the pantry floor. Then he left, wondering if the workers had any idea they would be eating like kings, and if any had ever gotten drunk on roman punch.

On the way back to his cabin he saw Alvah Dunning pull up in his canoe and wave William over.

"Mr. Doo'Rant," Alvah said as he disembarked from his canoe, "I was looking for you."

As usual, Alvah was well dressed for the weather. Even at his age — William assumed he was in his mid-seventies by now — Alvah was not one to allow a cold wind to keep him from canoeing on the lake. The trip from Eighth Lake must have taken him a couple of hours. He was wearing a coat made of otter fur. He had on a pair of rubber boots and a wool ushanka cap lined with mink that reached down the side of his face until it met his clipped, grizzled beard. He had his rifle and a fishing rod along with a pack in his boat, as if he was going camping. William wondered where else he was headed that day.

"Hello, Alvah. What can I do for you?"

"Was wonderin' if you knew when Doc Gerster would be showin' up?"

"I'm not entirely sure. The Gersters don't usually open their camp until mid-May."

"Well if you don' mind tellin' him, I think the spinners will hatch out early this year and he best get here early. I'm gonna be busy with the damn New Yerkers that'll be clamoring for me to take 'em fishing." Alvah spit tobacco juice out of the side of his mouth onto the ground next to him.

One paradox of Alvah's personality was that as he held his hand out to men of wealth to be paid for guiding them into the interior of the woods, he never hid his disgust that he was obliged to do so. But Alvah had a soft spot for certain people, Arpad Gerster included, because, from what William knew, he never complained about Arpad to the other guides, who were notorious for gossiping about their clients.

"I'll be heading to the city in a few days and will be sure to send word," William assured him.

"Fine," Alvah said, and turned to get back into his canoe. Then he thought better of it and said, "Say, not sure if you're interested, but there's a trio of loons stuck in a patch of open water in the bay. It iced over last night."

William's eyes lit up. "Can you take me?"

"Sure," Alvah said.

William retrieved his rifle and got in the canoe with Alvah. They paddled to South Bay and found the loons. They were swimming in a small patch of open water surrounded by a thin layer of ice that extended across the bay.

"Must've iced over on 'em last night. Probably been swimming in circles all night to keep the water open till the wind picks up," Alvah said.

William nodded. Loons were heavy birds; they needed a long flyway of open water or strong winds to get airborne. It was not their lucky day. He lifted his gun and shot at them. They immediately dove under water. He missed.

"Deuce it all!" he said. He set his gun on his lap and waited.

Within a few minutes they were back up, bobbing on the water and wailing in fright. William took his time, aimed, and shot at them again. He hit one and it flattened on the water while the other two took a desperate dive, hoping to find open water somewhere away from their predator. When they came up for air a second time William shot again and successfully hit another. The third took a dive. They waited. He never came back up. They scanned the horizon of ice. They assumed he either drowned or found open water. Seeing no sign of him, they broke the ice with their paddles and worked their way to the two dead loons.

"These will make good decorations once they're stuffed," William said, holding up the limp bodies by the scruff of their necks. The glossy black plumage dappled with white was a prize possession for mantels.

"Humph." Alvah neither agreed nor disagreed with him.

When they got back to Pine Knot, William offered Alvah money for his efforts.

"I could use some ammo," Alvah said when William pulled a few coins out of his pocket and extended them.

"I'll have Ike fetch some for you," said William. Another interesting fact about Alvah was that he'd rather barter if you had something of more value to him than money.

A few days later William set his belongings in a skiff to return home. It was still too dangerous for his steamboats to ply the icy waters, and it would take a whole day for him to get to his cousin's hotel on Blue Mountain Lake by skiff. After a night's stay at Prospect House Hotel, he would travel by coach to North Creek. From there, a train would take him to his home in Saratoga. It was a long journey, but always worth it. The nursery was complete and ready for Janet and baby Lawrence. It was time to return home.

Days later, he was in Barbour's office in Saratoga. "Sutphen may have found another buyer," Barbour said.

"Who is it?"

"We'll get to that in a moment. First you need to see this. It's a letter from a solicitor in London, addressed to you, and sent to my office asking for an account of the estate and a request to revoke your power of attorney over Ella." Barbour handed William the letter.

William skimmed over the perfunctory greetings and got to the meat of it.

> *Dear Sir, Miss Durant, your sister, has requested us to act as her advisor and we have undertaken to do so...... Miss Durant believes you hold her power of attorney, which she wishes cancelled, and we are told that we may shortly expect a statement of property and accounts from you, giving all details...*

It went on from there stating Miss Durant had only the best wishes for him, and good will, etc. etc. *Yours Faithfully, Mason and Edwards.*

"Confound it!" William slammed his fist down on his desk. "Do you think she knows about the sale?"

Barbour shrugged.

"But how the devil would she know? And who would advise her to seek out counsel to take the power of attorney away from me?"

"I was going to ask you that," Barbour said.

"My only correspondence with her since she left was about trying to un-wrangle father's affairs. She showed no interest in it, has not asked me about it at all. My mother corresponds with her, but I haven't even told my mother about selling the company."

Barbour clasped his hands together and placed them across his chest as he leaned back in his chair. "One of your friends who knows about the sale must have told her then."

William thought back. About a month before, he had dinner with Andrew Carnegie at the Union Club and had told him about the potential sale of the company, but he hadn't revealed much about it, just mentioned someone had made an offer.

"I'll remain silent about it from now on," William said. He picked up another letter that had been waiting for him. This one was from Ella.

"What does she say?" Barbour inquired.

"She's asked my mother to set up an account for her in London to deposit money and since she has been 'drifting around' she feels it necessary to have a solicitor in London take care of her affairs. 'In case of accident, illness, engagement or marriage.'" William slunk down in his chair and tossed the letter across the desk for Barbour to read.

"For God's sake, my father's been dead less than a year and she is talking about engagements and marriage. Who the devil is courting Ella? Worse, she's running out of cash," William said gravely.

Barbour put his hands up defensively as if to say, it is Ella after all. "You know, however," he said, placing his hands on the desk between them, "Ella getting married wouldn't be such a bad thing for you."

William was only half-listening as he sat steaming in his chair. His sister had always been needy, even as a child. And usually William, or his mother, gave in to her. Would it never end?

"The only way you'll be able to keep track of Ella's comings and goings is if you have someone living in London who can report back to you," Barbour suggested.

William thought for a moment, and then his eyes lit up. "Poultney Bigelow is a correspondent for the *London Times*. He recently contacted me about a Baedeker for the Adirondacks."

Barbour looked at him questioningly.

"The Europeans are always looking for good hunting grounds. People travel to India, Egypt and Siberia for big game hunting. Why not a travel guide aimed at foreigners to entice them to the Adirondacks?"

"Brilliant idea. That's something your father would do."

"Exactly what I was thinking," William said.

"While we're speaking of it, you'll be pleased that Phineas Lounsbury wants to make an offer for more acreage on Long

Point."

William was not enthused. "It's getting crowded on Raquette Lake. Bennett is building a casino across the channel at Antlers. Pine Knot will be squeezed in between hotels and Lounsbury's sprawling compound," William said.

"There could be worse things than being a neighbor to the Governor of Connecticut," Barbour said. "Besides, the land commission's rash decision to declare the Adirondacks a protected forest preserve has created a land grab. Since the Adirondack Railroad Company has parcels with good lumber, we will do very well if we sell or lease some of those lots as well."

William reflexively stroked his mustache, then caught himself and quickly rested his hand on his lap. "Will selling land lower the price for the sale of the company?"

Barbour shook his head. "No, actually, this delay has proven to be a godsend. The longer we wait, the more the company appears to be worth."

William listened absently as he shuffled through more of the papers waiting for him. One letter in particular caught his eye. He slit the envelope open.

"Fancy stationary, who is it from?" Barbour asked.

"Interesting," William said. "It's from Collis Huntington. He would like to meet with me."

"Huntington? He must take you for a duffer then. You know your father and him never got along? What would he want from you?"

"I have no idea," William said. "Maybe he's interested in buying the railroad?"

Barbour grunted. "I highly doubt it. He's up to his eyeballs in court proceedings. The government wants to be paid back interest on the bonds it lent to the Central Pacific. It's a blessing your father isn't around to have to testify himself. I don't think he could handle the government prying into his affairs again. The Credit Mobilier scandal was about all he could handle. I swear it was their hounding that exacerbated his demise. Why can't the public leave well enough alone?"

William ignored Barbour's rant about his father's corruption and continued to read the letter from Huntington. "He says he wants to dine at Delmonico's. I'm heading to New York City next week and I'll plan to meet up with him. There can't be any harm in that," William said.

"Yes. In the meantime, I'll craft a response to your sister's solicitors. I don't trust you to remain level headed about her. Until we know more, let me handle it," Barbour said.

William nodded in agreement.

It was quiet when he arrived home later that evening. He was grateful no one was awake and he didn't have to listen to a crying baby being lulled to sleep. He was so used to the solitude of Pine Knot where the only night sounds were the peepers calling for their mates. He went into his smoking room to pour himself a drink before finding Janet. Sitting by the fire and basking in its glow, he let the alcohol calm his nerves. The brandy put him in a better mood and aroused him. He placed his empty glass on the table and headed to his wife's bedchamber.

Janet was still awake, reading by her oil lamp: sitting up in bed waiting. Her soulful blue eyes landed on his. He walked over and kissed her lightly on the head.

"I'm so glad that you're home," she said.

"Yes," William said and stroked her hair.

Her face went flush as she smiled awkwardly at him, and started to untie her nightgown: she knew what he was expecting. William sat on the side of the bed and watched as Janet fumbled with her gown before he reached to assist her. Her awkwardness reminded him of their wedding day and first night together.

They had married in Stottsville-on-Hudson, Janet's hometown, named after her grandfather who had successfully built and operated a number of textile mills.

When William had looked around at the witnesses in church, he recognized close family, friends, and acquaintances that his mother and Mrs. Stott had invited from New York society. The Durants and Stotts had many business connections in New York and even though the Durant railroad investments had taken a turn for the worse, nobody would dare insult Dr. Durant by not showing up to his son's big event. He remembered catching a few of Ella's unmarried friends looking at him with a mixture of regret and surprise.

At first, William was somewhat shocked himself. When his mother informed him she had arranged the marriage to prevent him from cavorting with unsuitable girls, and to save the family's reputation from the financial debacles his father had contrived, he felt it was his familial obligation to do so. The Stotts and Durants went back many years; family business ventures kept them in touch. His father helped the Stotts gain their parcel of land on Raquette Lake from the state. Francis Stott was on the Board of the Adirondacak Railroad Company. It made perfect sense for William to marry into the family.

But he often questioned whether it was the best idea. He found himself daydreaming about what it would have been like if Louise had not been killed by a mountain lion. He had thought that Janet might replace his affections for Louise. He had high hopes for their first night together.

It had been a disaster. When he entered her bedchamber the first night, she was sitting up in bed, much like now, with a robe laced to her neck and the covers of the bed covering up most of her body. Then as now, he sensed that she was scared by his presence in her bedchamber. Hadn't *anyone* explained *anything* to her?

William had walked over to a chair in the corner to sit down and take off his shoes as she continued to stare at him as if he was a foreigner.

"Why don't you come over here?" he had said.

She pulled off the covers and walked over to him.

"Stop right there."

Shocked by his request she stopped in the middle of the room. He rose from his chair and walked to meet her. He untied the laces of her robe and let it cascade to the ground around her feet. He then undid the ties of her camisole and took pleasure in seeing her youthful, soft, plump flesh unfold from the confines. She gasped slightly in surprise as he caressed her breasts and then slipped his hands down to her backside.

Janet just stood there staring up at him, like a deer at a jacklight, entranced and unmoving. So unlike Louise, who would have reached for his shirt buttons and helped him undress.

"Go over to the bed and I'll meet you," he said.

Janet obeyed him, walking half-naked back to the bed.

"You might as well take off your undergarments," he said.

She blushed and then slipped them off before climbing into the bed.

William had undressed quickly. Janet appeared to be horrified by his nakedness which he found annoying. Louise was brought up in close quarters with her parents and siblings all sharing one large living space and was not embarrassed by the human body. She reveled in their love-making. He could tell this was not to be the case with Janet. She had no idea what she was doing and feared what *he* was about to do next. William lost his patience. After a few perfunctory caresses, he entered her. She yelped and he hesitated for a moment, looking down at her, and then continued. It was over in minutes.

The only change in their conjugal relationship since that night a year ago was that Janet had borne his child.

SIX

England

Everything had gone swimmingly at Anny Ritchie's dinner party. Anny had astutely placed Gabriel to Ella's left, and Andrew Carnegie, directly across from her. Poultney was exiled to the far end of the table where Ella thankfully never had to lay eyes on him, although she could feel his penetrating gaze on her all night long.

"Here's to auld lang syne," Carnegie said to Ella from across the table as he raised his glass to toast her.

"Yes. When was the last time we had dinner together? In New York City I'm sure. My father's birthday celebration? How time flies. Are you visiting family in Scotland?"

Ella could sense that people were watching her. She was drawing a lot of attention, having been seated next to the most dashing looking man at the party and across the table from the wealthiest.

"I'm here on business," Carnegie said.

"I hadn't known you were friends with Mrs. Ritchie."

"Mrs. Ritchie welcomed me because we have a mutual acquaintance. If I'd known you were the company she kept, I'd have asked for an introduction long ago."

"And you have lost none of your charm." Ella laughed. "I'm told your new book is causing a stir in London?"

The woman next to Carnegie shot Ella a look of surprise mixed with indignation.

Carnegie grinned. "Yes, I don't think my suggestion to eliminate the monarchy is very popular with the aristocracy."

"I'd say that was an understatement." The woman next to Carnegie glanced at her companions and rolled her eyes.

Gabriel, who had been carving his meat, stopped.

Anny Ritchie eyed Ella and Carnegie suspiciously from the other end of the table. There was a brief moment of tension as people turned toward Ella to hear how she'd steer the conversation. She could feel Gabriel's eyes on her.

"I imagine being invited to a hunting party with the Prince of Wales was not on your mind when you wrote *Triumphant Democracy*," Ella said with a slight laugh. "Although I'd agree the American way of governing is indeed a good model and you have a right to your opinions about such things."

Carnegie guffawed and let it go at that. "I hear you are also working on a book?"

The mood became more relaxed when an opening in the conversation allowed them to move on to less controversial subjects and someone asked Ella to elaborate on her writing plans. Later, while Gabriel helped Ella into her mink, he said, "You are the ideal guest."

Ella blushed at his compliment.

He smiled as he gazed down at her. "How long have you known Monsieur Carnegie?"

"Mr. Carnegie and my father were in business together years ago. He made the first luxury sleeping cars for my father's railroads." Ella was giddy from the champagne and port.

Gabriel brushed a wisp of hair from her brow. "Would you accompany me to the Royal Opera tomorrow evening?" he said.

Ella said yes without hesitation.

The next evening, Ella had her arm linked around Gabriel's elbow as he escorted her into the richly adorned auditorium of the theater. One glance at the women around her, basking in rubies and emeralds, and Ella realized she needed new jewelry. Instead of enjoying the performance as she should have, she sat stewing in her seat the whole evening feeling deficient wearing Aunt Sylvia's borrowed pearls.

She deserved new jewels, she thought. Indeed, her mother's diamonds would have been perfect for this evening if she still had them. As the performers sang their arias, her thoughts wandered back in time to the day her father had given her mother the diamond necklace and earrings. He had bought them at Tiffany's and Ella recalled how he had presented the gift to Hannah one evening while they dined at Delmonico's, a few nights before departing by steamship for London. Ella was very young at the time, only seven or eight. The Peace Conference held in Washington, D.C. that winter had failed to prevent what most believed would turn into a civil war, and her mother was anxious to leave New York City and return to her homeland with William and Ella.

Ella remembered those diamonds dazzled as her father placed them around Hannah's neck. Ella had always hoped someday she would inherit them. Their fate, along with the rest of her mother's jewelry, was to be sold off when the family went bankrupt in the financial panic of 1873.

During intermission the ladies and gentlemen met in the grand hallway on the pretense of needing refreshments, but in reality using the break as an opportunity to evaluate each other's attire. It was then Ella felt her inadequacies exposed while she stood amongst the other theater goers under the glare of the massive crystal chandeliers. Was it her imagination or was every woman in the hall swishing her skirt and batting her eyes at Gabriel?

She was not going to take any chances that Gabriel would abandon her for some well-to-do, over-coiffed socialite. She went straight to Harrods the next day to buy herself some diamonds. It was an extravagance. The cost, sixteen hundred dollars, was most of her savings. But she justified it knowing that William was selling the railroad and she would be receiving the rest of her inheritance any day. She had been denied long enough under the stifling grip of her father's miserly ways, and her room and board were taken care of by Aunt Sylvia, which left her a monthly allowance to dally in shopping sprees, tea outings, theater and the occasional dinners.

Afterwards, she waited patiently for the chance to show the diamonds off to Gabriel. But the chance never came. Over a month went by and she hadn't heard from him since their evening at the opera. She was doubting her ability to attract him. Did he think she was not well off enough to warrant his attention? Was she too old? Had she not dressed correctly for the opera?

One day while filtering through the mail in the summer room, Aunt Sylvia brought up Gabriel's absence.

"Whatever happened to that handsome man who took you to the opera? Count de la Salle?" Aunt Sylvia said as if reading Ella's thoughts.

Ella shook her head. "I'm not at all sure. The last I heard he was heading to Paris on business."

She sifted through her pile, hoping to find a card from Gabriel and instead found a letter from William. She slit it open with Sylvia's silver paper knife.

My Dear Sister, I had a letter from you some time ago which I should have answered had I not been away from home. I do not, I am afraid, quite understand what you mean when you say you feel the necessity of having some legal advisor in London.
...nearly a year must still elapse before, according to the law, Father's estate will be settled. And as it looks now, the indebtedness seems to exceed enormously the assets.

It went on for two more pages, a listing of the Adirondack Railroad Company's mortgage bonds, their value, and the fact that because the company was not earning any money or dividends for the investors, they couldn't even make necessary arrangements to repair the tracks. Of course, he said, the salary he receives as President is unpaid some months. And any money she was receiving as an allowance was really a 'gift' from mother. It finished:

> *You entirely ignored my references to business prospects in previous letters so that I ceased making any, nor shall I repeat them after this letter. Janet nor I go out in society so soon after poor father's loss. ....The baby thrives and his eyes are like father's. Your affectionate brother, William W. Durant*

Ella put the letter down and sighed.

"What is it, dear?" Aunt Sylvia said.

"Oh, it's nothing," Ella replied, hastily putting the letter back into its envelope. This was not welcome news. Had Poultney been wrong about the sale? And how could the estate have that much debt attached to it? How then, were William and Janet faring? And although he was trying to fool her into believing it, she highly doubted her gadabout brother was becoming a shut-in. She picked up the next letter in her pile. This one from the London solicitor she hired to look into revoking her power of attorney. It reiterated what William said. The estate was mired in debt, but if she wanted power of attorney William said he would revoke it. "Hmm," Ella said under her breath. There was one letter remaining, from her mother. Hannah chided her for not having any faith in William.

> *I don't understand, dear, why on earth you would want to revoke William's power of attorney. He has our best interests in mind no matter what decisions he makes regarding your father's estate. I'm afraid I won't be able to trust you with your allowance if I am not sure that William is looking after your welfare.*

It was a veiled threat. If Ella revoked the power of attorney and took it away from William, her mother would stop sending checks.

"Well, I can see whatever the news from home, it has put you in a bad mood. I, however, have something that will cheer you up." Sylvia held up the letter she had just opened. "Alfred Locock has invited us to his summer home in Brighton for a visit. Won't it be lovely to get away from London?"

Ella's face fell. If they left her aunt's home, Gabriel would never find her, and she had no idea how to reach him in Paris. Come to think of it, he had never once told her where in Paris he was from, much less anything about his family connections there.

"Good heavens, dear, whatever is the matter?"

"Oh, it's nothing." Ella attempted to sound cheerful. She had to admit her aunt was right. As the air was heating up and the winds were dying down, the air around Chelsea was putrid. And when she went on a stroll, she came back feeling as if her skin was covered with a thin coat of filth from the smog that hung in the air like a pall over everything. Maybe the sea air in Brighton would be good for her. She continued reading the letter from her mother. It said she was not feeling well, had been ill for some time, and that she would send her one thousand dollars to be delivered to an account at Lloyds Bank in London.

This improved Ella's spirits tremendously. "When shall we leave?" she said.

Her aunt smiled and started to fuss about their travel plans and what they should pack.

They arrived at Alfred Locock's residence in Adelaide Crescent by mid-July. Ella was glad Aunt Sylvia had talked her into going. The seaside town boasted elegant townhouses, graced with terraces. The Locock residence had a terrace on the first floor that provided an unobstructed view of the sea. Ella would sit with her morning tea watching people promenade by her window.

Anna Maria Locock had chosen to keep the summer home light and airy. There were no heavy brocades draping the furniture. White wicker easy chairs were scattered about the terrace. Small crystal oil lamps were set on lace doilies to provide lighting once dusk fell. The house lacked bric-a-brac. "It will only collect dust and salt," Anna said.

In the mornings Ella woke up disoriented, forgetting where she was when she heard the sounds of the waves crashing onto the shore. At first, she thought she was at Raquette Lake, but then she would smell the salt air, and hear the screeching cries of the gulls instead of the lonely wails of the loons, and realize she was at the seaside. It was one of the few things that made her homesick for the mountains.

If it wasn't the sounds that reminded her where she was, it was the smells. How different the salt air smelled compared to the pine that lingered in the Adirondack air.

Thankfully, there were no biting insects to contend with at the sea. Because of that, the windows had no screens. They were opened in the morning by the maid when the weather was mild, so that Ella woke up to find the drapery fluttering in her bedroom windows like a silk nightgown gently blowing on a laundry line.

In this uncluttered environment, Ella was able to focus on her writing. Anny Ritchie had talked her out of the novel idea, for now anyway, reminding Ella of her more serious devotion to the life of Dante. Ella hadn't touched the long dramatic play on his life since 1881, when Longfellow had read the beginning of it and provided a critique.

She had cast it aside, like so many things, when she had her fall-out with William, and then her father, over her unbecoming behavior with Poultney Bigelow. After spending a year working in the convent with the Sisters of St. Mary, her repentance was complete and she might have picked it up again. But when Longfellow died in 1882, she lost all interest in the project. Until now.

Their days in Brighton were lazy and uneventful. Alfred was a vicar and attended to his business at St. Andrews while Ella, Aunt Sylvia and Anna Maria strolled through the gardens in Palmeira Square. Many times, Ella left the two ladies so she could walk alone to think and stroll along the West Pier. A favorite of the tourists, the pier was laced with cast iron balustrades and anchored by lampposts in the shape of serpents. Whenever the weather permitted, Ella would end up sitting in the glass-enclosed house at the end and watch the gulls dive into the milky-white waves. She would pull out her journal and write.

One morning, while the women were discussing whom they might call on for a visit, Alfred was reading the *Brighton Herald* and tutting over the recent scandals at the racetrack outlined in the race hill cases section of the paper.

"These poor workmen are targets for the welshers!" he said. "They bring their small wages with them and are sucked into believing that they can beat the odds. And if they actually do, the welshers run for it with their money."

"Well, it's not as if the upper classes are free of the same vices," Anna Maria remarked.

Alfred flapped the top half of the *Herald* down and stared pointedly at his wife through his pince-nez. "For goodness sake, Anna, you'd hope if they have enough money to waste on gambling, they would know what they were doing. You won't find men of good station losing their fortunes at the racetrack."

Anna Maria rolled her eyes but didn't protest.

Ella was fascinated. Her father and William used to go to the race tracks at Saratoga, but she was never invited to attend. She was not aware of how bets were made on horses, but she had caught snippets of conversation about the races here in England at Anny's dinner table. And Gabriel, who owned thoroughbreds, took a keen interest in racing.

She wondered if he would be attending the races here in Brighton. Maybe she could find a way to attend herself. Going alone was out of the question, and although her Aunt Sylvia and Anna Maria were good company for some things, they were hardly the types to take her.

She soon became obsessed with the idea of finding a way to go racing. She took daily strolls on the pier thinking who might escort her to the tracks. It was at times like these when she really missed William. He would take her anywhere she wanted back in the day. And she knew intuitively Gabriel was at the tracks. It was the height of the tourist season and the Brighton racetrack was one of the main attractions.

She was scheming up ways she might make a trip to the tracks when she happened to see one of William's old friends, Mr. Arkwright, on the pier one afternoon.

"My word, if it isn't Miss Ella Durant!" he exclaimed.

Arkwright's excitement over anything was infectious. He was the last person Ella would have expected to find in Brighton and the first to make her feel thrilled to be there.

"Mr. Arkwright. Wait until I tell William I've bumped into you on the pier!"

"How is the old chap?"

"Doing just fine. A father now you know."

Arkwright laughed. "Yes, I may be the last bachelor left from our group of friends."

"It suits you fine," Ella said. Even when she was younger, she always found it easy to flirt with him.

"And look at you!" He held her at arms length and eyed her up and down as if she were in a window display. "I think the last time I saw you, you were making your debut and Basil Napier was waltzing you about the dance floor at Binstead."

"Yes, I remember." Ella felt a familiar sadness at hearing Basil's name. It had been so long.

Arkwright registered her faltering and realized he had made a mistake in bringing up Basil, who had died while serving in the Royal Navy. "Enough about the old times. I heard you were back. So what brings you to Brighton?"

Ella placed her arm around his outstretched elbow and as they strolled the pier she told him about her comings and goings over the past few months, including the invitation by Alfred Locock to holiday in Brighton. At the end of her story she made sure to emphasize that although she was grateful to her aunt and Mrs. Locock, she was becoming a tad bored with the routine in Brighton, and how, just the other day she thought, wouldn't it be fun to go racing? She knew Arkwright would take her. William had told her once that Arkwright appreciated any sport, but especially those that involved gambling. Playing cards at the clubs on Piccadilly was his favorite pastime. What else do you do when you have loads of money and nobody but yourself to spend it on?

It was a bright sunny day when they arrived at the Brighton racecourse. Ella was taken aback by the throngs of people jostling each other to get to their seats in the grandstand. The excitement in the air was palpable. People were milling about on the lawn, some so close to the track itself that Ella wondered if they might be run over by a horse. The view from the stands was breathtaking: sheep grazed lazily on the rolling downs against the shimmering backdrop of blue-green sea.

They took their seats midway in the stands. Ella lifted her spyglasses up to peer at the horses being traipsed around the track by their riders. She scanned the crowds with her glasses. When her view landed on Count de la Salle, she wasn't surprised. He was sitting next to a woman who appeared elegant in an understated fashion. Ella couldn't tell if she was his companion, or if she was with the man sitting on the other side of her.

"Who is that woman over there?" Ella nudged Arkwright and handed him her glasses.

"That's Lillie Langtry," he said and handed the glasses back to her.

"The actress?" Ella had heard about Lillie Langtry. Her beauty was renowned. She had seduced the Prince of Wales, although from what Ella had heard it wasn't hard to do. It was said that Lillie's marriage was a sham. Her husband, Edward Langtry, didn't do anything about her numerous affairs with royalty and wealthy Americans as these men provided the only income she had while he spent his time drinking away his inheritance.

One evening, at a dinner party, Lillie over-indulged in champagne and mischievously dropped a small ice cube down the Prince's back. The Prince was not amused, and immediately dismissed her as his mistress.

"She buys thoroughbreds specifically to sell them at a profit.

Quite the entrepreneur that one," Arkwright said. "Though I have no idea who that dandy is sitting beside her. Probably another starry-eyed admirer," he continued, speaking about Gabriel. "The young man on her left is her American lover, Freddie Gebhard."

Ella began to fidget in her seat. It took every ounce of effort to pay attention to the racetrack. She discreetly put her spy glasses to her eyes once more and pretended to look out at the horses but quickly brought them back to the object of her attention. Gabriel was gone.

"Tsk," she sighed.

"What is it then?" Arkwright said.

"Oh, it's nothing. I'm just amazed that one woman could have so many lovers," Ella said, hoping to deflect her disappointment at losing sight of Gabriel.

"No surprise there. Gebhard loves wine, women and horses. Lillie likes the attention and money she attracts. They're in business together I believe."

"Yes," she said absently, not really caring about the spoilt American heir, Freddie Gebhard, sitting next to Lillie. *Where had Gabriel gone?*

"Come on." Arkwright took her by the arm. "I'll show you how to place a bet."

They walked down to the lawn in front of the grandstand where the bookmakers pitched their tents and vendors hawked their wares. Ella smelled the aroma of street food as she passed men holding out greasy bags filled with fried fish and jellied eels to anyone who would buy them. Women paraded by in flouncy gowns of pink and muted yellow, clutching large, fringed parasols dancing in the sky above them. Hundreds of tents were pitched with banners proclaiming the names of bookmakers willing to take a bet and assuring prompt payment to those that would make them.

"This is not a place for the amateur punters," Arkwright said to her as he expertly guided her through the throng of people to the tent of a bookmaker he trusted.

"Stay here," he instructed. "Keep your belongings hidden under your shawl, and don't talk to anyone. I'll only be a minute." He ducked inside the tent to get the racing lists for the day.

Arkwright came back shortly and showed her the program, which listed the horses' names and their odds of winning.

"You wager on a horse based on his odds of winning. You have a choice: show, place or win." He showed her the list of horses and their odds.

Ella's head was swimming. It was rather complicated. And the din of the crowd was making it hard for her to concentrate.

Men with hats and badges with the names of bookmakers on them were weaving in and out of the crowds, collecting wagers. They were holding up programs and shouting, "Fivedaone!" and "toodawun!", competing to receive bets from people like Arkwright. And the wealthier, more dressed one was, the more likely they shouted in your face.

Utterly confused, Ella looked at the list and pointed at the name of a horse.

"Dante? To place?" Arkwright said. "But, Ella, he has no chance of winning. Do you see his odds?"

"I like the name," Ella said.

"Of course you do, silly girl, but that's not a reason to choose a horse. See here." He bent over the program with her to scan the list of names and the odds of each horse. "This one, Cleopatra, has good odds."

Ella shook her head firmly and placed a sovereign in Arkwright's palm. He looked down at it and then her before setting off for the bookmaker's tent.

She lost that race but was not deterred. Glancing through the program she found another horse that caught her fancy: Shakespeare's Folly.

"Let's try our luck on this one shall we?" she said.

"Oh no you don't. I can't have your brother accuse me of taking advantage of your naiveté. You must look for better odds and not chance your arm on a horse because his name has some literary significance."

Ella opened her mouth to protest when Gabriel came up to them. Caught off guard, her heart fluttered and she felt her blood pumping.

"Madam Durant," he said and bowed slightly. "It's so good to see you enjoying yourself at the races. I take it you are learning how to place a wager?"

Arkwright eyed Gabriel suspiciously. "I think we have it well under control," he said.

"Oh, excuse me, sir." Gabriel said tersely.

"Mr. Arkwright, may I, I, introduce you to Count de la Salle. Mr. Arkwright is an old family friend, a dear really. He was gracious enough to escort me today to the races." Ella found herself stammering.

"I thought I might offer you a tip." Gabriel smiled warmly at Ella.

"Why of course." Ella smiled back.

"I hear that Shakespeare's Folly will surprise everyone, although the odds are against him."

"That's nonsense," Arkwright said. "I heard he has added weight."

"It's a rumor." Gabriel stared at Arkwright as if he were a dolt.

Ella hoped there would not be a scene. When Arkwright scowled, Gabriel was visibly annoyed.

"I may be wrong, sir," Gabriel said. "But that is unlikely."

He turned to Ella and lifted her hand. She noticed he wore a large ring made of onyx circled by gold filigree.

"It was a pleasure to see you again. I hope it will not be the last time while I am visiting in Brighton," he said.

"Are you visiting friends?" Ella didn't want to miss the opportunity to find out more about him.

"I am letting a cottage near Adelaide Crescent," he said.

"How curious," Ella said.

He raised his brow at her.

"Well, what I mean, is that I'm staying there as well. With friends. The Lococks. Perhaps you know of them?" She hoped he did and would not have to guess or do too much detective work to find out where she was staying. Arkwright cleared his throat and took hold of her arm protectively, but she ignored him.

Gabriel shook his head no, and much to Ella's chagrin, said farewell.

"Well I never. Isn't he a bumptious fellow," Arkwright said. They watched Gabriel become enveloped by the crowd.

Ella pressed another sovereign into Arkwright's hand. "Shakespeare's Folly," she said determinedly.

Arkwright scowled again, but he knew Ella too well to waste his breath arguing. He placed her bet with his bookmaker and they took their seats back in the stands to watch. People were shouting out the names of their favorite horses; bookies were calling out for last minute wagers.

The horses were led onto the tracks and placed on the starting line. Ella tried to find Gabriel.

When the horses took off the crowd cheered wildly. Ella couldn't help herself either, and she shouted out her horse's name. Arkwright joined her. A man to their right, most likely an owner of one of the horses, was gesticulating so wildly he fell forward and was caught by the people in front of him.

It was a close race, but Shakespeare's Folly came in second and she won some money. She and Arkwright jumped up and down with glee.

"Hey, that dandy might have brought us some good luck after all," Arkwright said.

Ella couldn't hide her smug grin as they went back to the bookmaker's tent to collect her winnings.

She came home from the races with a few more coins in her purse than she had brought with her. She made sure not to gloat about it with her aunt or in front of the Lococks when they asked her about her time at the racetrack. It was one thing to attend, another matter entirely to bet. Alfred would not have approved of a woman placing bets on horses.

The day at the track made Ella restless for more excitement than the daily strolls with her aunt and Anna Locock. She hoped Gabriel would find his way to her.

He did. One day, Ella arrived back from her daily stroll on the pier to find he had left his calling card at the Locock's residence. He requested her to meet him for high tea at the gardens the next day. She clutched the card to her chest and ran to her room to find an appropriate gown.

When she arrived at the tea garden, Gabriel was already there, waiting for her. Ella took a moment to watch him from her position at the entrance. His composure was debonair, seated at the table in the tea garden, waiting patiently. He was wearing a light grey morning coat with tails and an ascot the color of dried blood, loosely tied around his neck over a crisp white shirt. Even in the heat he did not appear to be sweating. His long legs were crossed casually and he was staring at the sea. Ella braced herself as the waiter came to escort her to the table.

Gabriel looked pleased as he rose and assisted her to her seat. She was glowing inside and wondered if her eyes were revealing too much.

"You look lovely," he said.

"Thank you." She blushed and played with her gloves.

"I hope you don't mind that I took the liberty of ordering a tray of tea and sandwiches for us," he said.

"Oh, thank you," she said, pulling her gloves off. Stop driveling like a fool, she thought, I must have something to say?

He saved her. "How is your writing coming along?"

"I'm finding that the salt air is doing wonders for my imagination!" she said too quickly and chastised herself internally. But Gabriel didn't seem to mind her exuberance at all. He actually encouraged it.

"Tell me everything you have been doing," he said as he reached across the table and took her fingers in his hands. Ella felt a jolt of excitement by his touch and launched into a description of her activities while visiting the Lococks in Adelaide Crescent.

Gabriel courted her during her stay in Brighton. For two weeks they set off everyday for the racecourse. He would pick her up in his carriage and take her to the course, where they would sit together in the stands and watch the races. Gabriel knew all the bookmakers on a first name basis and would instruct her on which horse to bet on based on the odds and his insider tips. One day she saw Anny's husband, Richmond Ritchie, sitting in the stands with Eleanor Tennyson. She knew Anny was in Aix-en-Provence to take the healing waters for her nerves, and Ella wondered if she knew her husband was with Eleanor.

Ella considered intruding on the pair, if only to remind Richmond where his loyalties lay. *The nerve of him bringing Eleanor to the tracks for everyone to witness.* Did he not realize their affair was the topic of tea parlor gossip? Could Poultney have been correct that they were having an affair? How could he hurt Anny so? She was agonizing about what to do when Gabriel said, "Isn't that Mr. Ritchie? Who is he with?"

"That is Mrs. Tennyson. Mr. Ritchie is assisting Mrs. Tennyson manage her estate after the death of her husband," Ella said.

"Ah. Entertainment is an effective distraction from grief," Gabriel said.

Noting the irony in his voice Ella replied, "Yes." And left it at that.

It was another change Ella perceived in England since she had last been a resident. The days when societal norms reflected Queen Victoria's prudery were being replaced with her son Edward's—the Prince of Wales—penchant for frivolity. Why she felt compelled to lie to her aunt about her visits to the racecourse, she wasn't sure, because everyone else around her seemed to be enjoying themselves without feeling any guilt about it whatsoever.

After visiting the track Gabriel would take Ella out in his carriage to view Brighton and the seaside attractions. Ella wished she knew more about his family. One day she asked him about them.

"Who lives at your estate in Paris?"

Gabriel put his hand over hers and patted it lightly while staring out the window of the carriage. "I manage the estate and my ailing mother still lives there."

Ella waited for him to look at her. When he didn't she said, "I see. And do you have any brothers or sisters?"

"One brother," he turned to her. "We don't talk to each other anymore. He has his own house."

"Why don't you and your brother speak to each other?"

Gabriel's eyes went dark. "I don't want to discuss it."

"I'm sorry to have upset you." Ella removed her hand from under his.

"One day I'll bring you to my home in Paris. But we will wait until the time is right." He smiled down at her. "I don't want to share you with anyone." He kissed her on the lips before she could open her mouth to ask another question.

Ella arrived back at the Locock's residence exhausted after a day spent with Gabriel. Although she knew she wasn't doing anything wrong by spending so much time with him, she felt as if she were leading a double life when she entered the dining room for dinner in the evenings.

"How was your day, dear?" Aunt Sylvia would ask.

"Oh, quite pleasant," she'd say.

"Gabriel took me for a ride along the promenade to view the rose gardens," she'd say.

"Wonderful day for that today," Anna Locock would add.

Alfred would eye her suspiciously and wouldn't encourage the dialogue. Ella knew he was skeptical of Gabriel's intentions, and protective of her. But Ella was thirty-three years old: she knew how to take care of herself and had the means to do so with her monthly allowance. She also knew what she wanted, and that was a life with Count de la Salle.

SEVEN

New York

It always amazed William how efficient the Stott women were at opening up camp for the summer. Janet had learned well from her mother. She ordered the maids to air out the cabins, sweep out the dust, and rake away the pine needles that had fallen around the doors and windows. And when that was done, she went right to work on checking inventory. A mouse had gotten into the supply closets and made a home in the linens so new linens needed to be ordered. Flower pots were filled with geraniums, ivies, and pansies. The footpaths needed to be raked, the sails checked. Janet had a list.

Once these chores were done, it was on to St. Hubert's Isle by steamboat to help her mother and cousins open up the Church of the Good Shepherd. Although it was only May, the churchgoers would be coming in droves by mid-July, and the pews and altar needed dusting, the chalices needed polishing and the vestments had to be cleaned and pressed. It was quite a production to start a summer vacation in the Adirondack Mountains, but the Stott women were up for the task.

While they busied themselves with domestic affairs, the men,

William, his father-in-law, and his brother-in-law, Louis, would engage the Stott family guide to go fishing. Sometimes William's friend, Dr. Arpad Gerster would join them, and sometimes, if she could get away from the domestic responsibilities imposed on her as a woman, Janet's cousin, Julia, would tag along. Julia was never without a fishing rod when she visited the Stotts in the Adirondacks.

Julia managed in one day to catch thirty trout at Brown Tract Pond. Her annual haul of fish was a proud feature of the Stotts' camp diary.

William enjoyed spending time with Julia. She reminded him of Ella, back before her temperament became too difficult, before Poultney Bigelow ruined her reputation.

Ever since Janet's marriage to William, Julia Stott had been coming with her aunt and uncle to help them open up their camp compound on Raquette Lake at Bluff Point. Julia stayed in the cabin the Stotts called the Spinsterage. The Stotts had been threatening to tear down the old cabin and rebuild it with a new name, but Julia insisted that if they were to do anything they must at least keep the name intact. She was proud of the fact she was still single, declaring to anyone that asked her that she had turned down at least a dozen marriage proposals. Julia was the same age as William and more mature than Janet in many ways. Her tom boyishness and natural athleticism had a lot to do with growing up in a family of boys. Unlike Janet, she had a positive attitude toward sports.

The summer of William's engagement to Janet, Francis Stott had decided he wanted to brush up on his skills as a Commodore and asked Julia, Janet, and some of the neighboring girls to be the crew on his large guideboat, the *Ariel*. "It would be such fun!" he had said.

He had them all dress as sailors and outfitted them with a large black, embroidered *A*, which Mrs. Stott had crafted and pinned onto their cotton jerseys. The Stotts were all about staging events, from theater to musicales. This was just another example of their fondness for such productions.

Janet, William recalled, didn't take to the idea of wearing the cotton jersey her mother had made for her.

"I feel like Hester Prynne in the *Scarlet Letter*," she said, pulling at her jersey with the letter *A* emblazoned on the front and pouting.

William put his hand under her chin and said, "Chin up now, your father has high hopes for you as his crew." He thought it would make Janet laugh, but it didn't.

Her father then lined them all up to have their picture taken before launching his boat on the water. They stood in a row saluting the camera. William would often glance at the picture that sat in a frame over the mantel at the Stott family camp. Janet appeared stoic in it, but her eyes gave her away, she was miserable.

The Stotts were not fussy, and they were well adapted to lake life. Mrs. Stott, unlike William's own mother, never let the bugs bother her too much. She rarely complained, unlike Hannah and Margaret, who always complained about the insects. Neither of them would step foot in Pine Knot until mid-August when the bugs were not as pesky.

During the summer months William and Janet closed their home in Saratoga and stayed at Pine Knot. Between William's cousins, Howard, Frederick, and Charles — all of whom had camps nearby — and the Stotts, William and Janet had plenty of social events to keep them occupied during the summer months in the Adirondacks. The Stotts were always extending invitations to visit them at their camp on Bluff Point. William and Janet would take the steamboat there in the evenings, have dinner, and stay up late playing card games such as euchre. Then they would sit back in the easy chairs on the porch to watch the moon rise while the women gossiped and the men burnt tobacco.

William and Janet would head back to Pine Knot by steamboat, often under a moonlit sky.

The Durant steamboat line was doing a brisk business, thanks in part to the hotels springing up on the lakes between Blue Mountain and Raquette. His cousin Frederick's Prospect House Hotel on Blue Mountain Lake attracted newcomers each year, many eager to tour the lakes. And the Durant steamboat line made it easier to travel from Blue Mountain Lake to Raquette Lake. William's life was mostly serene; things were going well for his family financially. His only concern was Ella.

Her recent letters were pleas to him for a bigger allowance and pestering questions about when the sale of the railroad would be finalized. Her letters to his mother provided more detail about her life in England, but he suspected she was glossing over anything that might appear scandalous. He tried to find clues in her letters that would hint at why she was in need of more than her monthly allowance and the occasional checks Hannah sent. But she never revealed too much, except to say that her social life was a 'whirlwind' and didn't he miss it sometimes? William would throw her letters aside whenever she tried to entice him to admit that he too longed to experience the social life in England again with some of his dearest friends. But that wasn't his life now. His life was this: his Adirondack ventures, Pine Knot, his wife, child, and extended family.

Poultney offered more details about what was really going on in England with Ella, thanks partly to his investigatory skills, and partly because he was, from what William could detect in his letters, jealous. Ella had found a new infatuation. Which meant her attraction to Poultney was finally waning. A good thing, considering he was married.

But Poultney's latest letter, which William had just received, was disturbing.

Dear William,

I hope all is well with you and your family. Please tell Janet I say hello. I have some news for you concerning your interests here in England. James Muirhead, the editor for Baedeker, is interested in pursuing your idea for a guide on the Adirondacks. I have told him that he might want to give prominence to such centers of natural beauty as the Adirondacks and am sure that sentiment echoes with you. It will prove to be a valuable article for you to use to promote your business interests to the gentry here as a tourist destination worth investing in.

Now as for Ella. I regret to tell you that her behavior is unbecoming a Durant. She has been seen quite frequently with a gentleman from Paris who claims to be titled; a man, I'm afraid, of dubious character. However, you know as well as I do that your sister does not like to be told with whom she can associate, nor what she should or should not be doing with her social life. Your Aunt Sylvia is getting on in age and is completely oblivious as to Ella's whereabouts half the time. I am afraid that Ella may have taken up with this French aristocrat. I am trying to discover more about him. All that I have been able to ascertain is that he has some family ties in Paris and is in the business of racing thoroughbreds. He surrounds himself with the theater crowd, something Ella finds highly engaging.

He is also seen quite often at the clubs playing cards. But then most men of his station are, so it is not something I can rightfully say alarms me. I have not yet heard if he owes any great debts.

As I said, Ella is completely smitten with him. She barely acknowledged me at a recent shooting party at the Napier's Manor home in Thirlestane. If anything changes, or I hear any other news about this fellow I will be sure to inform you.

Yours sincerely, Poultney Bigelow

William put the letter away in his desk when he heard Janet's footfall on the steps leading to his cabin.

"Are you ready for church, dear?" she said as she entered.

William always assumed the reason his father had commissioned building the Episcopal Church on St. Hubert's Isle was to attract and keep people like the Stotts content to spend their summer months in the Adirondacks. Why else? Except for the obligatory Christmas and Easter visits, his parents were never church-goers. It was one of the reasons why his father had an apoplectic fit when Ella went into the convent to do charity work. Philanthropy and church work were not what the Durants were known for. There could only be one reason she entered the convent, his father would say: "because she was disgraced."

William glanced around the church. Besides the tourists in town for a summer holiday, the usual cast of families was there: his cousins Charles, Frederick and Howard with their respective wives, the Stotts, and the Lounsburys—whose family seemed to be growing exponentially.

They came flocking every Sunday once Mrs. Stott rang the church bell.

"And let us not forget that in these dark days we can trust in God to see the light." The Pastor woke William out of his day-dreaming.

"Amen to that," Mrs. Stott whispered as she waved a small fan over her face. "This smoke shuts down on us like a pall."

Over the past few days the sky had taken on a dull yellow appearance, and the sun was never seen. People were blaming it on the sparks that flew out of the smoke stacks of the railroad engines. The layers of accumulated duff on the surrounding forest floor were tinder for the flames that quickly got out of control. The recent streak of dry weather didn't help matters either.

On the way home from church in the steamboat, the ladies complained as ash fell from the sky and landed on their finest skirts.

The next day, William and Arpad left at 4 a.m. with their guides for a hunting and fishing trip. Their destination that morning was the South Inlet where they knew they'd find deer wallowing in the shallows. A swift breeze cleared the smog from the forest fires, and the morning air was fresh for the first time in days. Looking over their shoulder they could see the red haze of the sun climbing over the foothills of Blue Mountain. There were few sounds in the air except the birds waking up and loons wailing in the distance. They meandered downstream along a winding waterway lined with pickerel and lily pads, with spiraling larch trees sprouting from dregs of soil in the distant swamp. A kingfisher swooped over them and dove into the water after a small fish. He grabbed it in his beak and landed on a tree limb to eat it.

Two deer came into view ahead of them. They slowed their boats and drifted without a sound. William lifted his Winchester rifle and fired. He missed. Arpad brought his rifle up quickly before the other one bolted. He hit his target.

"Good show!' William congratulated him.

They pulled over to the dead animal, and Alvah lifted it into the boat.

"Jerome, if you would, row it back to Big Island. We'll meet you at Sumner Lake," William said to his guide.

"I'll do it," Alvah grumbled. "I ain't too old for it ya know."

Arpad got into William's boat and they let Alvah take the deer.

"He's in one of his sour moods," William said, as they watched him row away.

"He lost his favorite timepiece this morning while we were rowing out here," Arpad said. "And as you know, he doesn't own many things. He was very fond of it."

They rowed until they reached a small waterfall, where they got out of their boats to portage around it. Jerome Wood carried the boat from a yoke attached to one of the seats—a design specific to these guideboats—while William and Arpad carried the packs with their supplies.

At Sumner Lake, they unpacked their things in the small cabin William had built for their overnight outings. While Jerome Wood set up camp and prepared their lunch, they dropped their lines and sat back to enjoy the sun which had been missing from the sky for the past few days.

"I've been thinking, Arpad," William said, "of building a proper hunting lodge on Mohegan Lake."

"Hmmm," Arpad said.

Mohegan Lake, which William named after the Indian tribe in *The Last of the Mohicans*, was a small, reclusive lake. It was where he thought at one time he would live with Louise. The lake was set back in the woods, miles from the nearest road, and unlike Raquette, the shoreline was entirely devoid of summer homes.

"Do you mean to build another camp that would rival Pine Knot?"

William took a moment to answer. "I'm thinking of something entirely different. More like a country manor."

"I'd enjoy that better then. Not that Pine Knot isn't wonderful. But all of these new places going up around Raquette with their turrets and gingerbread trim strike me as out of place," he said in his thick Hungarian accent.

William didn't say anything. That was one of the many things Arpad and Alvah shared in common: a disdain for the tourists descending on the region and disturbing their solitude.

"And the gimcracks and what-nots they insist on buying to fill up the space on the walls and mantels! It's ridiculous," Arpad said in disgust.

William smiled. His own cabin was sparse, but Janet and her mother had decorated one of the main lodges at Pine Knot, the chalet, in such an eclectic manner. One could find the latest craze in décor: Oriental parasols and fans hanging from the ceiling, deer head mounts, or snow shoes lining the walls. Admittedly, it was rather an odd combination.

They continued to fish, not saying much of anything. When the sun hit the center of the sky, they sat in the shade along the shore to picnic on cheese, bread and wine.

"Let's hike over to Mohegan and I'll show you where I'm thinking of building a camp." William looked at Arpad hopefully.

"Oh alright," Arpad said, "you've twisted my arm." He took his right arm in his left hand and mock-twisted it. William clapped him on the back. They hiked on flat ground through an ancient trail made by deer and the first hunters in the region that tracked them. Jerome Wood walked ahead of them, thwacking away at the low hanging branches and brambles with his machete to clear the way.

When they got to the shore William said, "This is where I plan to build it. I'm going to call it Uncas. I own over one thousand acres of land around here."

That evening, Alvah joined them for a dinner of fried perch, fresh asparagus, and wine. They sat around the campfire and listened to Alvah tell one of his many tales. This one was about a bear he'd single-handedly killed.

"It was late spring, and the bears were comin' out of hibernation and looking for food. Mrs. Carter was all worked up cos a bear had been gettin' into her garbage and tearin' up the yard looking for scraps of food. She'd had enough of him already when one day he started chasin' after her cat. Now that cat was a good mouser and she didn' take too kindly to this bear trying to eat him for breakfast. She gone and grabbed her pots and pans and like a crazy woman she chased him out on the ice." He turned and spat a gob of tobacco juice onto the ground next to him.

"That lady's fearless, no doubt," Jerome Wood piped in.

"Either that or crazy," William laughed.

"Well her husband was away at the lumber camps but one of her neighbors heard her hollerin' out on the ice and came runnin' out with his rifle and took a shot at the bear. Was only able to hit him in the leg though." He poked at the fire with his stick, and they watched as the coals glowed red and sparks flew into the dark night sky.

"Someone comes and finds me in my cabin and tells me there's a bear loose on the lake. I grab my rifle and snowshoes and take off looking for him. He wasn't hard to track; he's dragging blood behind on the snow. I get close up to him and he rears on his hind legs." Alvah stood up, lifted his arms in the air and put his hands in a claw-like posture. He made a frightening spectacle in the glow of the fire.

"I didn't have time to think, or shoot. I just hit him in the head with the butt of my gun, like this." He picked up his rifle that lay on the ground beside him and gestured in the air with the butt of his gun. "Flattened him." He spat again.

The men sat silently taking it in. *Had he actually pummeled a bear to death?* William was skeptical. Alvah's yarns were amusing, but one never could tell what was made up and what was real. Either way, it didn't matter. The night sky was twinkling with starlight, the fire was glowing, and William knew it was times like these when he felt most akin to Alvah and the other guides, a moment, however brief, when they were all on equal footing.

John Barbour came to visit Pine Knot a few weeks later and brought with him so good news: Sutphen had found a buyer for the Adirondack Railroad Company.

"The Hudson Delaware Railroad is interested," Barbour told him over an after-dinner coffee on the porch of the chalet.

"And what price are they willing to pay?"

Now that the Adirondack Railroad Company was debt-free, its value to a prospective buyer had increased considerably. Sutphen used the money obtained from mortgaging the Durant lumber mill to expediently and anonymously purchase Adirondack Railroad Company stocks in Janet's name. As Barbour had predicted, the stockholders were willing and eager to unload their stock at less than half of its original value. Unknowingly, Janet became the company's second biggest creditor after Hannah. William had to admit Sutphen and Barbour were right. Their plan to rid the railroad of the debt was ingenious.

William felt Janet needn't know the role she played in the whole deal. She obediently signed the relevant documents on William's instructions without question, vaguely aware of what was occurring but unwilling to ask too many questions, knowing William would only become annoyed with her for doing so.

Not that Janet had time to worry about his business anyway. If she wasn't tending to baby Lawrence, she was with her mother or cousin planning another minstrel show at Bluff Point, or the annual church festival.

William looked from Barbour to the lake. He had plans with the money he would make. He wanted to build his hunting cabin on Mohegan Lake and to do it right would require funds. He was also making some deals with colleagues to sell off parcels of land. Members of the Association for the Protection of the Adirondacks, who met once a month on Wall Street, had invited him to one of their meetings. They were interested in setting up preserves where they could hunt and fish without running into tourists.

"Will the sale of the railroad net me enough profit to continue with my business enterprises here?"

"The price will depend on how much land you are willing to sell along with it," Barbour informed him.

"I'd like to expand the steamboat line. Perhaps have a couple more boats built for it."

"It's a risky proposition, William, to put all of your eggs in one basket, as they say. Although the region is quite popular with tourists, you'd be better off leasing your land for the rights to the lumber interests. There is a new technology that can turn pulp into paper using any type of tree. A German has patented it. With the new state restrictions, your land becomes more valuable as a resource than a place to build a vacation home. I heard that Anson Blake sold his rights to cut the trees and made a cool three hundred thousand. After the lumber company has harvested," he continued, "Blake can sell the land to whoever wants it next."

William contemplated this. He was meeting Collis Huntington again for dinner. Unlike his father's fortune, Huntington's investments were relatively unscathed from the financial panic of 1873. It might be wise to ask his father's competitor his thoughts on the subject.

"I'll think about all of this and get back to you on it in a month or so," William said and turned to Barbour. "In the meantime, Mrs. Callahan has made a lemon meringue that she insists is your favorite. Let's find our wives and join them, shall we?"

PART THREE

1887

EIGHT

England

Ella was in her room pacing the floor, furious. Poultney Bigelow was meddling in her affairs and she had had enough. It had to have been Poultney who informed William about Count de la Salle. How else would William know about her courtship with him?

> *Dearest Ella,*
>
> *I understand you've been making a fool of yourself publically with some Frenchman. Dear sister, please try not to repeat your past mistakes. For God's sake, if you have to go out socially request an escort with one of our family friends or cousins.*
>
> *In regards to your request for more money, I confess that for the life of me I cannot understand why you would need it. Have you already spent your savings? The monthly allowance Mother sends you should be more than enough to cover your expenses. I will consider your request and discuss it with John Barbour. But*

*given the circumstances of your latest social escapades I am not
certain you can be trusted with more money.*

*Janet sends her warmest regards. She is once again in
confinement. The baby is due in June.*

Your brother affectionately, William W. Durant

She flung the letter into the coals. It was Poultney's fault that her
brother thought her a fool and all so apparent why: the grouse
hunting party at the Napiers' country manor in Thirlestane.

Unbeknownst to her, when Bill Napier invited her to the party,
Poultney was also on the guest list. She was sure he had wheedled
his way onto it by asking William to send an introduction to Bill.
Ella now wished she hadn't attended, but when Gabriel left for
business in Paris, she couldn't stand the idea of being left to do
nothing but sit with Aunt Sylvia reading by the fire. So she went.

Her visit started out well enough. The autumn weather was
brilliant. On the morning after her arrival, they waited on the moors
with their breechloaders for the men on the ridge to flush out the
birds. They lifted their guns and took aim. The birds came raining
down, and the dogs howled with excitement as they ran into the
moors to retrieve the prey. The air was crisp and lovely. Billowy
clouds drifted across blue skies. It was a perfect day. And then there
was dinner, which was when Poultney showed up. The guests were
working their way into the parlor, and all eyes turned when he
swept into the front hall with a flourish.

"So sorry to be late," he said, as if his arrival was what everyone
had been waiting for. He stood before them, taking in the crowd,
his sandy hair windblown, his eyes sparkling, and his complexion
ruddy, arrogantly tossing his frock coat and top hat at the startled
butler. When Poultney's eyes landed on hers, he broke out in a
devilish grin. Her heart leapt, and then sank, when she reminded
herself he was married.

She reprimanded herself for gaping at him, and then turned
quickly toward the parlor. Why had *he* been invited? When he

ended up beside her at the dinner table she knew it was a conspiracy. Napier's wife Harriet shot her a guilty look, and Bill appeared downright embarrassed when Poultney sat down for dinner.

"My, Poultney," Ella plastered a false smile on her lips as she addressed him, "I had no idea you were so friendly with Bill Napier."

"Oh, yes, we're acquainted through your brother. He may have told you that I'm assisting with a Baedeker for the Adirondacks? He suggested I talk to Mr. Napier about how best to market it."

Ella acted nonchalant although inside she was seething. William never told her about the Baedeker, or that he was corresponding with Poultney. Why on earth he thought a travel guide would entice wealthy landowners in England to invest in his Adirondack schemes was beyond her. From what she was hearing at the tea parlors, they had enough financial worries to contend with at home: tenant uprisings, downward spiraling prices for agricultural crops, and country estates that were falling apart. Besides, why involve Poultney when William knew how much she detested him?

"I've heard all about it," she lied. "I can't imagine it will do any good," she added with spite.

Poultney just laughed at her. "So I guess you haven't heard about William's land deals?"

His superior tone of voice infuriated her. But she refused to take the bait. Reaching for her glass of claret, she sniffed and said, "I know all about the Durant business, thank you."

"Really?" Poultney took his glass up as well and raised it to her in a toast. "Congratulations then."

Ella cocked her brow.

"You have no idea do you?"

Ella gulped, looked ahead of her and remained silent. She could feel a bead of perspiration forming on her upper lip. She put her glass down and raised her napkin to dab it away.

Poultney waited for a reaction and garnering none, put his own glass down and sighed.

"I know you too well. You're bluffing and I can't keep it from you anymore. William sold some of the landholdings and I hear it turned quite a profit for the family." He waited for a response. When she still refused to give him that satisfaction he took a sip of his wine and said casually, "How is that friend of yours? The Count?"

Ella glanced sideways to see if anyone was listening. Thankfully, they were all engrossed in their own conversations and no one was paying any attention to her and Poultney, not surprising, as they were the only Americans at the table.

"I would prefer not to discuss my private life," Ella lowered her voice and leaned into Poultney, "especially here." She glanced around the table to emphasize the need for discretion in front of her brother's closest friend and acquaintances.

Poultney eyed the dinner table guests as well, then turned his gaze back to her. "Very well. But we need to talk."

Good lord, she thought. Not again.

And so it went. When dinner was over, and while the women were ushered back into the parlor to gossip, and the men retreated to the drawing room to smoke their cigars, Poultney took Ella by the arm and escorted her into the library while no one was looking. It was becoming all so familiar.

"Poultney, you cannot keep dragging me about whenever you feel the need to accost me! Our friends will catch on and think it undignified of you," she said in an attempt to make light of his boorish behavior.

"Shut up and sit down," he said, pointing to a chair.

Ella was horrified. "Don't speak to me that way!" she said.

"I do so for your own good Ella," he continued. "You were always a spoiled girl and never listened to anyone, including your brother. But I'm not him, and I'm telling you, you must listen to what I have to say."

Ella was frightened and sat down.

"I've been doing some digging into the affairs of that Count of yours."

"Pfft." Ella immediately got up to leave.

"Hear me out, I say!" Poultney practically shouted at her. "He's been implicated in some racketeering at the betting parlors on Williamson Street."

Ella curtailed her exit to the door and stood looking at him.

"We all know those parlors are illegal. I hardly think Gabriel would get involved in such shady practices as the bookmakers that prey on the innocent drunks in those establishments. He buys and sells horses. That's probably why you've heard his name cast about in those crowds." Ella waved her hand at him dismissively.

"Don't be so naïve, it doesn't become you." His eyes bored into hers and she diverted her gaze to the book shelves.

"I'll be sure to bring this up with him the next time I see him," she said absently.

"When will that be?"

Ella whirled around. "You are not my keeper. You missed that opportunity when you seduced me and then scampered off, ashamed, like a dog with his tail between his legs, after we were found out."

His face fell. She had hit her mark.

"I was just a college boy then. Don't you think we could bury that hatchet and remain friends? There was a time when I found favor in your eyes."

She felt herself soften but shook off the thought of reconciliation.

"You're a man now. A married man," she reminded him. "I must return to the party. People will be wondering where I am." She gathered her skirts and strode toward the door.

He beat her to it and blocked her way. "I'll always love you, Ella," he said, gently pulling her toward him and kissing her lightly on the lips. She held back tears as she pushed him aside and fled the room.

If William was going to try and hold her inheritance hostage for what he deemed her inappropriate behavior, he could go to hell. The London solicitors she hired were unsuccessful, but an American lawyer might hold more sway with William. Ella had found another lawyer to take care of her affairs; this one had an office on Wall Street. She planned to inform William via John Barbour; *two could play at this game.* She rang the bell for her maid and sat down at her desk.

Her maid, Trixie, appeared at the door. "You rang, Miss Durant?"

"Yes. Draw a bath for me, I'll be dining out tonight. And press my red, no, violet, gown."

"Yes, Miss Durant. Will you be wearing any of your jewels tonight?"

Ella thought for a moment: diamonds or emeralds?

"Yes, you can take my emeralds out and dust them."

When Trixie left with her gown, Ella lifted her pen.

> *Dear Mr. Barbour, William wrote to me last May that nearly a year must elapse before Father's estate could be settled, and advised me to select a lawyer of unblemished reputation to examine any interests of mine. I have therefore, selected Mr. T. Ritch of the firm of Arnoux, Ritch and Woodford, 18 Wall Street, as he was strongly recommended to me. I should always be glad to hear from you socially as well as professionally 'Uncle Jack' and hope you let me know the results soon.*
> *Sincerely Yours, Heloise (Ella) Durant*

William would not hide the sale of the Railroad Company from her. She would insist he reveal the accounts of the recent land sales as well, and deposit her share of the profits into her London bank account. Satisfied with what she had written, she sealed it and placed it on the desk for tomorrow's post. Her bath was ready, and so was she for a night at the theater and then dinner with Gabriel.

Sarah Bernhardt drew a standing ovation for her role in *Camille.* There was not a dry eye during her death scene. Ella could understand why American audiences considered this particular play vulgar. If one did not understand the French language, the tragic love story about the courtesan, *La Dame aux camélias,* and the whimsy of the actors' tête-à-tête, could be misinterpreted. The play was, at one time, banned in London. All the more reason that American audiences flocked to see it when the production came to New York City.

"Pierre Berton invited us to Madam Bernhardt's dressing room afterward," Gabriel whispered in Ella's ear while they applauded.

When they arrived at the door to Sarah Bernhardt's dressing room, Gabriel's friend, Pierre Berton, welcomed them. He was the actor credited for launching Bernhardt's career when nobody else believed that her brilliant blue eyes would be enough to attract audiences.

The dressing room was full of famous people: Lillie Langtry, Sir Henry Irving, and his assistant, Bram Stoker, Oscar Wilde, and Bernhardt's husband, actor Jacques Damala.

Damala sat in a chair in the corner of the dressing room watching the people come and go with his dark glowering stares in what Ella guessed was a morphine-induced stupor. Sarah was engrossed in a conversation with another actor. She had changed from her stage costume into a pale green evening gown made of velvet and long gloves that almost reached her shoulders. On her head sat a small band made of the same velvet material planted with a large ostrich feather.

Ella felt she had been lifted up into the sky, where she was a spectator looking down on the party. When the Prince of Wales and his entourage entered the room, she was awestruck.

Wait until I write to William about this, she thought. He will not be the only one to have met the Prince.

The guests parted to make room for the Prince's wide girth as he swaggered over to Sarah to offer her a bouquet of flowers. He brushed her cheek with the back of his hand in a gesture that suggested more than brotherly affection, said a few words to her discreetly, and then left just as abruptly as he came, acknowledging the small curtseys and bows from the company, but not interested in small talk.

The night couldn't have been more perfect. After the theater, they dined at the Café Royal, a favorite of the French expatriates in London, where they feasted on foie gras, lamb with a mint sauce, and champagne. While finishing their meal with a glass of port, Gabriel finally noticed her new emeralds.

"Those emeralds look stunning against your black hair. Are they an heirloom?" he inquired as he lit a cigarette.

"These? No. They are a gift, from my brother." Ella fingered the emerald pendant self-consciously.

Gabriel was pleased. "They are beautiful, but they cannot compete with your own beauty."

He extinguished his cigarette, took her hand in his and said, "Where shall we go next?"

Ella had expected this question. For months now their flirtations were becoming more serious. When an evening was coming to an end, they would ride around the city, fondling each other in the back of the cab and delaying their inevitable separation. Ella knew Gabriel wanted to consummate their relationship just as much as she did.

But it was impossible for them to go to his place. He shared a townhouse with a colleague Ella had never met. "A family friend," he'd tell her. And going back to Aunt Sylvia's was usually out of the question—except tonight. Ella hadn't told him yet, but Sylvia was away visiting a sick relative in Portsmouth. The only people at the Chelsea townhouse were Ella's personal maid, Trixie, and the butler. If they waited long enough, both would be asleep. Ella had told them not to wait up for her.

She sipped her wine and found the courage to say what she had been waiting to all night. "I think I know a place we can go, at least for tonight. My aunt's house."

Gabriel's eyes lit. She had surprised him.

Ella backtracked a little. "Only for an hour or so, until my Aunt Sylvia returns from her own evening out."

"It would be my pleasure," he said.

The house was quiet when they entered.

Ella watched tentatively as Gabriel examined the family portraits and porcelain figurines her aunt collected and showcased.

Without saying a word, he walked over to the settee, sat down on it, and patted the seat next to him, gesturing for her to sit down.

Ella was suddenly nervous. The room was dark except for the glow from the candles she had lit. She took a seat across from him instead. He had an unusual smile on his face, which made her stomach twist.

"Your aunt. She's not coming back tonight, is she?"

When Ella nodded yes, he patted the seat next to him again and said nothing. His eyes were hidden by shadows and appeared hooded, forbidding and inviting at the same time.

Ella felt her legs tremble as she walked across the carpet to sit down next to him. He took her in his arms and kissed her. First gently, then urgently. Ella was pliant in his embrace. He reached for the buttons behind the neck of her gown and undid each one expertly until her bodice lay loosely around her bare shoulders. He slid it over her breasts, revealing her camisole.

He handled her corset with the same dexterity. While he reached for her breasts, she found herself undoing his shirt buttons. Her hands trembled in expectation and she fumbled with them. He helped her and they held each other close as they kissed. After so many years of denying herself any pleasure, Ella felt the pure bliss of his warm skin against hers. Gabriel's deft, assured hands seemed to know her body better than she did herself, as every touch magnified her pleasure until her need for him became almost painful. When Gabriel finally moved her under him on the settee and finished what he had started, she felt released.

Aunt Sylvia's stay with her sick relative was extended, and so for a couple of weeks they met clandestinely at the townhouse. But both of them were tired of trying to avoid the attention of her butler, and the settee was inconvenient for making love. When her aunt sent word she was on her way back, Ella was determined to find her own place.

"I've been meaning to anyway," she said one night to Gabriel, after they had made love and were sitting by the fireplace on the Oriental rug, both of them naked. Gabriel stood up and found the mink coat she had carelessly discarded on the floor, impatient as always to make love as soon as they entered the parlor. He draped it around her.

"You look divine in mink," he said.

He uncorked a bottle of wine, then poured and handed her a glass. The butler was taking a short vacation and Trixie was snoring away in her bed, discreetly oblivious to the lovers.

"But can you afford to?" he asked as he lifted a spray of hair from her eyes and placed it back on top of her head. He looked at her adoringly.

"Now that my brother's affairs are settled I'll have the funds to pay the rent and afford a maid," she said.

Which was true. She had received a note from her New York lawyers that William had deposited five thousand dollars into her account. He sent a note along with it stating it was her share of recent transactions on the estate and not to anticipate more for months to come as the sale of the railroad might take years. It would do, Ella thought. Because now she could move into a place on Cavendish Square and lead the independent life she had been longing for since she left her father's home in North Creek.

NINE

New York

William's attention was focused on a map of plans for Camp Uncas when Janet knocked lightly on the door and then entered his study. He rolled the map up quickly and put it in his desk drawer so that the only thing on his desk when she came up behind him was a layout of the new cottage he and Janet would share at Pine Knot.

"What's this, dear?" Janet said. William felt her taut, expansive belly bulging through her gown against his shoulder as she leaned over him.

"It will be the ceiling of our cottage," he said.

"I don't understand. Why are all of these limbs crisscrossing like that?"

"Those are trusses. They are needed to hold the ceiling up and I like the exposed style," he said, looking at her, and then down at the paper.

"Hmmm, I see," she said.

"What is it? You don't like it?"

"No, dear, it's nothing." She smiled weakly at him.

This was a Stott trait. She would avoid saying what she really meant by posing it as a question instead: "Why are you doing it *that* way? Do we *really* have to attend dinner at the Barbour's house tonight?" And whenever he tried to prise out of her the exact meaning of her question, she would look at him as if he would never understand anyway, so why bother? William found this irritating. The Durants usually made their opinions known, often forcefully.

He folded the paper and placed it back in his desk drawer, returned a wan smile, and waited for her to say something else. She picked up on his cue that he no longer wanted to be disturbed.

"Dinner will be in an hour," she said. She waddled across the floor to the door, closing it firmly behind her.

A few days later, William was in Sutphen's office once again. Thankfully they were finished with the unsavory business of buying the company stock in Janet's name. This time, William was on a mission to discern the prospects for selling the railway.

"I did have an interested buyer," Sutphen said from across his enormous desk. He sounded ill at ease, which caught William off-guard. Sutphen was usually so composed.

"Who is it?" William asked.

"Collis P. Huntington." Sutphen studied William as if gauging his reaction.

William was surprised. When he met Huntington for dinner a while back, Collis had inquired about the railroad, seemingly out of polite curiosity, nothing more.

"And what is he willing to pay for it? Does he have plans to take it all the way to Canada as my father envisioned?"

"I'm afraid I can't say what he envisions. I highly doubt he is in a position now to make any negotiations with us while the Pacific Railway Commission is grilling him and other colleagues of your father's about what is owed to the government for building the transcontinental line."

William looked past Sutphen and out the window at the skyline of Manhattan. *The man certainly had a high priced view of New York City.*

William brought his attention back to Sutphen. "But what about it?"

"About what?" Sutphen said.

"What are the chances of taking the railroad to Canada?"

Sutphen canted his head to one side and stared up at the light dangling from the ceiling. He smirked as if something were wrong and removed his spectacles. "In the current investment climate, highly unlikely," he said, taking a handkerchief out of his waistcoat and rubbing his glasses. "Besides, the state and public in general are not too keen on deeding over any more land to the railroads. Anti-railroad sentiment is at its peak, you know, especially in the Adirondacks where everyone is blaming the smoke exhaust from the trains for the massive forest fires in the region."

He placed his glasses back where they belonged above the bridge of his nose and clasped his hands together before resting them on his vest. "Besides, the state won't exempt corporate lands from taxation anymore. Those days are over. Your father knew it was coming one day; he just never got the chance to unload his landholdings before his death. You do realize the Company now has a considerable tax bill?" He eyed William.

"Of course, of course." William wished he could slap the condescending look off Sutphen's face. He decided it was time to get some answers out of him. "So why would Huntington have a meeting with *you* then? And not talk to *me* about his plans?"

Sutphen averted his eyes. "I have absolutely no idea," he said.

William recalled what his father had once said about Sutphen: he worked for the highest bidder.

Sutphen pulled out his pocket watch. "I have another appointment. Is there anything else I can do for you?" He smiled pleasantly at William.

"No." William lifted himself off the chair. He knew when Sutphen was stonewalling him; it had happened many times before. Instead, he sent a message to Collis Huntington, asking him to meet for dinner at William's hotel suite.

"Railrogue! That's what the press is calling me! To hell with them all," Collis blustered while they sat drinking their port after dinner a few days later. "I'm telling you, William, if your father were alive today he would never stand for this! These commissioners appointed by Cleveland are idiots. Asking the most asinine questions. Did you know they're making seven hundred and fifty dollars a month to pour over the Central Pacific books? Why, I can make that much in a day." He gulped his port and slammed the glass down on the table.

William reached over with the decanter and filled Huntington's glass. He had hardly gotten a word in through dinner. Huntington spent the whole time fuming about the Railway Commission hearings at which he'd just testified, and was in a mood to vent.

"Father was hardly healthy enough to withstand the scrutiny before he died," William said.

"It may have been a blessing that he died when he did then. Pardon me for saying so." Huntington took up his glass and nodded his thanks to William for refilling it.

"Which brings up an issue I wanted to speak to you about." He leaned closer to William. "Your father's files. Did you ever hear him talk about a particular set of files he kept regarding his involvement with the Credit Mobilier corporation?"

William felt his pulse quicken. He would rather forget about his father's role in the Credit Mobilier scandal that tarnished the family's reputation. The construction company, which his father set up for the Union Pacific, bribed congressmen to look the other way while he swindled the government out of millions by over-charging for construction of the transcontinental line. It had made his father very wealthy as a result.

"My father was never legally implicated in the scandal, you know that," William said.

"We both know he was in it up to his ears," Huntington said as he sliced the air with his hand. "That's not the point. I want to know what he did with all of the documents."

"Even if that were true, what makes you think my father would keep evidence that might implicate him in any way?"

Huntington laughed shortly. "You know your father. He was always a risk-taker. Do you think he would have gotten rid of anything that might prove useful in defending himself if it became necessary?"

William considered how to phrase his next question and decided to take his cue from Huntington's directness. "Surely that might be said to apply to you also."

"Yes, but I was in a more," he paused briefly, "delicate position over Central Pacific. I disposed of any papers that I deemed *distasteful*, shall we say. Your father, on the other hand, kept it all. He had an artillery that could bring down any politician that dared to cross him."

William was perplexed. "Why not ask Sutphen? He has been in charge of my father's railroad affairs for years."

"I already did," Huntington sighed and then leaned back once he realized William didn't have what he was seeking.

"And he said what?"

"He has no idea where your father kept these documents. He told me there were many things your father kept from him. A sly man, your father, that's for sure." Huntington rubbed his chin thinking back about his days working to beat his adversary to win the most land and gain the most wealth from laying tracks across the western frontier.

In the silence, William wondered if this was the true reason Huntington was taking an interest in the Adirondack Railroad Company: to get access to documents he could use to blackmail the people who were persecuting him.

"Now, let's discuss you and your future." Huntington changed the subject. "What are your plans for this camp beautiful I keep reading about in the New York papers?"

"You mean Pine Knot?"

"Yes. My wife is insisting that I look into buying some property in the Adirondacks. These railroad commission hearings are making her quite distraught, as you can imagine. And she thinks the best thing for my health would be to find a quiet place to escape."

"I understand," William said.

"Well, anyway," Huntington continued, "I've been meaning to

look into it and just haven't had the time. What do you say? Do you have any property in mind that might suit me and my family?"

William rested his glass down on the table and thought for a moment before answering. He did own parcels that would fit his needs, Mohegan Lake for instance, and Sumner Lake, where he and Arpad Gerster kept a hunting cabin.

"I'd have to take a look at the railroad company's maps," he said.

"Heavens, what for? You don't own the land outright?"

"Most of my father's landholdings are in the company's name. You, of all people, should know that was how he was able to acquire so much land in the Adirondacks. He had to promise to use it for the railroad construction."

"Ah yes, at tax sales from what I've heard. Brilliant move on his part, I must admit. I should have been doing what he was during the construction of the railroad. But alas, instead of land speculation, I spent my fortune in shipping and rail."

He paused. "So tell me then, William, what are your plans?"

At first, William didn't know how to respond, because he was so unsure himself. Now that the company stocks were mostly in Janet's and his mother's name, he was in a more secure position to move forward with plans to expand the railroad. But, as Sutphen said, it was hardly likely he would be able to find investors willing enough to risk this venture, and there were others trying to do the same thing from the western end of the mountains. William wasn't trained in the business of rail; he reluctantly adopted his position as head of the company after his father insisted he do so. And the last thing he wanted was to have to deal with Sutphen anymore.

"I'd like to sell the railroad and expand the steamship line, that, and incorporate on Raquette Lake. I've put in a telegraph line, and I'm obtaining permission to put in a Post Office, and—"

"That's all? You're staking your future on the development around Raquette?" Huntington interrupted him.

"Well, with what land we do own anyway. There are numerous hotels going up around the lake. People are flocking to the area."

Huntington did not seem impressed.

"I'm sure your father had grander plans than that?"

William looked askance. "He did want to subdivide some land along Eagle Lake at one time."

"Bully for him! That's what I'd expect to hear. Now, tell me, how do you plan to go about developing all of this land if you don't own it outright?"

William had no answer.

"Just as I thought," Huntington said.

"I suppose Sutphen will deed over some of the parcels to me to do what I want with them. They can't all go with the new owners."

"Not if you don't let that happen," Huntington said. Huntington got up from his chair and said, "Look at the time," as he consulted his watch piece, "I've got to catch a train back to Throgg's Neck. Thank you for a pleasant evening."

William reluctantly escorted him to the door. There hadn't been enough time to discover what Huntington had meant by his last comment.

A few weeks later, William opened up Pine Knot. Without Janet, it was a lot more work, but she was in confinement. Once he felt the most important tasks were accomplished, he took off on his boat to Brown Tract Pond with Julia Stott to go fishing. They were sitting in the still waters waiting for a nibble on the end of their lines when William broke the silence.

"Have I ever told you the story about my fishing trip in Norway?"

"No. You've been to Norway?"

"Yes, twice. I was young; late teens."

"How was it?"

"Very good. I was with some guides, and I landed a very large trout. The biggest they had ever seen. I couldn't quite understand the language, but I believe they were trying to tell me it was some type of mythical monster I had on the end of my line," he said.

Julia laughed.

"Anyway, I had the fish close enough to the boat in clear water, and one of these blokes comes along with an enormous iron hook, plants it into the mouth of the fish, and hauls it out of the stream. He was quite proud of himself."

"Really? That would take all of the fun out of catching a fish, I'd think," Julia said.

"Indeed, it did. So I told the man to put it back in the water," William continued.

"And did he?"

"Oh yes. And then the fish took off, it pained my arms I tell you, he was bending my rod and straining my line. He shot underneath a bank and then the next thing I knew he was flipping out of the water. He had broken the line and took my tackle with him."

Julia laughed heartily and William chuckled, remembering his consternation at losing such a prize.

They drifted lazily in the quiet breeze, and time went by slowly, as it tends to when there is nothing to occupy it but looking out on still waters. Julia must have thought it her turn to break the silence and said, "How is Janet faring?"

"She's feeling quite well. Her friend, Cornelia, is staying with her until her mother finishes opening up camp and arrives to help. The baby should arrive in a few weeks," William answered as he cast his line. The misty morning was giving way to the rising sun. It was going to be a warm day.

Julia watched as William's bait sank out of site. "Uncle Francis plans to demolish the Spinsterage and replace it with a more modern building," she said.

"I know. He's asked me for my opinion." William smiled. He knew Julia was upset about it and found it amusing she held onto that cottage as if it was her birthright to remain single. A stuttering scream pierced the sky, and a large winged shadow passed overhead. They watched as an eagle landed on a branch of a dead tree and gazed down on them.

"We had some very good times there," Julia mused, turning her attention back to her line. A dragonfly stopped to rest on it briefly before resuming his attacks on the mosquitos and black flies hovering in the air. His translucent wings reflected the sun. "I remember quite a few evenings when Janet, Dora and I would sit up giggling all night long." Julia paused for a few moments. "You know, she's quite young."

"Who?"

"Janet. She was quite young to marry when she did. Not yet twenty. I thought for sure she'd stay with me in the Spinsterage until I was an old woman."

"She'd be your companion you mean? I suppose that's not what her mother wanted for her," William said. He was unsure where this conversation was going.

"Aunt Elizabeth was so upset when she lost Dora and Lawrence, not even a decade after poor Bertha."

Without having to say it, William knew what Julia was implying. Janet's mother, having lost three children to diphtheria and consumption in less than a decade, was glad to see her surviving daughter married off to procreate and bring some joy into the family after so much sorrow, even if it was arranged.

"Janet was as happy as her mother when the engagement was announced," William said.

"Yes, I suppose she was," Julia said. William watched her cast her line with ease and grace off to the far reaches of water and remained silent, although he vaguely felt he should be defending himself against something.

The conversation ended abruptly as something tugged at the end of Julia's line and brought them both to attention. She struggled with it expertly.

"He's running away from you," William cried. He reached for her hand to help reel in the large trout.

She brushed him off and struggled with the line as the fish dashed under water. It jumped, then turned. William watched as she expertly pulled back and laughed at its antics. When she finally hauled it in, she sat back breathing heavily, admiring the fish flopping around on the bottom of the boat.

"My word, that's one of the biggest I've ever landed," Julia said.

"And you handled it well," William said. A stiff breeze picked up, and William raised a small sail. It caught the wind and shortened their trip back to the Stott camp by half.

Ike Lawrence was waiting for him in the trapper's cabin when he arrived back at Pine Knot. His nephew, Nate, was with him—his sister Sarah's son. William shook the young lad's hand, guessing he was about seven years old now. On the floor beside Ike sat an Adirondack pack filled with furs.

"Not as many furs this spring?" William asked. It was then that he finally noticed Ike. He wasn't his usual self. He wasn't smiling, and he was holding his hat in his hand looking downcast.

"Ike, what is it?" William asked.

He turned to Nate when Ike didn't respond right away. "Nate, you go to the dining hall and see if Mrs. Callahan has any maple candy left for you."

Nate ran from the cabin with a spring in his step.

The men waited until he was out of sight. Ike sat down in a chair and kept his eyes on the floor while he spoke.

"Mr. Doo'Rant, something awful has happened," he said. He raised his head. His eyes were red and rimmed with tears.

"My sister Sarah's dead."

"Sarah? How? What does Nate know?" William asked.

Ike blew the air out of his mouth and turned away so William wouldn't see his tears.

"It was a month ago now, April, when it happened. It had been a rough winter, and the children were hungry. We ran out of supplies. Even maple sugar. We hadn't heard from Sarah's husband Jeff or my brother Jake. They were at one of the lumber camps, but it was too far to send word to them. I keep thinking if I had snow shoed to find them…"

He choked on his words. William handed him the handkerchief he'd kept in his vest pocket, and Ike wiped his eyes with it. Then he continued with the story.

"Sarah insisted we take some furs to the Antlers Hotel to barter for some food supplies. We needed lard, sugar, flour—everything. There was still ice on the lake, about two feet thick in some parts." He sounded as if he was trying to assure himself that he wasn't negligent and had thought it through.

"It was only me and Sarah that could go."

Since Ike's father Isaac had died, there was no one else to help him. His other sister, Emaline, had married and decided to live on her husband's farm, and his own wife had a newborn and their other children to look after.

"It was the weight of her pack that did Sarah in," Ike continued. "She had too much in it."

Ike warned her. But she'd insisted that they get as many furs as possible to the hotel.

"I was the first one to hear the ice crack," he said. He'd turned around swiftly to warn Sarah. "We better get off the ice," he said to her. Ike told how she'd nodded in agreement and they started for the shore. But the pack strapped to her back was weighing her down, and the crack in the ice caught up to her.

"When she fell through, I ran to pull her out. But that damned pack was so heavy, and we couldn't get it off her. I lay down on the ice in front of her and reached into the water to cut the straps with my knife." He went on to describe how he had cut the leather straps holding the pack to her back, but she had also strapped it around her waist.

"When I realized she had it strapped around her waist too, I reached for the strap. My hands were so cold, Mr. Doo'Rant, they were numb. I could hardly feel 'em."

William stayed silent as Ike described how Sarah had lost her grip on the ice and groped for him.

"She was screaming at me. I'll never forget that. She was crying and screaming at me to save her from drowning. She was screaming so loud it echoed across the mountains. I can't get that sound out of my head. It haunts me at night."

Ike began to sob. William was stunned into silence at Ike's grief. He shifted uncomfortably for a moment and then reached his hand out and placed it on the young man's shoulders, offering what small comfort he could. He waited.

"The ice cracked around her. I held onto her hand as long as I could, and then she let go. If she hadn't I would have drowned with her. She would've dragged me down with her."

He dropped his head into his hands again, completely

shattered.

William shuddered. He had lost a horse and sled once to the dark lake, much the same way. But he could hardly imagine what it would be like if he lost his own sister Ella like that.

Ike lifted his head up and sighed. "The worst of it is when Jeff got word about it at the lumber camp. I heard he was wailing and crying like a baby. They couldn't calm him down. He started tearin' up the camp. They sent for a doctor at Long Lake. But before he could get there, he up and left the lumber camp, and no one has seen him since."

"Who is taking care of Nate and his sister?"

"Me and my wife. We've adopted them. No choice."

"But where did he go? How could he abandon them so easily?"

Ike shrugged wearily and looked out at the lake through the glass window of the cabin. "I just don't reckon I know, sir."

"But my wife and me, we can barely keep up with the place, and now all of these kids. And she hasn't been well since the last baby was born. My father and grandmother both are dead, as you know. With Emaline married and living with her family somewheres else, and Sarah dead, I'm not sure if I can trap as much as I used to for you, sir." He sounded exhausted.

"Ike, that is the least of my problems, I assure you. Those furs you bring me are for your family to profit by. Are you sure you can't entice Emaline to come home and help out?"

Ike shook his head sadly.

As William contemplated what to say next, Nate came running back with a piece of maple candy wrapped in paper. He jumped with both feet on each step until he reached the doorway, and then he grinned from ear to ear from his accomplishment. Simple pleasure, to conquer the steps one at a time, William thought.

"Don't fret too much about this, Ike. I may be able to find a local girl to come and help while your wife recovers from having the baby. At least until you can get things in order."

William increasingly found himself assisting his workmen and their families in their struggles to survive in the Adirondacks. It was one of the reasons he thought it important to bring in the Post

Office and incorporate a town, to bring some semblance of civilization to the region, even if people like Arpad thought it was getting too crowded. There were always places like Mohegan Lake if one needed to get away from the tourists.

His empathy for his workers may have been why, when the prospect was presented to him, he allowed himself to be cajoled into building a Catholic Church on Raquette, after Mrs. Callahan brought the lack of a proper worship site for them to his attention.

He had just returned from mass at Church of the Good Shepherd and was in the kitchen checking on dinner plans.

"I've invited Dr. and Mrs. Gerster to dine with me this evening. What's on the menu?" he asked Mrs. Callahan.

"Well," she huffed, brushing past him on her way to the sink to wash some potatoes. "You might 'ave told me earlier."

Catching herself she said, "I'll send one of the boys to look in the icehouse for our meat supplies, sir. I'm sure we'll find something suitable."

"Fine," William said, and made to leave.

"How was church, sir?" she asked from the sink.

"Very good. The new reverend gave a wonderful sermon."

"Humph," she said and continued to scrub the potatoes.

"Mrs. Callahan, is there something you want to say to me? I can tell when there is something bothering you and the mood never suits you," William said.

Many things bothered Mrs. Callahan. The boys didn't bring the right amount of mutton out of the icehouse. The mice were getting into the cupboards, and "By God, if they're putting all this effort into the new cabin, why not upgrade the kitchen walls while they're at it?" Usually, she said these things to herself, or the dog, or whoever happened to be in the kitchen, although never when it was his mother. Hannah wouldn't stand for it and would show Mrs. Callahan the door if she heard half of the things coming out of her mouth. But the young lads William hired to tote things back and forth between the icehouse and kitchen usually heard an earful.

She turned around, wiped her hands dry on her apron, and placed them on her hips.

"Well since you're asking. I've been thinking that if you're putting up a Post Office, and trying to set up this town, why not give us Catholics a church?"

William smiled. He had thought of just that, a long time ago, when his father first suggested they build an Episcopal Church. His father, of course, dismissed the idea.

"Do you think there are enough people to attend? And who would we get to run the services?"

"You let me take care of that, sir. And yes, there are quite enough of us around here. We meet at my nephew Maurice's when there is a priest traveling through."

"Very well then. I'll look into it," William said.

"You will, sir?" Her face visibly brightened.

"Yes. Now let's get back to the menu for tonight, shall we?"

He knew he had to appease Mrs. Callahan. Not only was she one of the few women in the Adirondacks that could read and cook properly, she was his only connection to the superb recipes coming out of the kitchens across the channel at the Antlers Hotel restaurant. Her husband, John, who managed the place, would sneak them to her. Charlie Bennett, the proprietor, got them from a highly regarded chef in New York City. William had yet to discover who he was. At first he had come right out and inquired. But Charlie laughed at him. So William tried every trick he could think of to get him to reveal his source. He even invited him over to drink some of his best imported whiskey, knowing Charlie had a weakness for alcohol.

It didn't work. Charlie remained tight-lipped. Even worse, Charlie had a propensity for what the Germans called *Schadenfreude*. In America they called it smugness. Bennett found satisfaction in William's frustration.

Until he found out which chef in New York City was feeding Bennett those recipes, he was beholden to Mrs. Callahan's husband John to keep Pine Knot's dining up to par. William didn't like to be outdone, especially by the likes of Charlie Bennett.

The Durant's guide and caretaker, Jerome Wood, surprised everyone when he arrived at Pine Knot after a long winter's retreat with a wife. They had met by mail. She worked at an umbrella factory in England and put a note in one of the packages sent to America. It had said:

> *To whoever finds this letter, I made this umbrella and I hope it keeps you dry. If you wish to, please correspond with me at the following address. Sincerely, Hannah Hodgson.*

She gave her address in London. William had recognized the neighborhood; it was in the manufacturing side of the city and the company she worked for was one that his friend Charlie Arkwright owned.

Jerome had answered her, and they had been corresponding for a year before he saved enough to buy her a ticket to America.

Like many of the guides-turned-entrepreneurs in the region, Jerome saved his money.

"Now that I'm married," he explained to William while stacking wood in the hearth of the chalet, "I'll be looking to start up my own business here on Raquette." He wanted to build a small lodge for tourists on Big Island where he could take in tenants and guide. All of which meant William would be in need of a new caretaker.

"I'll still guide for you, Mr. Doo'Rant, when you need me to. Your father and yourself have been very good to me."

"And you've been good to us, Jerome. I wish you all the best in your next adventure. But I do have a request for you. While you're building, would it be possible for me to hire your wife to help out at the Lawrence household? Now that Sarah is dead, Ike's wife could use assistance with her new baby."

"I'm sure she'd be glad to help out, sir. I'll speak to her about it and get back to you," Jerome said.

William left Jerome to finish his task and started walking back to his own cabin to get dressed for dinner with Arpad, when he saw Charlie Bennett landing on shore in his small boat.

William stopped and waited to see what he wanted.

"Mr. Doo'Rant," Bennett walked up the path to greet him. "I've been meaning to talk to you."

"What about, Bennett?"

"John Holland and me, we want to move that mill you own at the foot of Raquette up the Marion River to the carry so we both can use it," Bennett slurred. "Holland's renovating his hotel and I am building some cabins for guests." He teetered in place and put his fist up to his mouth to suppress a belch.

"It's a bit early to be imbibing isn't it, Bennett?"

Bennett swayed and narrowed his eyes on William as if trying to stay in focus.

William thought for a moment. His mill was one of the few remaining in the area. It was not much of a burden to William to allow them to move it. He could always access it when needed.

"And what will I get in return if I allow you to move the mill up the river?"

Bennett shrugged. "I hadn't thought of it."

"I could use a new caretaker. Jerome Wood is setting up his own place to take in tourists on Big Island."

Bennett's eyes widened. "Unbelievable! Does he think there's enough tourists to go around?" He teetered as he gesticulated.

"I was thinking of asking John Callahan to help me out this summer," William said.

"I went to Paris this year you know." Bennett folded one arm on his chest, propped the other with it, and placed his hand on his chin to tug at his beard. He eyed William suspiciously. "Discovered some wonderful recipes at the restaurants there."

This was not Bennett's first trip abroad. He was unmarried and managed to save all of his earnings so that he could travel in the winter. William was amazed that a man as uncouth as Charlie Bennett managed to travel the world and extract some of the best recipes from the top chefs. He tried to hide his envy. William wished he was doing the same. It was a lifestyle he missed but could no longer afford the time.

"That's wonderful, Bennett. Maybe you could share with me. I've always been fascinated by French cuisine."

"How about that mill then?" Bennett zeroed in on his bargaining chip.

"I get Callahan for the summer. You provide me with the latest recipes from Paris. And it's a deal," William said with an outstretched hand.

"Deal then," Bennett shook it.

William left him, still swaying, and scratching his beard, probably wondering if he had given away too much. William smiled to himself: two deals struck in Adirondack style. It had been a productive day.

Janet was sitting up in bed cooing at the infant swaddled in her arms. She beamed at William. He placed his pinky finger into the small palms of the little girl's hands.

"What shall we name her?" Janet asked.

"I was hoping to name her after my mother—Heloise Timbrell," he said.

"Of course, dear." She cooed at their baby. "We'll call her Leila, so she's not mistaken for your sister."

"Yes, I like that." He sat down next to them and admired Leila's pink skin.

"John Barbour inquired for you," Janet said.

"Hmm," William continued to look down at the baby.

"And you've received another letter from Margaret," Janet said.

William sighed and lifted himself off his chair.

"I think I'll take some tea in my library," he said. He kissed her head and left the room.

As soon as he got to his library, he pushed aside some papers, made room for his drawings of Uncas and contemplated his plans. Spending time in the woods meant his senses were fulfilled and this made him want to create something to match the beauty he witnessed. Whether it was the natural light filtering through the trees and dappling the forest floor; or the aroma of balsam and pine that permeated the air; or the wind whispering in the treetops; or the lake water slapping the shore, William always returned from the woods inspired by the sights, smells and sounds. And he didn't want to interrupt the flow while he knew he had the time and opportunity to take advantage of the muse.

His valet came in with a tray of tea and handed him his mail. On the very top was a letter from his mother's companion, Margaret. He put it aside and went back to his drawings. He lifted his pen, but was distracted by the letter.

"It's no use," he said aloud, and slit it open.

In Margaret's usual acerbic fashion, she wrote that Ella had written yet again, requesting more money from Hannah, and she wondered, why does Ella need the money if she is companion to her Aunt Sylvia?

Why indeed, William wondered himself. He finished reading the letter, which described his mother's ill health and household accounts, then threw it down in disgust at Ella's continual need for more money. He heard his son Lawrence screeching and the governess trying to shush him in the hallway.

"Papa, papa!" his little voice cried.

TEN

England

It had been a trying few weeks. Aunt Sylvia didn't take Ella's news about leaving very well.

"But I thought you liked it here?" Aunt Sylvia said, when Ella told her about her impending departure.

"Of course I do, it's lovely. But I feel the need to start up a new life here in London, and now that I have the funds to do so, I want a place of my own. I intend to write," Ella assured her.

"But dear, why couldn't you stay and be my companion?"

Ella winced at the word. "Aunt Sylvia," she said and reached for her aunt's hand, "rest assured, I will come visit every week. And when you travel in the summer, I can join you as your companion."

This placated her aunt somewhat although she was no fool. Ella imagined Sylvia knew about Gabriel's comings and goings, if not the butler, Trixie may have revealed something. All the more reason for Ella to find her own place, so as not to draw too much attention to her private affairs, all of which Aunt Sylvia could relay to her mother since they frequently exchanged letters.

Still, she had not heard from Gabriel, who had left on a business trip to Paris weeks earlier. It was breaking her heart. Her recollections of their lovemaking left a gnawing pain in the pit of her stomach. She couldn't sleep at night.

She should have been excited about her freedom to come and go as she pleased once she moved into her flat, but the emptiness of it haunted her. She found herself walking through a room, gazing at a chair and picturing Gabriel, sitting, reading, or drinking his morning coffee. Her bedroom was no haven either; instead it was a reminder that he was not there to share her bed.

An invitation to attend a dinner party at Anny's was an opportunity to get him out of her head. It was an evening of readings and performances. Each invitee was instructed to select a favorite poem or reading from a novel or play. All the guests would be asked to read a piece, chosen randomly, aloud.

The only thing holding her back from attending was the thought of the unspoken questions that would linger on people's faces when they saw her arrive alone. She wanted an escort. Charlie Arkwright, who was proving to be her lucky penny, showed up in her life once again when she was shopping in the West End.

"Ella!" He hailed her down as she was admiring a dress in one of the windows.

He approached her and they exchanged a peck on the cheek.

"You look smashing, as always," he said.

"You're a flirt," Ella laughed.

"Always."

She loved that he readily admitted it. "Say, I received an invitation to a dinner party at Mrs. Ritchie's house for next Saturday. Would you like to escort me?"

"It'd be my pleasure. No Count then?"

Obviously Arkwright had heard the rumors of their affair. She wondered if he still communicated with William. As long as she didn't reveal too much about her private life, she had nothing to fear from Arkwright. He was not one to waste time with idle gossip, knowing his indiscretions with young maidens made him a target as well.

"Count de la Salle, I'm afraid, has been called away on business," she said prosaically.

"Very well then. We can't have you attending one of Mrs.

Ritchie's events alone, can we? Not when you have one of the most eligible bachelors in all of London to take you," he joked.

"You have cheek!" she laughed and gently tapped at his arm. "Of course, I'll be the envy of every woman there."

"Next Saturday then. Let me hail you a cab," he said.

Anny had assembled an eclectic group of friends that evening: the author Henry James, George du Maurier—a satirist made famous for his cartoons in *Punch*—Sir Henry Irving and his personal assistant Bram Stoker, as well as a few of Richmond Ritchie's colleagues. Richmond stayed with his own crowd most of the evening, glumly glancing in the direction of Henry James, who everyone knew was openly affectionate toward Anny.

Served him right for his dalliance with Eleanor Tennyson, Ella thought, even if, so she'd heard, it had cooled considerably since last summer when Eleanor found another lover.

What really shocked Ella, however, was to see Poultney with his wife Edith. Curious to learn more about the woman who had managed to pin down her errant lover, Ella sidled toward where they were standing and pretended to admire a portrait hanging on the wall while straining to catch snippets of their conversation. It was one-way, Poultney-style conversation. He was talking with Henry Irving about a recent dinner party at the Beef Steak Club while his wife stood by complacently as if she had no idea what her husband was talking about. Once in a while, Ella noticed, Edith's eyes would dart about the room, probably hoping to find a familiar face.

"Gentlemen." Ella wormed her way over to them and caught the surprise on Poultney's face. She turned to the actor. "Hello, Henry." He bowed slightly. "Poultney, shame on you for not introducing me to your wife," she said.

"Miss Ella Durant, let me introduce you to my wife, Edith," Poultney said.

Ella took Edith's limp hand in hers and said, "Welcome to London. I hope you're enjoying your stay."

An awkward silence followed before another guest, a young man who knew Henry Irving, came up to their small party and interrupted them, focusing his attention on Irving to brag about his recent novel.

"I meant to tell you, I have several publishers asking me for the first chapters," he told Irving, his back to the rest of them.

"I presume these publishers and their periodicals are offering immense quantities of money to match their admiration?" Poultney said to the man.

The debut author gasped and wheeled around to face Poultney. "I'd say that was none of your business, sir. No more so than asking me which tailor I use to cut my trousers."

"Then why, sir, do you bore us with your fairy tales of fame?" Poultney retorted.

After a painful pause, Henry Irving glanced at Ella, imploring her with his eyes to rescue them all. *This young man had no idea with whom he was dealing.*

"The competition is stiff these days to capture the attention of the reader, I'd say a bit of self-promotion can go a long way," she said to shut Poultney up. "I myself am writing a play, I'd love to talk with you about the business."

The young writer, grateful for the chance to escape, held his bent arm out to Ella and said, "May I escort you to dinner? I'd love to hear more about it."

The dinner was perfectly orchestrated, and afterwards the guests took their places in the parlor in preparation for the evening's entertainment. Ella wished she had chosen a different piece of writing. She had brought 'Friends', a sardonic poem addressed to Poultney when he first threw her over. She scolded herself for choosing it in a moment of self-pity. It was too late to take it back now, as Henry James stepped forward and started reading it aloud in a thunderous voice, finishing with a flair:

Mere friends? Why does the warm blood creep into my cheeks when thou art near?

A hush went over the crowd and all eyes fell on Ella sympathetically, and then Charlie Arkwright, thank God, started clapping. The rest joined in and Ella's dread dissipated when the satirist, George du Maurier, stood up from where he was seated to read another passage.

"It's the writer's curse," Anny Ritchie leaned in and whispered to Ella. "People can't help but believe that when we write something, it is part memoir."

"I suppose you're right, but I'd be a fool, wouldn't I, to allow my poem to be read if it was about someone here," Ella said.

Anny nodded her head in agreement.

George du Maurier started reading. The excerpt was from a novella, chock full of breast heaving anxiety and secret lovers. When he announced the author this time, people looked around confused.

"Who is Edith Bigelow?" Ella heard somebody whisper. Poultney was stoically standing behind his wife Edith who was seated directly across from her. Ella couldn't tell if he was embarrassed or in a rage; his cheeks went from pale to positively puce.

"Now in her case," Anny nodded at Edith, "I'd guess it's true."

"Who could blame her really?" Rhoda Broughton, the novelist sitting on the other side of Ella leaned over to address them both. She was wearing long gloves, just like the ones Ella had seen Sarah Bernhardt wearing only weeks before.

"I hear since their children were born, they rarely share a bed this side of the Atlantic," she added dryly and in a low voice so no one else would hear.

Ella politely applauded with the rest of the crowd, and when she caught Poultney glaring at her she smiled tritely. The applause ended abruptly when the door to the parlor opened and the butler announced the arrival of Count de la Salle.

Although many in the crowd knew him, his entrance caused that predictable stir when a party has to readjust to a newcomer. He was impeccably dressed, as usual, wearing a black suit, with a cream-colored shirt and black tie.

He bowed slightly to Anny, apologized for his tardiness and begged her forgiveness for interrupting the theatrics before taking a place amongst the crowd of men hovering near the waiter and his tray of glasses containing after-dinner port. Ella wasn't sure if she was the only one who felt the air charged with a current of energy that had been missing until he arrived.

The night was full of surprises.

After the brief interruption provided by Gabriel, the readings resumed. Ella attempted to refrain from looking in his direction. The few times she did, he was enraptured in the readings and ignoring her presence. She became so caught up with inner turmoil at his presence that she was unable to focus on the readings and wished she could leave.

When the readings were over and the applause had died down Ella found Arkwright. "I'm not feeling all that well. Be a dear and take me home, please." She hoped to escape before confronting Gabriel, unsure if her nerves could handle it.

"Of course. You look peaked. Are you all right?" Arkwright asked.

"I'm feeling faint at the moment," Ella said.

He led her to the door where the butler helped her into her coat.

"Please tell Mrs. Ritchie I'm sorry to leave so abruptly. I'll be in touch with her tomorrow," Ella said before they left.

"You'll feel better in the morning, I'm sure of it," Arkwright said on the carriage ride home.

"Thank you," she said as they stood on the stoop of her flat.

"Should I wait for you?" he said.

"No, no, I'll be all right. My maid is home this evening," Ella reassured him as she reached for the key in her bag.

"I'll be off then. I'm meeting some boys at the club for a game of baccarat," he said with enthusiasm. He coughed. "Now, er, you're sure you're well enough to make your way?" he said with a concern that barely masked his anticipation of the card game ahead of him.

Ella smiled, nodded as she opened the door to her flat and pecked him lightly on the cheek. "I'll be fine. You go and enjoy your card game."

He jumped back into the waiting carriage, waved at her and then instructed the driver to take off.

Ella watched as the carriage disappeared into the night and was closing the door when Gabriel stepped out of the shadows.

"My heavens! You startled me! How long have you been standing there? Are you spying on me?" Ella couldn't tell if she was angry or frightened.

"I didn't want to disturb your evening," Gabriel said sarcastically. "I had the cab drop me off up the street," he gestured behind him, "and walked. When I saw you at the door with that *man* Arkwright, I thought it best to wait until he left."

Ella's eyes narrowed. "Your behavior is unacceptable." She made to shut the door but he put his hand out to stop her.

"You're not going to invite me in?" he said.

"Why should I?"

Gabriel didn't wait for her response, instead he stepped into the doorway, blocking her from keeping him out. Ella unclasped her cloak from around her neck and placed it on the rack in the hallway. She left him standing at the door and made for the parlor where she lit a small lamp. She was glad she had told Trixie not to wait up for her.

Gabriel had taken his own coat off and followed her into the parlor. He walked over to the mantel and leaned against it. Ella was at a loss for words. At first she was angry at Gabriel for showing up at the dinner and not telling her he was in town. But then, once she knew he was there, she longed for him to acknowledge her presence. Which he didn't. All evening. Until he saw her leave with Arkwright. Now here he was, acting like a jealous lover.

"What do you want from me?" she demanded.

"The same thing you want from me, ma chérie."

Ella raised her brow and sat down. "What I want is to know where you've been these past few weeks. You become my lover and then you vanish into thin air. I won't stand for it," she added with what she hoped sounded like conviction.

His lip curled as if amused. "I've told you before that my business calls me away quite often. There is no use telling you where I go or where I am. I travel all over," he said.

"You could at least send me a post," she said.

"A love letter? Why should I when you have men like Mr. Arkwright waiting in the wings for your attention?"

Ella flung herself off the couch. "How dare you question my relationships. What do you think I am, a courtesan?"

"Maybe that is what Mr. Arkwright has in mind for you," Gabriel taunted.

"Is that all I am to *you*?" she snapped. Her fists were clenched as if ready for a fight, but she kept them at her side.

The room was dead silent when he finally spoke. "Don't ever raise your voice to me," he said.

"Don't run off from me and not tell me where you've gone then!" Ella said.

Instead of replying he walked over to the candleholder, picked it up and lit the candle with a match. Then he extinguished the oil lamp, darkening the room. He came over to where she stood. The candle he was holding cast a warm glow over his face, making it hard for her to tell if he was still angry.

"My absence doesn't imply I don't care for you, my dear. Why don't we return to where we left off?" he said as he held out his free hand for her to take.

Ella couldn't stop herself from placing her hand in his. "I miss you terribly when you're gone," she confessed.

He led her up the stairs to her bedroom.

When they got to her room she started to say something and he put his pointer finger to her lips and whispered. "Shush. Don't say a word." He put the candle on the table next to her bedside. The flickering light cast ghostly shadows on the walls. He turned her around and undid the buttons of her dress, lifted off her chemise and undid the stays of her corset. He caressed her shoulders, leaned over and kissed them. "So lovely, ma chérie." He moved his hands down her back and helped her out of her petticoats and drawers, caressing her gently.

She turned around to find him, "Gabriel, I—"

"Shhh." He gently pressed his finger to her lips. "Get into bed, I'll meet you there."

Ella stayed silent and walked over to the bed and slid under the silk covers. He stood near her by the dressing table, his dark figure barely visible in the dim light. He undid his necktie and took off his coat, then draped both over her dressing table chair. He was taking an agonizingly long time to undress.

Finally, he came to the bed and slipped in beside her. She felt his arousal as he lay on top of her and kissed her gently, then more urgently. When he thrust himself inside her, it took all of her self-possession not to cry out. But in one explosive moment all was right again. Her lover was back.

For two weeks they rarely left the flat. Ella would send her maid Trixie to the market for fresh food, the things that Gabriel liked. They did nothing but eat, drink a lot of wine, sleep and read the papers. Ella had Trixie pick up the *Sporting Life* for Gabriel. He would pour over it every afternoon. She wanted to ask him which thoroughbreds were his but decided not to pry because whenever she did, he seemed to get annoyed, much like William did whenever she asked him in her letters about her inheritance.

And Ella was afraid he would leave if he found her annoying. The thought of losing him again frightened her. Their love-making was becoming more and more exciting. He was a passionate lover. Sometimes he was rough with her. While fondling her breasts he would pinch them, hard. Or while he was nibbling at her flesh he sometimes bit her in the most tender spots, such as her inner thigh. When she cried out, he would only smile deviously at her, like a child who enjoyed playing with fire. But his rough foreplay always turned tender, and he knew exactly how to touch her in the right places.

Gabriel was knowledgeable about many things of which Ella had little experience. He might like to bet on horses, but he would not risk his wealth on an unwanted child, or so he told her. He was therefore well-versed in contraception methods and taught Ella about all of them.

One afternoon, Ella had her head propped on Gabriel's lap as she lay on the divan in her silk nightgown, reading a letter from Margaret Molineaux. They had not dressed for the day yet. They were waiting for their lunch to be served in the bedroom first. As if it would matter, Ella thought. They hadn't attended an evening social function together since Anny Ritchie's dinner party. Gabriel however insisted they dressed every day if only to pretend they were leading some semblance of an ordinary life.

Gabriel was stroking her hair as he read the paper. He stopped when he heard her sigh in disgust.

"News from home?"

"It's my mother's companion," Ella said and sat up. "She sent me word that money will be deposited into my account here in London." Ella flicked the letter in the air. "She told me not to expect more for a very long time."

"But your mother sends your allowance monthly?"

For a moment Ella thought he looked alarmed. She refused to believe it. He had no need for her money.

"Yes," she said casually. Gabriel rarely asked her outright about her financial affairs. Only once, when she had first confided in him about her regretful decision to grant power of attorney to William, did he offer his advice that she seek counsel. She turned her attention back to the letter.

Margaret wrote that her mother was too ill to write herself. They were visiting family in Florida, and she enclosed a check from her mother for one thousand. She hoped this would be enough. And concluded her letter with:

> I can't imagine what more you would need from your mother or why, at least until Christmas. As a companion for your aunt Sylvia I am sure she is attending to your daily needs. Try not to spend this money too quickly, as you have a propensity to do so.

She had signed the letter Aunt Peggotty, a term of endearment Ella used as a child when Margaret was her governess, before Margaret's true nature revealed her to be the evil woman she was.

The letter Ella sent to her mother weeks before must have crossed in the mail. Otherwise, Margaret would have known Ella was no longer her aunt's companion.

Ella lay back down on Gabriel's lap. "It's just that I am, after all, entitled to one third of the estate and have yet to get an accounting. I've heard through mutual friends that William is on the verge of selling the company and has already sold some land. I deserve some of that money."

"How much are you expecting, ma chérie?"

"William told me once the estate could be worth over one million."

He paused for a moment. "I have an idea," he said, and lifted her off his lap so she was looking directly at him. "Why not ask a friend to intercede on your behalf and inquire about your inheritance."

It couldn't be Poultney. Ella would never talk to him again. Bill Napier wouldn't do either. He was far too loyal to William. Charlie Arkwright wouldn't want to interfere; it was not his style to do so. That left Alfred Locock. He might be able to persuade William to reveal what was coming to her. Thinking about it gave her renewed energy.

"I need to go out," she said and rose from the divan to sit at her dressing table. "Anny Ritchie left two calling cards while we were 'busy'. She will think you've kidnapped me if I don't call on her today."

Gabriel stood up from the divan and stretched his arms over his head. "I will not keep you then. I've been meaning to call on a few friends at the clubs as well."

Ella smiled at him, picked up her brush, turned toward the mirror and tried to coax her hair into a bun in anticipation of her tea with Anny.

"Dear, if you don't mind me saying so, you look tired," Anny told her later that afternoon. "Are you feeling well?"

Ella had never felt better, although she was tired. Exhausted actually, and ashamed when Anny asked her how her writing was progressing.

"Well, I, um. I haven't written anything for a while," she said, averting her eyes and taking the teacup to her lips.

"Good heavens, why not? You have that spacious flat of your own now and no one to bother you but your maid," Anny said, looking confused. When Ella didn't answer immediately Anny cocked a brow and guessed. "He's staying with you isn't he?"

Ella remained silent but her eyes gave her away.

"And you've gained a reputation with your friends for not following up on invitations. What? Does he hold you prisoner in your own house?" Anny wouldn't let Ella avoid explaining.

"I've been quite busy, yes. Gabriel and I have been busy planning a trip." Ella couldn't think of any other excuse.

"Really now? Where to?"

Ella had to think quickly. "The stables," she said. "He rents out stables in Newmarket, and he wants me to see the horses he keeps there."

"Hmmm, Newmarket. I see," Anny said, and took a sip of her tea. She set down her teacup and waited to hear more.

"Are those new drapes?" Ella said.

"Now I know you're avoiding the truth," Anny said. "Those are the same drapes I've had for years. What is really happening?"

Ella knew it was no use trying to hide anything from Anny. She told her about her affair with Gabriel after extracting a promise not to reveal the details to anyone else. Anny listened without once interrupting. It was too good a story.

At the end, she withheld any judgment, only saying to Ella, "Don't let that man get in the way of your writing. Insist on having at least three hours a day to yourself. Discipline is the only way you will finish that play of yours."

"I know you're right."

"What do you know about him?" Anny questioned.

"I know he owns thoroughbreds. His family estate is in Paris. He loves the theater and good food."

"That's all?"

"Well you did introduce us," Ella said. It sounded more accusatory than she intended.

Anny leaned back in her seat and assessed Ella. "You know how these things are, I receive many requests to introduce people into

London society, especially from people that knew my father well. Goodness, even Andrew Carnegie was an introduction from a publisher in London who asked me to invite him to a dinner."

"Are you saying you know nothing about Gabriel's past?"

"What I'm saying, Ella, is that he was introduced to me by Lord Thompson. Once he became part of our social set, he remained. He seems well connected enough, especially with the theater. But going back to his introduction to me, one would have to assess his reputation based on Lord Thompson's judge of character."

Ella thought back to that first evening at Anny's dinner party. Lord Thompson was too drunk to notice anyone at the party, much less Gabriel. Dark thoughts began to enter her mind creating waves of anxiety. She didn't want to feel this way.

"Ella," Anny said, bringing Ella back into the present. "Who coiffed your hair today? If you don't mind me saying so, dear, it looks absolutely horrid."

Anny was right. Ella was becoming a prisoner in her own home, and in her mind as well. The only thing Ella could think about during the carriage ride home was how much she missed Gabriel in the brief interlude during tea. She knew her constant thinking about him was becoming obsessive. At times she wondered if their desire would burn itself out.

When she walked into the front entrance, she could see Gabriel sitting by the window, his aquiline features silhouetted against the waning evening light filtering through the silk curtains. He was smoking a cigarette and reading the racing news.

"Hello, dear," he said without looking up.

She walked into the parlor to greet him. "Hello," she said and started unpinning her hat.

"How was your visit with Mrs. Ritchie?"

"It went well. She insists we get out more. She misses us."

"Does she?"

"I was thinking that maybe we could go out tonight," Ella ventured.

"Of course, why not? My friends at the club were asking about you." Gabriel smiled.

Ella let out a small breath, relieved. She wasn't sure why, but she thought he might protest the idea. "Fine then. I'll tell Trixie to press my lavender dress. I've been wanting a reason to wear it."

"I'd prefer to see you in the red one tonight. We'll dine at the Café Royal."

"Red one? Well don't be silly. It's too late in the season for that dress, lavender is more spring-like." Ella assessed her hair in the mirror, Anny was right; it did look horrid. She began fiddling with the pins that were holding the bun. "I must do something about this hair."

Gabriel stood up and walked over to her. He took her hands away from her head and stood in front of her. The lighting in the room was dim as the day had turned to dusk and his face was in a shadow. She couldn't read his expression when he said, "I want to see you in the red one tonight."

He said it with such authority Ella jumped.

"Come," he said, leading her out of the parlor toward the stairs. "You can fuss over your hair in the bedroom."

She followed him, chastising herself for feeling afraid.

Thereafter, Ella kept her word to Anny. Every day after lunch she told Gabriel to find something to do while she wrote in her bedroom. He would reluctantly leave her and return before dinner. Eventually Ella's anxiety about his commitment to her started to ebb.

But after weeks of a blissful courtship, dinners with friends at the Café Royal, and attending the theater together, Gabriel informed her that he had to leave again.

They were eating dinner at the flat. Ella rested her fork on her plate and tried to remain calm, but inside she was desperate. This time when he left, would he come back? She wasn't even sure why she doubted he would. She didn't dare tell him how she felt, and knew it would only anger him if she reacted badly to his news. They had spent every night together for the past four weeks. She had hoped it would be enough for him to propose they marry. But if that was what he was thinking, there had been no hint of it so far.

"How long?" she said as she reached for her wine glass with

trembling hands.

Gabriel shrugged. "Two, maybe three weeks. It won't be long, I promise. I leave tomorrow," he said. Ella could not read any emotion in his eyes.

She suppressed the urge to cry.

"I'm done with my steak. Why don't we finish our wine by the fire?" he said, and rose from the table.

Ella didn't protest the fact that she had hardly eaten. She had lost her appetite.

ELEVEN

New York

William was sitting in a velvet-backed chair at the Union Club in New York City with his cousin Howard, waiting for an early supper.

"So when do you plan to join the Yacht Club?" Howard asked as he reached for a Cuban cigar in the humidor on the table in front of them and clipped the end. He leaned back, crossed his legs, propped one elbow on the arm of the chair and lit the cigar with his free hand. William watched with a mixture of curiosity and admiration as his cousin inhaled deeply, shaped his mouth into a circle, and moving his jaw like a fish gulping for air, blew smoke rings into the space above his head.

"Once I buy a boat," William said, lighting his own cigar.

"But you have a boat, a fleet of them, in the Adirondacks," Howard said.

William ignored his sarcasm. "I don't think my steamboats would qualify as proper vessels for the New York Yacht Club."

"Yes, well, when you need a sponsor, let me know," Howard said.

"I think my father's prior membership status will land me a seat, even if he is deceased," William said.

Howard could be such an arrogant son of a bitch, but William refused to let the Durant competitive spirit get the better of him. When the time was right, William would enter the club on his own terms.

"Speaking of your fleet of steamboats. The guides around Forked Lake are not pleased that you dammed up their favorite trout stream to launch another vessel." Howard flicked an ash into the tray beside his chair.

"The guides are becoming persnickety and their concerns are baseless. It was a small stream to begin with and the only one near a road. They should be happy. My new boat can carry up to twelve people. Potential clients for them," William said.

"Don't shoot the messenger, old boy." Howard held both hands up in the air. "I'm just telling you what I've heard from my men. They don't want Forked Lake to become another Raquette or Blue Mountain. They want to keep the clients to themselves, and they think a new steamship means a new hotel. They think their small shanties and cabins provide enough accommodation for the tourists and they don't want to compete with any newcomers."

William didn't argue with him. He leaned back and thought about what Howard said. He thought perhaps his cousin was exaggerating; he had never had trouble with the natives before.

"Speaking of hotels. Frederick needs to borrow money from me again," Howard said.

"For Prospect House?" William lifted his head. This wasn't good news. Howard had lent his brother money for his hotel on Blue Mountain Lake only a year before.

"He can't keep it afloat. It was the worst idea to build such a monstrosity to begin with. I blame your father for that." He stared levelly at William, as if daring him to contradict him.

William couldn't conjure up a thing to say in his father's defense. Dr. Durant had goaded Frederick on, living by the motto 'think big'. Unfortunately for Frederick, thinking big and making it work were not the same things. He didn't have his brother Howard's business acumen, for one, and the season in the Adirondacks for hoteliers was short.

"There's a lot of competition with hotels right now catering to tourists."

"Yes, but the clientele Frederick attracts are finding it just as easy to purchase land and build their own damn summer home."

William didn't disagree. He should know; he was the one selling land to these people. "How much does he want this time?"

"Thirty thousand," Howard responded.

"Good God! Why so much?"

"The roof is leaking, the plumbing in the three hundred or so odd rooms needs upgrading, and oh let me see," Howard added, "the weather in the Adirondacks is not exactly conducive to keeping wood from rotting. The veranda needs a new floor."

William took a gulp of his port. "I don't know what to say."

"Neither do I," Howard said. The men took a deep drag of their cigars and went silent.

An hour later, William was meeting Collis Huntington for another round of after dinner drinks. He stepped into the lobby of the Fifth Avenue Hotel. The room drew his attention with its high ceilings framed by gilt crown molding and windows flanked by dark velvet draperies dripping to the floor. Palm plants were scattered about in large cream-colored porcelain containers, lending an airy feel to what would otherwise be a heavy atmosphere.

Men in black tuxedos roamed around talking with each other, or making their way into the reading room to smoke. He followed a few of them to find Collis. He was sitting in a chair in the corner reading *The San Francisco Examiner* but glanced up as William approached.

"Good to see you, young man," Collis said as he smiled warmly at William and placed his paper aside.

William shook his hand and sat down across from him. A waiter appeared and asked for his order. "I'll have a Madeira," William said. The waiter bowed and left.

"So tell me, William, how is Sutphen doing with his negotiations?"

"I spoke with him briefly. The Delaware and Hudson are showing an interest in acquiring the Railroad."

"Excellent." Huntington slapped the arms of his chair with glee.

"They'll want the land along with the company," William said.

"We can't have that," Huntington said, shaking his head.

"And how do you propose I sell the company without one of its greatest assets?"

"Has Sutphen sent them a list of the landholdings yet?"

"Doubtful. They just recently sent a letter of inquiry. He only told me about it this morning," William replied, taking up the glass of aperitif the waiter left on the table in front of them.

"Good. I suggest we strip the bulk of the landholdings from the sale of the Railroad Company. Leave enough for them to believe they have received a fair deal."

"Look here," William said. "If the Railroad Company sells any of the landholdings we're obligated to pay the proceeds to the shareholders, or put it back into the railroad for improvements."

"I suppose you're right. That was your father's dilemma. However, we could 'transfer' the deeds to someone, then once the company is sold, have them transferred back into your name."

William didn't understand.

"You find a buyer before the final sale to Delaware and Hudson. He purchases the land at a reasonable price; a price less than its actual value, mind you. And then he transfers the deeds to you. After the sale."

William was intrigued. There'd be no one able to accuse him of wrongdoing at the expense of the company's potential profits. But something wasn't adding up.

"I don't understand. You're on the Board; wouldn't it behoove you to ensure the company obtains maximum profit?" he said.

"I will. Profit I mean. I'll lend you the money for the transaction. Once you take ownership of the land, sell most of it to the highest bidder. I already have a willing buyer in mind."

Huntington sat back in his chair and lit a huge cigar. "You must keep my name out of it though. I am up to my eyeballs with investigators and disgruntled investors. I don't need another journalist with a penchant for hyperbole digging up more dirty laundry about me to air out in the *New York World*," he grumbled.

"And what do you get from this?"

"Once you sell the land, you can pay me back, with interest."

"The company owns at least half of a million acres," William reminded him.

"I know that. I'll arrange the transfer with one of my clerks. He'll approach Sutphen to purchase a certain amount, say three hundred thousand acres. Instruct Sutphen to allow the transaction; he'll know what to do. Once that's done, sell the railroad with whatever land is left."

"And then what?"

"As I said before, we have the land deeded back to you."

"And I sell it for a profit?"

"Yes," Huntington leaned back in his chair and relaxed. "Of course, you will want to keep some of the land for yourself. And I would like a stake in your development plans as well." A sly smile crossed his face. He brushed an ash that had fallen onto his dark blue colored waistcoat and puffed on his cigar.

Astounded by his adroitness, William watched the lingering smoke circle Huntington's balding head and thought, why not? Not only would this allow him to keep some of the land he coveted, but he could dispose of his obligation to Ella as well. She had been hounding him about it long enough, now she was getting desperate, enough so that she had asked their old family friend, Alfred Locock to intervene. Once the railroad was sold, he'd be able to pay her off and continue on with his life without having to worry about her wily antics anymore. She'd be more than satisfied with her inheritance, and he could take his time developing the landholdings to his satisfaction, dribbling money to her as an allowance.

A few weeks later, William was seated on the porch at Pine Knot enjoying the September sunshine, when his tranquility was disrupted by the sudden appearance of Charlie Bennett.

Before William had a chance to invite him to sit, Charlie had worked his way into a wicker chair and started babbling. William indulged him.

"I miss the Doc. He told some of the best stories about his days on the transcontinental." Charlie leaned back in the rocker.

"We were right here," Charlie pointed at the floor of the chalet porch, "your father, me and my brother Ed. It was before you got here and developed this." He gesticulated at the surroundings.

"Me and my brother used to guide your father and his friends. We had a few small shanties on this spot of land, and some farther back in the woods. The Doc'd come up here with the other sports, all railroad men themselves, and entertain us with yarns about his feats."

William remained silent, waiting for the rest of it.

"So anyway." Charlie glanced over to make sure William was paying attention. "He tells us about the ruckus between the Union Pacific and the Sioux Injins. Tells us he hires the Pawnees to wipe 'em out, git rid of them. They was causin' all types of trouble for your father."

William knew this much. And he remembered tales about the Pawnees from his father. In 1866, Dr. Durant transported over one hundred dignitaries and businessmen from the east coast to see, firsthand, the construction of the railroad in the western frontier. His father had employed the Pawnees as entertainment for the event. They did war dances and re-enactments of Sioux raids on the railroad, where the Pawnee warriors fought back, and were, of course, the victors. The sight of the Indians, dressed in their scant wardrobe and feather-dress, caused a stir with the audience, especially the women. The festivities went on well into the morning. His father sent newspaper articles to the family while they were abroad, and William read firsthand accounts of the event by those in attendance. He remembered how proud he was of his father then because he did everything with panache.

"So he tells these Pawnee Injin chiefs, you bring me back Sioux scalps. And for everyone of 'em, I'll give you $25.00," Charlie continued.

William lifted his eyes off the lake and paid more attention to Charlie's rant. He hadn't heard about this part of his father's dealings with the Pawnee.

"And one day, this chief shows up with a basket full of 'em."

"Full of what?" William wasn't sure he was hearing the story correctly. Did Charlie say that his father condoned the taking of scalps as a war prize?

"Scalps!" Charlie laughed. "Boy he was surprised! He said he hadn't expected to pay out that much in one day!" He slapped his knee as he laughed.

Christ, William thought. That's monstrous.

"How are the plans coming to move the mill?" William steered Charlie to another topic.

Charlie stopped tittering and coughed. "Oh yeah, well I think John Holland and me are gonna move that mill next week, and we could use some help with it," he said.

"What more do you need from me?"

"Well, we was thinking if we could use one of your steamboats to drag it, it might go quicker."

"Alright then. But I expect some payment for the use of the boat at least."

"Sure thing Mr. Durant," Charlie said, and raised himself up to take his leave.

"I'll tell you why Jerome Wood is setting up his own boarding house on Big Island," Arpad said later that evening over coffee, brandy, and tobacco, while they sat by the fire in the chalet.

"They all think they can be like the Bennett brothers and board tenants. The hotels have a monopoly over the guides now." He tapped the ash from his pipe into the ashtray stand next to him.

"I suppose it's better this way. Hotels are more alluring to tourists than those shanties the guides build wherever they want," William said.

"Well, I would agree that the days of squatting are over for the guides. But I cannot condone what Charlie Bennett is doing over at

Antlers. He's told all of the guides in the area, including Alvah, that if they want work from the guests of his hotel, they have to work for *him*. He's taking a cut of their very small profits."

"I don't think Alvah needs to worry," William assured Arpad. "As long as the sportsmen that come here are willing to overlook his ill-manners, he'll always be in high demand for his skills."

"I suppose," Arpad grunted his agreement and placed more tobacco in his pipe. He lit a match, puffed and a fruity smell filled the air. "He'll not work for Charlie Bennett. He says it's highway robbery."

"I think I'll play now, dear." Anna Gerster, who had been sitting and listening to the men, got up to play the piano.

They stopped talking to listen to the tinkling sound of the piano playing to the backdrop of the crackling fire. Their moment of peace was shaken, however, when they heard a terrible crash and scream come from the kitchen.

William grabbed his rifle from the gun rack and ran to the kitchen. Mrs. Callahan was swinging her arm around wildly. Attached to her wrist was a raccoon. She flailed, banged it against the wall, screamed, shook, and cried.

Arpad arrived behind William. "It won't let go. It may have lockjaw," he said.

"Get her to stand still," William said. He had been trying to aim his rifle at the raccoon, but her wild flailing prevented him from getting a good shot. Suddenly, she ran out of the kitchen. They followed her and watched as she banged the animal against the trunk of a White pine.

"Stand still, woman," William hollered as he aimed his gun at the raccoon.

"It's no use William, she's hysterical," Arpad said. His wife, Anna, was there and he directed her to go into the kitchen and boil water.

Arpad then went up to Mrs. Callahan and took a hold of her arm. "We'll get this thing off of you, but you have to stand still." He directed her attention at William who was holding the gun.

She looked up, frightened beyond belief, whether because

William was aiming a gun at her or because of the raccoon, William didn't care; he needed to end this riotous scene. When Arpad lifted her arm in the air with the raccoon dangling from it like a monkey swinging from a tree, he aimed, hitting it in the gut. Once he knew it was dead, Arpad wrapped his hand in his coat and gently pried the jaws loose from her wrist.

He took her arm gingerly and led her to a seat in the kitchen. She was ashen.

"William, get me a blanket, immediately. This woman is in shock. Anna, find me some linen to wrap this and find me that bottle of brandy."

He cleaned the wound with hot water and dabbed it with brandy.

Arpad's skills as a doctor were always welcomed at Pine Knot. Whether it was a fever, scraped knee, or a bad bout of stomach flu, he always had a remedy.

"Now tell us, Mrs. Callahan, what happened?"

"I heard a noise!" she said weakly. "And when I went out to check that the bear box was secured, I saw a raccoon snooping around. I grabbed a pan and tried to chase him away and he came after me!" she said.

Arpad examined her arm gravely. "This will need stitches."

"The steamboat is waiting for you. I'll have the captain take you to your camp and bring you back," William said. He walked Arpad to the door as Anna stayed behind to comfort Mrs. Callahan.

"Let's just hope that raccoon wasn't rabid," Arpad said to William once they were out of earshot.

Arpad reassured William that his disinfection of the wound should prevent tetanus, but he insisted it would be up to three-week incubation time before Mrs. Callahan showed any signs of rabies.

"And William," he added, "you have so many people working for you now. You've created a small town. Maybe it's time you consider setting up medical supplies as well. I can't be everywhere at once, and some basic supplies such as antiseptics and proper bandages are of the utmost importance in situations like these."

The next day William was giving instructions to his workmen when he was waylaid by another problem: John Holland appeared, with his jaw set in a frown and eyes downcast.

"Mr. Doo'Rant," he said, taking his hat off, "may I have a word with you, sir?"

William stopped what he was doing and waved his workmen away so he could speak to Holland in private.

"What is it Holland? I'm busy as you can see." The weather was closing in on William; he had lingered too long this fall at Pine Knot. He had stayed because it was the only place he could go and spend time planning Uncas. It was noisy at home with the children scampering about and Janet peppering him with questions about one thing or another, and at his office in New York City he had to contend with daily telegraphs from Sutphen. Given all of the interruptions and emergencies of the last few days, however, William was beginning to wonder if he would have had more peace at home.

"Well, ya see, sir. I just can't afford to pay ya for using the mill, sir. And I was wondering if you could find it in your generosity to allow me to use it for a bit without payment until next summer when I get more money from the tourists."

"Holland, I don't have time for this. Get to the point. What are you talking about? I never asked for any money to use the mill. I told Bennett you both could use it on loan. I only requested he pay for transporting it with my steamboat."

Holland's dour expression changed to shock. "That's not what he told me."

"What the devil do you mean?"

"He said I'd have to pay him every week for use of the mill, and that he would be paying you for the both of us. He was going to charge me five dollars a week."

"Why, that's outrageous!" William said.

"I know, sir, I was thinking the same thing. See'n how we're just moving it up river so we alls have better access to it, and you not usin' it much, I was wonderin' why he'd say you was asking for money. And I never knew you to be *that* miserly, if ya excuse me for saying so," Holland said.

"We'll move the mill tomorrow. Bennett is out. I won't let that man extort you. Or me for all that matter." With that declaration, William dismissed Holland to get back to the matter of closing the camp. This inconvenience, along with waiting to see if Mrs. Callahan started foaming at the mouth, would mean a delay in his returning home for his son Lawrence's birthday celebration, but there was nothing he could do about it. He was not about to let Charlie Bennett take advantage of his good graces, and God forbid his poor cook took ill with rabies.

The next day the steamboat was waiting for him on the dock, with Holland onboard.

The mill was tethered to a barge, with a strong rope tied to the steamboat. As they passed Antlers Hotel they could see Bennett pacing the beachfront, raising his fists in the air and blundering on about being dealt a raw hand. He'd caught wind of it no doubt from one of William's own work crew. There was no need for a press to print anything of value to anyone around Raquette Lake; gossip spread faster than wildfire, and by the time it did reach the press it would be second-hand news. They ignored Bennett and chugged on.

Everything was going smoothly until the barge hit a snag of dead wood in the river. It jolted the steamboat and snapped the rope. William and Holland saw it all from their seats on the boat. The barge became stuck. The steamboat careened ahead until William told the captain, "Let's turn around and try to untangle it."

They pulled over to the barge and tried to lift it off the snag with oars.

"It's no use!' Holland yelled. "She's stuck like a cat in a tree."

"Bloody hell," William said.

William handed one of the men helping another rope. "Attach this to the barge. When I give the go ahead, you try to dislodge it."

The captain added more wood to the engine, and with a loud creaking, the steamboat strained while the men poked and pushed at the barge with the oars. Their prodding caused the mill to escape its tethers and start pitching around on the barge.

"Slow her down!' one of them yelled. But it was too late. William and Holland watched in dismay as the mill slid off the back of the barge into the river where it sunk to the bottom with one big gulp.

They turned the steamboat around with heavy hearts and chugged back to Pine Knot.

Bennett came out of the Antlers' Casino and stood on the deck watching them pass by with his arms folded across his chest in a defiant manner. William couldn't shake the suspicion that this tragedy was somehow Bennett's doing.

The next evening, when he passed Antlers Hotel once again on his way home, Bennett lit fireworks in the air. It was a birthday party, or so his workmen told him. William knew better. Bennett was celebrating William's failure.

TWELVE

England

Ella felt as though she were in purgatory, waiting for salvation in the form of Gabriel, but he never came to take her to that place she called heaven. He had left town weeks earlier and there was still no word from him. What did arrive in the post was a bill. It came from the Café Royal, where they often dined.

The first few letters from the Café she left unopened, hoping he would be back to retrieve them soon enough. But when the last letter came, it was marked URGENT in red letters, with her name attached to it, so she finally opened it. Unbeknownst to Ella, he had placed their last three meals at the Café on credit and told the management to forward his bills to her address at Cavendish Square. The amounts were staggering. She hadn't realized how much they ate and drank with their friends.

There was the French wine, the champagne, the sumptuous meals. It all added up. It didn't help that Gabriel, and she for that matter, were used to the best. So only the Veuve Clicquot would do (and they drank a lot of champagne) and the red wine had to be from Château Haut-Brion. The bills were astronomical. Ella did the math quickly in her head: the wine bill alone was over one hundred dollars, the equivalent of three months rent.

Ella was aghast and didn't know what to do. Her name was associated with the bills. The last thing she needed was a creditor coming after her. William would take it as proof he was right about her inability to look after her inheritance, cut off her allowance and demand she return immediately. She also had a reputation to maintain if she were ever to publish her play on Dante. She had no choice but to pay the bills. It left her with very little of the one thousand her mother had sent, and it plagued Ella to think of Margaret clucking her disapproval and telling her mother 'I told you so' on the other side of the Atlantic if she dared asked for more.

Worse, she had received word from Alfred Locock that William was not forthcoming about the estate, and so she was still in the dark about her future finances. It was all too much for her.

She sank into a state of despair. She never left her house and barely wrote. She spent her days sitting in her parlor window, pining away, recalling the lovely hours she had with Gabriel. Although Trixie would bring food, she couldn't eat it and she lost weight.

Her melancholy was at its height and she hadn't bathed in days when Anny showed up at her door, brusquely pushing aside Trixie, who insisted that Miss Durant would not see visitors.

"What are you doing here sitting by yourself, wallowing in self-pity?" Anny said accusingly. She stood by the entrance to the parlor, Trixie cowering behind her with a look that said, "I couldn't stop her."

Anny's hands were planted firmly on her hips as she assessed the squalid conditions of the room: food scraps mingled with papers strewn everywhere, empty wine bottles, and items of clothing draped over the furniture. Since her depression set in, Ella wouldn't let Trixie clean the parlor. She just wanted to be left alone to brood.

Ella looked at Anny despondently and said nothing.

"You look like a ghost. Good heavens, Ella, when was the last time you bathed? It smells in here." Anny swished her hand back and forth across her nose, walked toward a window and opened the sash. A cool breeze came into the room. She turned to Trixie.

"Go start a bath. And for goodness sake, clean this place up!"

It was the first command Trixie had heard in weeks, and she was visibly relieved to be doing something useful.

"Ella," Anny sat down next to her and took her hand, "you must pull yourself together. I have some very good news for you."

Ella brightened. Maybe Anny knew where to find Gabriel.

"I have a publisher. Kegan Paul and Trench is interested in your play. I showed them a copy of what you've done so far."

"How did you get it?" Ella asked.

"You gave it to me. Don't you remember? Last time I came to visit. Before that Count of yours left and you started circling the gates of hell."

Ella had to smile at the metaphor. Then she realized. Her work. Someone wanted to publish her work. It meant something to look forward to, to live for.

Suddenly the room was filled with activity. Trixie was clearing plates, picking up papers, and dusting. And then Anny was taking her by the hand to her bed chamber.

Anny coaxed Ella into a bath and held up her face to wash away some of the dried tears that had been plastered on her face for days.

"Oh dear," she said. "This will not do. I have invited Mr. Kegan Paul to my house for dinner this Saturday, thinking you would be ready for him. I think it would do you good to get out of here. You may stay with me for a week until you get yourself back together. And my French maid can save this mess of hair. One twirl around with the curling iron, and we'll have you looking like a princess for Saturday's dinner party."

She turned to Trixie who had by now finished cleaning the parlor and was waiting for more instructions by the door to Ella's room. "Go fetch two of Miss Durant's evening gowns, some tea gowns, and her night things. I'm taking her home with me."

Ella didn't protest. She felt like a child whose mother had finally come to save her from some evil monster, which was, for Ella, her own mind.

"Everything will be all right." Anny said with unending optimism.

The dinner event with Mr. Kegan Paul saved Ella, not only because she remembered her place in society and took it back, but because he offered to read the rest of her manuscript. Ella went right back to work on it. She threw herself wholeheartedly into the work. As Anny said, "writing does wonders for abating grief." Anny should know; she had her fair share of it in her own family.

When Anny asked Ella to travel with her family to the Isle of Wight for a summer holiday, Ella accepted enthusiastically.

The Isle of Wight was everything she remembered from her youth. They stayed at Anny's cottage in Freshwater Bay. The cottage had a view overlooking the sea and the towering chalk downs that jutted out into it like a beacon, daring the ocean to encroach on the land. Ella wrote every morning in a small porch that had windows running the length of the room.

The days passed, measured by the tides. The lobstermen timed their lives by the swell of the sea. In the mornings at high tide Ella watched them put on their oilskins and boots, and drag their brightly painted boats into the water. They laid out their lobster traps in designated spots and left them for the day. They'd come back within a few hours, take off their oilskins and drink their tea, staring out at the graveyard of ancient rock left behind when the tide retreated for the day, and wait for their bounty. Then in the evening, when the tide rose again, they'd drag their boats back out to retrieve the traps, laden with lobsters.

Ella understood why Tennyson wrote poems here and why Longfellow came for inspiration. Indeed, writers flocked to the Isle of Wight to set pen to paper, artists to paint on canvas, and photographers to capture on film the raw beauty of the place.

Anny's daughter Hester and son Billy were there as well. Ella woke to the sounds of their voices in the morning, planning the upcoming day's events.

Besides family, friends were present constantly. There was always someone coming or going, but tea time was reserved for just Anny and Ella. It was the one time of the day—mid-afternoon— when they would talk about their writing.

Usually they talked about the progress Anny was making on her father William Thackeray's biography. The eminent writer and novelist was the reason Anny was so well connected with the literary set in London and Isle of Wight.

She admired Anny for her devotion to her father's memory. It never crossed Ella's mind to write a biography about her own father, famous for his business in railroads, and the scandals that ensued. The newspapers had done enough damage to the family's reputation, she thought.

Anny's mother, poor thing, suffered from severe depression, and Anny rarely talked about her. It may be one reason, Ella thought, why Anny was trying to save her from the same fate.

After tea they would stroll the beach, or if the weather were inclement, they would call on one of the many family friends that lived in the area. Lord Tennyson always welcomed them at Farringford, his house on the bay. Anny's numerous connections and friends amazed Ella, among them the essayist Oliver Wendell Holmes and the authors Lewis Carroll, George Elliot and Henry James.

If only Ella had had the same connections in New York, she may have been a famous writer by now. Her father's friends and acquaintances were more interested in pursuing the dollar than anything as fanciful as the written word. Indeed, her father had actively discouraged her from pursuing her art.

It was under Anny's guidance that Ella found her voice again and managed to produce a decent manuscript to show to the publishers. When the summer ended, she was reluctant to go back to her flat, where she knew she would have to face the lonely void left behind by Gabriel. It would be such a change from the love and bustle that filled the space in Anny's household, with family and friends, interesting both to talk to, or about.

On one of her last days there, Anny took the children to the beach for a picnic. Ella had declined to go and instead took a coach ride into Freshwater. She stopped at a café for coffee and saw Poultney Bigelow. He was drinking his coffee, alone, at a small table, and writing. At first she was startled to see him, and then she reminded herself how popular the Isle of Wight was, and

Freshwater Bay in particular, with the literary set. It shouldn't surprise her to see him here. She tried to ignore him, but he caught her eye, and she was obliged to talk to him.

Poultney stood and helped her into the seat across from him. "Goodness," she said, "what a surprise to see you here."

Poultney smiled and motioned a waiter. "I'm doing an essay for *Harpers*. It's a follow-up to a piece they did in 1870, 'South Coast Sauntering'. They thought the Isle of Wight might have changed since then. I'd say it's like the Adirondacks, wouldn't you? Everyone complaining about too many tourists."

Ella smiled at the reference to their old stomping grounds. "That doesn't sound like your type of article," she said.

"It's not," Poultney said. "But neither is writing pieces for a Baedeker, which I'm doing for your brother. I'm doing these side jobs for one reason only: to have an excuse to communicate with you. I made the pitch to *Harpers* when I heard you were here with Anny." He waited for her reaction.

Ella turned away and watched a pair of young lovers sitting next to them. "You are full of surprises," she said, turning back to meet his expectant gaze. "Were you planning to just show up on Anny's doorstep one day like a lost puppy?"

Instead of answering her, Poultney picked up his coffee cup and took a long draw, an indication to her that was exactly what he planned.

"How is your Count?" he said, putting his cup down.

Ella blushed. "Well, if you must know. I haven't seen him in a while."

"Hah. No surprise there." He studied her for a moment before continuing. "If you think I'm gloating, I'm not. I sincerely wish you happiness."

"Thank you," Ella said.

"That's why I've done some investigating into his reputation."

"Poultney, really! Are you going to dig up dirt on the men who find me attractive? Who has put you up to this? William?"

Poultney shook his head. "No. I took it on myself. I do care for you, Ella. I know it's hard for you to believe, but it's true."

Ella was moved by his contrition, and she knew by his steady gaze that he wasn't lying.

Furthermore, her curiosity was piqued. She hadn't thought about Gabriel in weeks. The stay at Freshwater had cleansed her of any more longings for him. But still. "Where is he then?"

Poultney's eyes registered alarm. She sounded too desperate.

"I don't know. I can't find out much. None of my French connections trust me enough to reveal anything about their aristocracy. I'm too close with the Kaiser. And the French are not too fond of the Germans right now." He laughed with a tinge of sarcasm.

"However, I did manage to find out he is a legitimate Count. His family estate is somewhere on the outskirts of Paris. It's gone to disrepair. That's all I could find out."

"Disrepair? Why?"

"You know as well as I do Ella, it's a common problem with the aristocracy in Europe. They're tied down to these crumbling estates and can't afford the repairs. Many are on the prowl for American heiresses with huge dowries to save them from ruin."

Ella pondered what Poultney said. She didn't dare reveal to him that the Count had jilted her and left her with a large bill from the Café Royal. He would only report it back to William. Best to keep that to herself. She did however want something more from Poultney before she left him.

"What's the news from America?" she said.

Poultney proved to be a trove of information. Not only was her brother negotiating the sale of the railroad, he had their father's old nemesis, Collis Huntington, appointed to the Board to help him.

Completely recovered and refreshed from her holiday at Isle of Wight, Ella returned to London and her flat. She had her manuscript in hand when she walked through the door. Everything was how it should be. She was writing; she had a lead on a publisher; she had a completed manuscript to show them.

And then she saw his long legs, crossed, and dangling over the side of a chair in the parlor as she unpinned her hat to place on the rack in the entranceway. Her breathing became shallow, her heart started to race. How could she have forgotten? She had given him a spare key. Where was Trixie?

"If you're wondering about your maid, she said she was expecting you home today, and I sent her for fresh flowers." His deep voice echoed across the room.

She thought quickly. Escape was impossible. It was time to confront him. She entered the room and found him sitting patiently, leisurely leafing through the latest issue of *Punch*. When he finally looked up from it, his gray eyes met hers, and she lost all resolve.

"You look refreshingly beautiful," he said, finally with a slight smile.

Ella had to decide how to respond. She was confused by her emotions. Suddenly, the deep hurt and anger she had been feeling for weeks was replaced by absolute joy at the sight of him. If she hid how she really felt though, and feigned indifference to his presence in her parlor, he would leave and she'd be done with him. She chose indifference. Walking over to her desk, she put her manuscript in a drawer and locked it. She slowly removed her gloves, one finger at a time, set them down on the table and turned to him.

"I'd like my key back," she said, holding out her hand.

He showed no emotion as he stood up, took the key out of his pocket, walked over to her and placed it in the palm of her hand. Then he closed her fingers around it and pressed them down. He held her hand like this for a few moments as he fixed his eyes on hers. Ella felt the strength and warmth of his hands travel up her arm and through her body. Suddenly she ached for him to hold her in his arms again but resisted the urge, and swiftly removed her hand from his grasp.

"I must go and freshen up," she turned away so he would not see the desire in her eyes, "you can show yourself out."

"I understand you were harassed recently by the management at Café Royal. I am very sorry for the inconvenience. I left them your name and address in case they could not track me down."

"It appears you don't like your whereabouts to be known by anyone," she said tersely.

"Given my station and profession, I try to avoid attracting too much attention," he said.

"And what *exactly* is your profession?" Her voice rose.

He didn't flinch. "You already know. I buy and trade thoroughbreds."

"And gamble with them I suppose?"

"What I choose to do with my money is up to me," he said with a touch of anger in his voice.

"Not when it involves my money as well," Ella snapped.

"I am a gentleman. I have the money for the bill at Café Royal." He pulled a check out of his frock coat and set it on the settee. Then he picked up his hat to leave.

Ella moved to retrieve the check, hardly believing him. When she saw the amount—exactly how much they owed, the amount she had paid—she felt remorse for doubting him. "Don't go!" Ella pleaded.

He ignored her and started for the entranceway, but she followed him and put herself between him and the door. He was about to brush her aside when Trixie returned with the flowers, and as she opened the door, propelled Ella into his arms.

"Oh dear me!" Trixie said. "I'm so sorry, Miss Durant."

Ella's eyes stayed fixed on Gabriel's.

"Take those to the kitchen and find them a vase with water," he said to Trixie. "You can leave them in the parlor. Miss Durant and I do not wish to be disturbed."

Intimidated, Trixie scurried to the kitchen without another word.

Gabriel took Ella's hand and led her upstairs to the bedroom.

He closed the door behind them, and not bothering with the buttons, he swiftly pulled her dress down over her shoulders, slightly tearing the material. He reached down to her neck and started kissing her playfully, and then more ardently, tugging at her skin until she gasped. Gabriel smiled knowingly. He lifted her in his arms and flung her down on the bed. They both quickly undressed; Ella fumbled with her petticoats and he helped her out of them. He was an eager lover, as though he couldn't get enough from her. Ella responded to his need, as it matched her own. How had she forgotten how much pleasure he brought her? They spent the rest of the afternoon together, never leaving the bedroom. When dusk crept through the window and the shadows began to form on the walls, Ella reached for the bell.

Trixie came up the stairs and knocked on the door softly. Gabriel rose from the bed to put on his trousers and shirt. "Tell her we're going out," he said. It was a command, not a request. He knew she didn't care. She would do anything he wanted.

PART FOUR

1889

THIRTEEN

New York

Although he never condoned Ella's behavior when she struck Margaret years earlier when the two were in the throws of one of their many heated arguments, William secretly believed his mother's companion deserved it. He remembered once as a young boy watching Margaret trying to braid Ella's hair in a most threatening manner.

"Hold still or I'll beat you with this brush!" She had raised her hand, holding the weapon over Ella's head. Ella sat glaring into the looking glass on her dressing table, her lips pressed in a tight frown. He could understand why Ella detested her so. The household became much more peaceful when his mother finally released Margaret from her duties as Ella's governess and made her a companion instead.

However, Margaret's disdain toward Ella never waned. Even now, while the Durant family was gathering in Saratoga for the New Year celebration, she had something venomous to say about Ella.

"She's been up to no good I'm sure of it!" she said, pulling William aside while the others played cards in the parlor.

"What are you talking about?" William sighed with annoyance.

"Ella's been writing your mother constantly requesting more money. Hannah's sent her at least five thousand already. Why on earth does she need so much money?"

William stared down into Margaret's pinched face. He could respect a woman like Julia Stott to choose spinsterhood because she was a beautiful woman who wanted her independence. Margaret, on the other hand, probably had no choice in the matter.

"Margaret. I am fully aware that Mother is sending Ella her allowance and, at times, some funds to tide her over. London is an expensive city to live in and Ella, as you know, is used to the finer things in life."

"Haha," she cackled. "That doesn't mean she deserves them. I thought Hannah had set her up in a position as a companion to your aunt?"

"I believe Ella is now living in her own apartment in London and helps my aunt when she is able. She is a writer now." He too was grieved Ella had left their aunt's house and was constantly begging their mother for more money. He was well aware of it all. As holder of the power of attorney for both his mother and Ella, he had all of the receipts and Margaret's constant badgering was beginning to anger him.

"Dear, we are about to play cribbage and my father is looking for you." Janet came into the hall and saved William from having to defend Ella any longer.

"I'll be right with you," he said to her. Janet scrutinized Margaret for several moments before leaving them.

"I will settle all of the family affairs when I meet with Ella in London. No need to worry about it anymore. I suggest you let me correspond with Ella from now on." And he left her fussing in the hallway so he could resume playing cards with his in-laws and wife.

That afternoon, when the guests were resting, William approached the dining room to check on the table setting. He found Janet arranging the name cards on the table and stepped in to see how she was managing.

"How are you doing?" he asked.

Janet jumped. "Oh, hello, dear." She held a small name card in her hand, absently tapping it in the palm of her hand.

William walked over and took it from her, read it and knit his brow in disapproval.

"Where did you plan to put this?" he asked.

"Well," Janet glanced around the table nervously. "I thought Father Kelly might like to sit next to your mother, she was the one after all that introduced you to him, and I—"

"That won't do," he said abruptly. "My mother is getting on in age. She may have made our introductions but that is only because my father, who donated some of the money for the Catholic Church in North Creek, was deceased by the time of the opening. No. Put him next to me. Here." And he placed the name card at the plate next to his own and moved the name card from that plate next to his mother. He put his hand to his chin and stroked it. Something wasn't right about the arrangements.

"Do you have a diagram?" he asked her.

"A what?"

"A layout for the dinner guests," he said.

Her face fell with confusion.

"For goodness sake, Janet, it helps to draw out who goes where in case one of the servants moves one of the guest's name card."

"I never thought of that," she stammered.

"My dear, you're tired," William took her hand in his. "You must be, with all of this company and the new baby. Let me take care of this." He led her out of the dining room and bade her go to her bedroom. Then he studied the layout of the table, went to his study and retrieved a piece of paper to draw out where everyone should sit for the New Year's Day dinner.

That spring was the first in a while that Janet was able to come to Pine Knot to help William open it for the season. The past two seasons she had been either in confinement or expecting. Now that Basil was five months old, they could leave him with a nurse while they made the journey to the Adirondacks.

They busied themselves with the help, she with the domestic affairs of opening the kitchen and checking for mice, restocking the pantries and airing the linens. He went around the grounds with John Callahan to make a checklist of things that needed to be repaired, or replaced: rotted wood, shingles for a roof, cracked windows. The chimneys needed to be swept out, new wood needed cutting and to be stacked at each hearth. When they were finished with their tasks, they set off on one of William's steamboats for the Stott camp on Bluff Point for a grand dinner celebration to start off the new season.

"William, I understand you're building a Catholic church?" his father-in-law asked him over dinner.

"Yes," William said while carving into his venison. "I expect it will be done by next summer."

"Splendid!"

"I heard they are planning a bazaar, much like ours, to raise enough money for vestments," Elizabeth Stott said.

Every year the Episcopalians hosted a church bazaar at the end of summer. His mother-in-law was in charge of the activities. Someone would agree to host the event and they would raise about three hundred dollars to pay for church repairs or new hymnals.

"That sounds like a good idea," William replied.

"Which reminds me. William, what do you say about hosting a pig this summer?" Francis Stott asked.

William thought about it. It was a huge distraction for Mrs. Callahan. Every year, someone hosted the pig, fattened it up, and then had it slaughtered for the roast at the church bazaar. They were disgusting animals, as far as William was concerned, and took up a lot of space. But he was one of the few that had it, and a crew of people that stuck around all summer to feed the pig.

"I'm sure we could do that. Couldn't we, dear?" Janet placed her hand on his arm.

"I suppose so," William reluctantly agreed.

Within a week, a pig was delivered by two of Stott's guides to the docks of Pine Knot.

William set the pig up in a pen hundreds of yards away from the main camp compound; still, Mrs. Callahan was unhappy about it.

"You don't have to feed it if you feel it beneath you," he told her one day, as she scowled over the feed bucket. "I can get Nate or one of the other kitchen help to do it."

"That's not why I'm complaining," she grunted, lifting the feed bag over the bucket.

"And you could just feed him scraps from the kitchen, you know."

"None but the best."

He noted her sarcasm. "Mrs. Callahan. What is it now?"

She stopped what she was doing and put her hands on her hips defiantly.

"We Catholics could use a place for our pig as well," she said.

"Oh for God's sake!"

"No need to blaspheme." She held her hand in the air to stop him.

"I thought Bennett was taking care of that," William said.

"He was, but this new construction project is causing the pig to get squirrely and he keeps running away from his pen," she said.

"What makes you think he won't do it here?" William said.

"I'll take care of it. Don't you mind. So can we bring him over?"

"Whatever you want. I don't want to see or hear from either one of these vulgar creatures," William said dismissively and left her.

Pine Knot was finally ready for the season, and they would return again once the black flies died off in mid-summer. Pigs were the last things on his mind when he got home.

Barbour was waiting for him in his office in Saratoga. "Sutphen has confirmed the sale of the railroad," he said immediately.

"Delaware and Hudson are willing to buy it?" William motioned for Barbour to sit down.

"Yes," he said.

"How much?"

"Several hundred thousand, with the mortgages you have left."

Barbour pulled a silver cigarette case from his jacket and extended it toward William in offertory. William signaled no, Barbour lit one with a striker, and inhaled deeply. "This," he said, sliding a piece of paper across the desk to William as the exhaled smoke filled the room, "is from Sutphen."

William examined the document. It was a deed to three hundred thousand acres of his father's land, currently held by one of Huntington's clerks, a Mr. Cromley.

"I'm not sure how you and Sutphen managed it, but Cromley paid for the land before it was sold off with the railroad company, and is now transferring it back to you."

William smiled at Huntington's handiwork. He had chosen someone he could trust, and far enough removed from the Railroad Company to make it look like a legitimate transfer of property.

"What will you tell Janet?"

"Janet?" William shrugged. "Nothing, I suppose. Why does she need to know anything? She has her maids and nannies and servants. She seems content enough to me. I'm more concerned about how much to reveal to Ella."

"You only need to give her a share of the company's profits. The rest, the land, the steamboat line profits, are yours," Barbour said conspiratorially.

"How so?"

"William, when are you going to start taking control of your sister's affairs?"

"How do you mean?" William shifted uncomfortably in his chair.

"I mean, have you ever actually *read* the power of attorney document Sutphen coerced her to sign off on? If she were under my wing, which she wasn't at the time," he said to assure William he was not complicit, "I would never have allowed it."

William was flustered. Had Sutphen put one over on him? What was Barbour getting at?

"I strongly suggest after you sign off on these papers, you hand them to Sutphen directly yourself. And speak with him about the familial obligations to your sister." He planted his cigarette stub in the ashtray on William's desk and lifted himself off the chair. "By the way, we're looking forward to visiting this summer. My wife tells me Janet and her mother are in charge of this year's church bazaar. She wants to make sure we can attend."

"Of course, of course," William said.

"And maybe you can show me this new Catholic Church, St. William's is it? I have a few bills for you to sign off on for its construction, including this one," Barbour took a bill from out of his coat pocket and slid it over to William's side of the desk.

"Four stained glass windows designed by Tiffany's. Awfully generous of you, isn't it?" He waited for William to explain the need for such extravagant windows in a rural church that was only going to be used for his workers and their families on Raquette Lake.

"I was charged a fair price for them," William said not meeting Barbour's eyes.

Barbour snorted as if what William said was an exaggeration and retrieved his topcoat and hat from the stand. "I'll see you at Pine Knot," he said as he left.

Once he was gone William pulled the letter from Alfred Locock out of his desk drawer. There was no end to the audacity of his sister. First she hires lawyers to badger him about the estate, and now she was dragging a good family friend into their private affairs. He resented the intrusion. He picked up the striker and placed it under the letter as he held it over the ashtray on his desk. As he was about to strike the light he hesitated, thinking about the Lococks, and their other family friends in England. How much they all loved Ella and William. They treated them like family while they lived there. Ella even got into the habit of calling Alfred 'Uncle' at one time. William knew Alfred was only doing what he felt right, looking out for the welfare of Ella. He had no idea the extent of Ella's whimsy when it came to managing money. Just as he was about to light the striker again his clerk knocked on the door.

"Mr. Durant, a telegram for you."

William put the letter back in his desk.

As usual, William tensed up the minute the porter opened the door to Sutphen's office building in New York City. He climbed the height of the building in the elevator and stepped out into the carpeted hallway on the fifth floor.

"Mr. Durant," Sutphen greeted him in his office.

"Mr. Sutphen." William shook his extended hand stiffly. He took the papers out of his satchel and placed them on Sutphen's desk.

"You needed these?" he said.

"Yes. Indeed. I will inform Mr. Huntington that the transfer is complete. He has an expectant buyer. A Chauncy Truax."

"The judge?" William was perplexed.

"And he has interests in a mineral and timber company in the Adirondacks. He will pay handsomely for the land," Sutphen said.

"How much?"

"Almost a half of a million." Sutphen managed to crack a smile.

"Indeed," William said somberly. He quickly did the math in his head. After paying back Huntington for the loan he furnished to buy the land from the railroad, with interest, he would profit handsomely. This, plus the sale of the railroad company, increased the Durant family fortune to over a million, and he maintained ownership of thousands of acres for himself to do with as he pleased.

"And now for the rest." Sutphen handed William some papers. "You need to sign these papers, approving the sale of the railroad company to the Delaware and Hudson."

William took the pen from the inkwell and examined the papers that would absolve him from any more responsibility for the Adirondack Railroad Company and, hopefully, any more meetings in Sutphen's office. He glanced down at the document and with mixed emotions signed his name: *William West Durant*. He lifted his head to find Sutphen picking lint off his trousers. William looked back down at his signature and added underneath it: *Esquire*. He smiled inwardly as he handed the paper back to Sutphen who picked it up, and noticing the signature line, harrumphed, before settling the papers into his desk drawer.

"Congratulations," Sutphen said with his usual lack of emotion, "you are now free of your obligations to maintain the railroad, and after the sale of the land you will be quite wealthy."

William wasn't sure if he should shake his hand or go find a club where he could open a bottle of champagne with someone who actually cared. Instead, he raised the issue of Ella.

"I plan to travel to London with my wife this fall. I will be meeting with Ella then. I'd like to hand over her share of the inheritance. I will need a breakdown of her assets."

Sutphen eyed him and rested back in his chair, brought his hands together forming an arc, then pushed his fingertips under his chin. "What would you like to give her?" he said.

"What do you mean?" William said.

"What I mean is that you are only obligated to dispense the amount based on the company certificates in her name."

"That's it?"

"Yes. Have you ever read the power of attorney document she signed?"

William clenched. This was the same question Barbour had asked him. William didn't bother to do so, and they knew it. He left them to do the lawyering. When he didn't answer right away, Sutphen guessed his response.

"Mr. Durant. As the company lawyer, I will advise you that your obligation to your sister ends after the sale of the railroad. You hold control over her inheritance. It is up to you to provide for her what you deem appropriate. Your wife Janet and your mother own the largest share of the stocks in the company. You and your sister each have shares as well. I have calculated the amounts." He slipped a piece of paper across the desk to William. "Your sister will inherit close to thirty thousand dollars."

William thought about this. After deducting the five thousand he had given her already, he only owed Ella twenty-five thousand. That, plus the monthly allowance she received, should be plenty for her to live on and be content.

"And Mr. Durant. You may not realize this as well, but once Ella marries, you are no longer the guardian of her affairs. She is on her own." Sutphen swept aside the paperwork from his desk and waited for William's response.

William was stunned by this revelation. He had thought his ties to Ella would never end. He hardly expected her to marry. From what he'd heard, she was cavorting with some French rake. She would never learn.

He picked himself off the chair, shook hands again with Sutphen, and left his office to find someone to share in his good fortune. By now it was lunch time, and the air in New York was becoming humid. William put his fingers between his collar and neck to try to get some air. He hailed a cab and went to the Union Club to find his cousin so he could gloat.

It was mid-July. The church bazaars were just weeks away, and Mrs. Callahan was concerned that the pigs wouldn't be fat enough, especially the Catholic pig, which she called Ic.

"Why Ic?" William asked.

"This one's Ic, and that one's Ep," she said as they watched Nate toss the pigs their dinner one evening. William had followed the two of them so he could see how much damage the pigs were doing to his land.

"Epic?" he said.

"Episcopalian and Catholic," she said. "How else am I to tell which is which if I don't name them?"

"Does it really matter?" he asked.

"Why, of course it matters! I can't have anyone thinking I would switch them if one turned out fatter than the other."

Nate sloshed the slop into a low trough he had built for pigs. They were the vilest animals William had ever encountered. The pig pen was nothing but trampled mud. They ate everything in the enclosed area. And when it got too messy for them, they had to move the pen to a new location just so they could furrow that up as well. Worse, the Catholic pig, Ic, had not cooperated since he landed at Pine Knot. After Ic's second escape from the pen, William began to suspect Bennett, who had insisted the pig be kept at Pine

Knot, was seeking revenge against William for shutting him out of the mill operation.

"Just make sure that Ic no longer gets out. Last time, Nate had to chase him out of Mrs. Durant's new rose garden." He checked to make sure the gate was secure and huffed off, leaving Mrs. Callahan to the beasts.

Ic got out that evening. This time, they found him in the gardens munching on the iris. Mrs. Callahan's husband, John, took a switch to his hind quarters while Nate bribed him with a biscuit to herd him back into the pen. An hour passed before the reluctant pig entered his pen. He then turned defiant, charging William when he arrived to secure the gate latch. William jumped back.

"Good God, I can't wait until it's slaughtered!" It was impossible, he knew, but he could have sworn the pig was sniggering at him.

"The Catholics think you are trying to poison their pig, dear," his mother said as he entered the dining porch the next morning for his breakfast.

"Oh for God's sake, that's preposterous," William said. He went to sit down next to Janet. She patted his arm and pointed her chin toward their son Lawrence who was startled from his porridge by William's outburst.

"Well, you must admit," his mother continued, "for some mysterious reason or another, only the Catholic pig escapes the pen and eats things that could hardly be called palatable."

"I can't help it if that damned pig has found a way to open the gate," William said.

"Dear, please. Not at the dining table." Janet gave him a disapproving look and then swept Leila up from her high chair. She went over to Lawrence, took his small hand, and removed the children.

"I think you should call on Father Kelly," his mother said, lifting a teacup to her wrinkled lips.

"Father Kelly? Now why would I do that?"

"He has been asking to visit Pine Knot, and he can say a mass for the workers here. Then he can bless the pigs. That should satisfy them. Catholics go for that sort of thing." She sniffed, put her teacup down and unfurled a handkerchief she had retrieved from inside her sleeve before bringing it to her nose.

His mother, William knew, was usually right about such things. He sent a telegram to Father Kelly that afternoon.

It was a few weeks, without incident, before Father Kelly could visit and say mass at Pine Knot. When the day finally came for his arrival, Mrs. Callahan was running about like a hen clucking at her chicks. She had made a special meal just for the priest. When the mass was over, the workers and their families planned to dine at Pine Knot on her chicken and biscuits and lemonade.

William greeted Father Kelly at the dock. He was a tall man, like William, but unlike William, rotund. His thinning hair was pepper red. He had the kind of skin color that turned crimson at the slightest embarrassment or after a short time in the sun. His eyes were as pale as the color of water, and they always appeared merry. Unlike other men of cloth that could sense a benefactor when they had one near at hand, he never tried to convert William into the Catholic fold.

"William!" Father Kelly's eyes glistened under his black-rimmed hat as he came off the steamboat and onto the dock.

William took his hand and motioned to Ike to retrieve the luggage. "Welcome to Pine Knot, you'll be staying in the chalet." William shook his hand in greeting.

Mrs. Callahan came walking down the lawn toward them.

"That would be my cook, Mrs. Callahan. She has been working very hard to make a meal that would please you. I'll warn you now that if you don't offer her a compliment on it she will be in hysterics the rest of the summer."

Father Kelly let out a hearty laugh that brought the blood rushing to his face.

The mass was held on the front lawn overlooking the water the following Sunday. A contingent of Catholics showed up, including Charlie Bennett and his sister, Jerome Wood and his wife, and some of the carpenters with their families. Father Kelly gave a wonderful sermon about the blessings of the Adirondack air, mountains and lakes. They took communion and feasted on the food Mrs. Callahan had prepared. It was during the feast that William brought up the pigs.

"Father Kelly," he started in as soon as the food was laid down at the table and the blessing was done. "I wondered if I might be able to make another request of you."

Father Kelly lightly tapped him on the back with a show of camaraderie. "Anything," he said.

At that moment Mrs. Callahan appeared with the gravy. She eyed William as if to urge him on.

"Well," William continued as Mrs. Callahan ladled gravy over their biscuits, "you see, we are hosting a couple of pigs here at Pine Knot, to be given up for the church bazaars in a few weeks. And well, we were—I was," he corrected himself, "wondering if you might be willing to bless them."

Father Kelly lifted his long translucent lashes up off his eyes and gazed questioningly.

"Bless your pigs?" he said.

Mrs. Callahan stood by, her ladle suspended in the air as if anticipating the worst.

"Why, of course I will, in the name of St. Francis!' he said. And then everyone relaxed.

When the supper was over, Father Kelly, followed by a few curious on-lookers who had to be sure the Catholic pig was still alive, marched to the pen and watched as he raised the aspergillum in the air and shook holy water over them while mumbling a blessing about bounty.

After the blessing, William thought the pig fiasco would be over, but on the day of reckoning, Ic would not be put down. William had heard the shots from his porch rocker where he was reading and was surprised to find Ike standing over him minutes later looking confused.

"He's still alive," he told William.

"How could that be? Did you load the gun or were you firing

wads?" William knew Ike was a good shot and would never miss at close range.

"No, sir." he said. "I put bullets in, I swear."

"Give me that gun," William said. Ike handed him his muzzle loader and a few bullets. William made sure it was loaded and stormed toward the pen.

Ep had already been delivered to his maker the week before. He was smoked and ready for the Episcopalian bazaar. It was Ic's time to go.

When they arrived at the pen, Ic was fit to be tied. He was squealing and running around in a rage.

"You've addled him," William said. He raised the pistol, aimed it at the pig that had given him so much trouble these past few weeks, and shot it dead. It took three men and a sledge to drag it to a waiting boat that would carry it to Jerome Wood's smokehouse on Big Island.

A week later, Mrs. Callahan received word that Jerome Wood's smokehouse burnt to the ground. A spark from the chimney fire had gotten loose and lit a piece of dry wood that lay about. Everything in the smokehouse, including Ic the pig, had burnt to a crisp.

"What are we going to do, Mr. Durant? The bazaar is tomorrow!" Mrs. Callahan fretted.

William couldn't believe this pig was still tormenting him. And from his grave no less.

"I'll take care of it," he said.

He instructed one of his workmen to load up the venison from Pine Knot's icehouse and have it delivered to St. William's for the bazaar the next morning.

Mrs. Callahan was forever grateful.

FOURTEEN

England

Aunt Sylvia asked Ella to travel with her to Thirlestane for the annual autumn hunting party, but Ella was reluctant to leave Gabriel behind. However, he didn't receive an invitation, and she was not in a position to bring him along.

"I have to go," she said to him one evening at dinner.

"Your aunt can't find another companion to take her?"

"My cousins are in the country and won't be back to London until Christmas," she said.

He lifted a piece of meat from his plate and chewed on it before answering her. "You mustn't go," he said. "I've made plans for us to attend the theater and dinner with Monsieur Berton and his friends on Saturday."

"You can attend on your own. I daresay they are all your friends anyway. Why do you need me there?" Ella laughed, trying to make light of the situation. She didn't want to fight with Gabriel tonight. It would only tire her and tomorrow she needed to shop for her trip to Thirlestane.

He put his fork down on his plate and excused himself from the table.

"Don't pout!" she said. "You told me you would be going racing in Ascot next week. You'll be gone the same amount of time that I will. The absence might do us some good."

He continued his retreat from the dining room.

Trixie came in to clear his dish. "Are you finished, Miss Durant?"

"Yes, Trixie." Ella frowned. She sat waiting for him to return. When he didn't, she sighed and reluctantly went to her bedroom where she knew he would be waiting for her.

He was sitting in a chair, sulking.

"You are acting churlishly," she said to him as she crossed the room to her wardrobe and began picking out dresses for her trunk.

"You're leaving me to see that man," he said.

"Who on earth do you mean?"

"Arkwright." His face was dark.

Ella shuddered and went back to her packing. "Don't be a fool!"

"I'm no fool. I've seen the way he looks at you. He'll be there and he will be flirting with you."

"You've had me to yourself for weeks now. As much as I enjoy your company, I think I deserve some time to enjoy myself with family friends. Mr. Arkwright is a dear friend. He treats me properly, and not like some possession," she said.

"What are you insinuating?" he said.

"I'm only pointing out a truth about our relationship. You want to control everything, and I am supposed to follow your every whim. You've been living under my roof for weeks now, eating my food, ordering around my maid, and have offered nothing in terms of a commitment to me. You haven't even offered to contribute to our household expenses. Maybe it's time I found someone that can appreciate my good graces and find it in himself to match them."

Ella felt her pulse quicken with rage. She was entering dangerous territory with Gabriel but couldn't help it.

He rose from his chair and stormed across the room toward her wardrobe. He stood in front of it, blocking her from taking any more of her dresses out.

"Move out of my way," she said angrily.

"Apologize." His voice was thick.

Ella winced for a moment. When he refused to budge, she slapped him across the face. "Get out of my way," she said.

For a brief moment he was too stunned to do or say anything while she trembled in place. She was about to push him aside when she caught the glint of his large onyx signet ring as his backhand came crashing down across her face, sending her staggering to the floor.

"*Salope*," he said between clenched teeth.

She held her hand over her cheek, which was starting to feel tender. "You are nothing but a worthless brute!"

There was a knock at the door, and then Trixie said meekly, "Miss Durant, are you ok?"

"I'm fine, Trixie," Ella said. "Please send up some ice." She glared at Gabriel. "No man has ever hit me."

"It is very obvious."

"Get out. Now," she said, rubbing her jaw.

He picked up his frockcoat that was hanging on a rack and slammed the door behind him without looking back at her.

The carriage followed a meandering route along the lochs and vales of the lowlands of Scotland. They arrived at the Napier country manor, Thirlestane, near Selkirk, in the evening. The sun was setting on the multitude of trees surrounding the estate, basking the landscape in a brilliant golden hue. Bill Napier greeted them as they descended from the carriage, accompanied by his wife Harriet.

"Ella," he said, kissing both her cheeks. "So good to see you, my dear. I hope the travel was not too arduous for you and your aunt." Ella hoped her cosmetics and wide brimmed hat, drooped partially over her face, would conceal the black eye Gabriel had given her.

Bill tried to hide his reaction to the sight of her when he finally got around to studying her face. Of course he was too polite to say anything, but his furrowed brows said enough.

A valet took their luggage, and a maid guided them to their rooms so they could refresh themselves before dinner.

Ella looked into the mirror, scowled and dabbed at the puffy eye with powder; Gabriel's wrath was not easily disguised. Aunt Sylvia had already asked her about it, and she hoped her explanation would suffice: she fell and hit her head on her dressing table. It was a partial truth.

Trixie was fussing about the room, taking her dresses out of the trunk and hanging them in the wardrobe.

"Leave the green one out," Ella said to her.

Satisfied she had done as much as she could to hide the remnants of her argument with Gabriel, she went to the parlor to wait to be called to dinner with the rest of the guests.

Charlie Arkwright was the first person she saw, leaning against the mantel with a drink in his hand. He was speaking with a young woman that Ella guessed was half his age. Poultney was also there, talking with Jack Napier.

"This is going to be a long week," Ella muttered.

Ella mingled with the other guests and avoided any questions about her appearance, although the polite nods and worried glances cast her way were more trying than she had expected. She was relieved when Arkwright found his way next to her and handed her a glass of champagne.

"I see you've copped a mouse," he said in her ear. "Who's the basher?"

"It was an accident," Ella said, moving away from him in an attempt to avoid his alcohol-tainted breath.

"Hmmmm. I see. Let me take a look at you then." He eyed her up and down. "The rest of you seems to have come out alright in the fight."

"I told you, there wasn't a fight. I fell," Ella said.

Arkwright just laughed. "I'd be sorry for whoever it was that tried to cross you."

Ella was saved by the ringing of the dinner bell.

Harriet must have decided to make amends for the last time Ella visited and was left like a castaway to fend off Poultney. This time, Ella was placed at the end of the table with the Napiers, and a few of the Napiers' neighbors, including the beautiful young lady who was the object of Arkwright's flirtations. Jack Napier was always a jovial gentleman and one of William's dearest friends. He reminded her so of his younger brother Basil, Ella's first love, killed in service. William had named his youngest son after Basil.

Jack started telling a story about a poacher on the Napier estate. "We rode this morning with the men to stake out a place for the drivers in the hunt tomorrow. Suddenly, there appeared a man with his dog and rifle."

"Did you recognize him?" the neighbor asked.

"No," Jack shook his head. The wine had greased his tongue enough so that his British accent was lost to a Scottish lilt.

"We called out to him: 'Hey there!' And he scampered away from us out of sight. 'What's that, I said?' thinking I heard a shot. And my man, MacDouglas, says to me, 'I dinna hear naething but the plover sir.' His imitation of the driver was spot on. Everyone laughed.

"So did you catch him?" Ella said.

"We found him with a stag standing at bay on a boulder, sweeping his big antlers at the man's staghound," Jack said.

"So I lifted my gun in the air and shot the stag for him. And we are dining on it tonight."

They all laughed.

Thirlestane was a modern estate by English standards, and Bill's father, Lord Napier, had invested considerably to keep it up. There was modern plumbing, gaslights in each room, and next to the fireplace was a brass fixture that when pulled would alert the servants in their quarters downstairs which guest needed assistance. Ella used it sparingly, trying not to draw too much attention to herself. But she heard from Trixie that some of the other maids were running themselves ragged up and down the stairs. The Napiers managed hundreds of acres including some woods, where they nurtured the deer the party would be stalking and driving all week.

The next morning, Ella got a taste of the thrill Jack was talking about at dinner the night before. They rose at dawn. It was dark and rainy in the morning. Mist lay thick on the brown heather. The drivers were hard pressed to discern the direction of the wind because the moisture-laden air refused to move the clouds. They mounted their Shetland ponies and took to their places amongst the hills, hoping the direction of the wind wouldn't shift suddenly on them and alert the deer they were coming, while the men and women rode out to stake a place in the moors by the river Yarrow.

"Keep low," Jack said as he pulled up alongside Ella on his horse. "Take off your bonnet. They'll be going to soil as soon as they catch our scent, so be prepared."

After dismounting her horse, she did as she was told and tried to find a comfortable spot on the ground, which was strewn with protruding rocks and boulders. She found a spot with a large tuft of heather and a rock she could hide behind so the deer wouldn't see or catch scent of her until it was too late. And then she waited. A small rock was digging into her side, but she dared not move. Her breathing became heavy as the minutes passed.

As there was nothing else to do but steal glances around her, she viewed the landscape. The undulating hills were tinged brown with heather. Clusters of trees dotted the landscape. Their only companions were the plover and occasional hawk or eagle soaring overhead.

They all lay still as the wind when the cries of the men and staghounds caught her attention in the distance; a herd of deer were descending toward the river. 'Going to soil,' she thought. There were a number of stags and several hinds.

They waited for a sign from Jack to shoot. When it came, in the form of him standing up and taking aim at the herd, the rest of them did the same. Ella took aim at a stag, hoping not to hit a hind. When the sounds of shotguns ringing the air died down, the sportsmen assessed their quarry: three stags and one hind. No one would lay claim to her, and an injured stag had taken off for the river, trying to escape the hounds.

Jack took off in pursuit of him while the drivers came down from the hills and collected the dead deer, placing their carcasses on the flank of their ponies. A few men followed Jack into the river and the rest, weary from the wait and rush of adrenaline, returned with the drivers and their ponies to the manor and the hearty meal waiting for them.

"Jack will be full of himself tonight," Poultney said, startling Ella as he came up beside her on his horse. She had almost forgotten he was one of the guests; he'd barely paid any attention to her since she arrived.

"Someone's been cutting it up rough with you," he said, gesturing at his own eye.

"It's nothing," she said, kicking her horse to fly ahead of him. She thought that would be the end of it, but she underestimated his temerity. After lunch, the sky brightened considerably, and while they were leaving the dining room, Ella asked Aunt Sylvia if she'd like to take a stroll through the plantations.

"No thank you, dear," Sylvia patted her arm. "I think I may retreat to my room for a nap."

"I'll join you for a stroll." Poultney had been right behind them and overheard the conversation.

Ella tried to ignore him.

"How kind of you to escort her," Sylvia said.

"Yes, how kind," Ella said pertly.

He led her into the gardens.

"Before you say anything." She stopped walking and took a stand in front of him. "I'll not discuss my affair with Gabriel."

Poultney shrugged innocently. "I wasn't planning to ask. I've seen the results of his love for you. I hope I never run into the man again because if I do, I dare say I'll not act like a gentleman towards him."

"Aren't you being cavalier?" Ella said and continued to walk. "Perhaps you've forgotten that you had me pinned to the looking glass in Anny Ritchie's library."

"That was self-defense. I know your temper. Your memory may be waning but mine's not. Don't you recall pummeling me in front of your brother when I tried to convince him that you and I were just friends?"

"Hah!" Ella threw her head back and laughed.

Poultney feigned innocence. "I was just trying to avoid any

scandal." He glanced at her sideways and added, "For your sake."

"I believe it was too late for that," Ella said.

"Well, at least I wouldn't strike out at you. Although, I believe, dear girl, you underestimate your ability to provoke preemptive attack."

"Enough of this," Ella scowled. "I'm beginning to believe all men are boors."

"I've never bored you, my dear."

"Stop teasing." She smiled and hit his arm.

"I'm not," he said with a sly smile.

"What are you doing here anyway?"

"Bill Napier invited me," Poultney said. He kicked a small pebble off the path. "I leave next week for America. Is there any message you'd like me to bring to your brother?"

"I thought you were spying on *me* for him."

"I wouldn't call it spying."

"No? What would you call it then?"

"Justified concern for your welfare."

"If my brother was as justifiably concerned as you, I'd have my inheritance from him."

"Be patient. I hear it may be coming soon."

"Really?" She stopped to face him. "How so?"

"The Delaware and Hudson has made an offer."

"When?"

"It's in the works. Soon, my dear, you will be the rich American heiress your suitor has been waiting for." He cupped his hand over her cheek gently.

"That's not funny, Poultney!" She pushed his hand away.

"I'm not jesting," he said.

They halted their conversation before it turned into an argument when Harriet and another woman from the party came upon them. Ella asked to join up with them and found refuge in their banter. Poultney tired of it quickly and found an excuse to head back to the Manor house.

Days later, Ella left Thirlestane with her aunt. At first, she was worried Gabriel would be waiting for her, as he had done before.

Then she remembered he had planned to go racing at Ascot, and it was with a mix of regret and relief that she opened the door to her flat.

He was not there. She sighed and picked through her mail. A letter from the publishing house was mixed in amongst her bills. Anticipating the worst, she tore it open anyway, and shrieked with glee to read they had accepted the manuscript for her play about Dante.

There was no greater joy than this affirmation of her talent. She was floating on air as she climbed the steps to her bedroom. If she hurried, she had time to send a message to Anny, requesting they meet for tea to celebrate. When she entered her bedroom she was taken aback. On the bed was a package wrapped in a silver paper with a big bow of blue satin.

She assumed someone else found out about her good news and was sending a congratulatory gift. She timidly opened the package. Inside was a long box, wrapped in black velvet. She lifted the lid to find a necklace of gold with a pendant of Madeira topaz. And a note from Gabriel, begging her forgiveness.

FIFTEEN

England

Ella was frantic. In a few weeks, William and Janet would be sailing across the Atlantic to bring her the news she had been waiting for about her inheritance, and they were staying at the newly opened, and very upscale, Savoy Hotel. Ella thought it a perfect cause for celebration, but knew she had to temper her enthusiasm.

When she suggested in her correspondence to William that they take in the opera before dinner he responded tersely:

> *I've never appreciated the humor in Gilbert and Sullivan's Mikado. Janet and I are looking forward to dining with you in our hotel suite at the Savoy. I expect you will be bringing your guest, the French gentleman?*

Ella re-read the letter while sitting at her desk in the parlor. From the tone, she knew she'd need a shield from his wrath. He was not pleased at all that she had written to their cousin Estelle in New York, inquiring about the sale of the railroad, telling Ella to *"keep friends and family out of our financial affairs."*

Ella knew cousin Estelle had a short leash on her tongue, and through her brother, Howard, would know about how much was gained by the sale. Indeed, she revealed to Ella that Howard had told her he thought it was close to one million.

She was in a quandary about what to do next. She could just imagine how smug William would be if he found out about her failed affair with Gabriel. He had warned her, he'd say, just like he had warned her about Poultney. And she couldn't bear it if he thought she was destitute in London without any prospects for marriage. He would insist she return to live with Aunt Sylvia.

So what to do about the dinner with William and Janet? If she didn't show him she could manage her affairs he would not be forthcoming with her inheritance. She was worried that Margaret, who was most likely intercepting the letters she sent to her mother, had poisoned William against her. And if Margaret hadn't yet accomplished this, she was sure Poultney would finish the job. If William suspected Ella was desperate for the cash, he would wonder why and question how she was spending her time and her money. He would give her a paltry sum and then promise the rest in dribs and drabs depending on his mood and her good behavior. It would be no better than when she was living under her Father's control. She would be held captive to his whims and prudish expectations of her playing the part of a proper spinster.

She hated that he had such power over her and wished to God she had never signed over the power of attorney. As she pondered her next move, a sharp rap on the door sent her maid Trixie scrambling from the kitchen to answer. Ella glanced at the clock on the mantel. It wasn't tea time, and she wasn't expecting visitors.

"Pardon me, is Mademoiselle Durant in?"

Ella heard Gabriel's friend, Pierre Berton, the actor and playwright, at the door. She quickly stood to receive him.

"Monsieur Berton, what a lovely surprise!' she said as she entered the entranceway. "Trixie, why don't you fix us some coffee?" She led him into her parlor and directed he sit on the settee. He was dressed rather lavishly for a late morning outing. His cravat was burgundy, his vest was made of velvet in the same rich color, and he was sporting diamond cufflinks.

She sat and watched as he deftly swished his frockcoat tails out from under him to take his own seat. Like all actors, he did everything with a flair for the dramatic.

He got immediately to the reason for his visit.

"I've come to speak to you about Gabriel," he said.

She was stunned he thought she cared. She opened her mouth to tell him so, but he continued before she could say anything.

"Please hear me out," he said, holding his hand in the air. "I do not offer excuses for what he did to you."

"He's told you then?"

"Yes," he said gravely. "Gabriel has a temper madam, and I am afraid you have brought out the worst of it in him. I do not blame you for this, I only state the truth."

Trixie came in with the coffee, and they settled into pouring it for themselves and stirring the contents before continuing.

"He is not used to a woman like me I'm afraid. I'm sure it is an affront to him that I will not answer any of his letters."

"So he has been trying to reach you?"

"Yes, he has written from the races. The last was addressed from Ascot. I never read the contents; I tear them up immediately."

Monsieur Berton raised his brows as if surprised by her gumption. Ella guessed why: the idea that a woman, especially one in her thirties, as Ella was, and beyond hope of marrying, would stand up for herself against an eligible bachelor such as Gabriel, surprised him. His own protégé, Sarah Bernhardt, was well known for demanding respect from men of all stations, then entered into a marriage that everyone knew left her a victim.

"I see," he said and after a pause continued, "I'll let Gabriel know this, as he was very concerned about you, which I am sure is compounded by the fact that you will not respond to his letters."

"You may also tell him that I have no intention of taking him back. If that is why he sent you," Ella said.

"No, no. He does not even know I am here today. I never told him I was coming."

"You've seen him then?" Suddenly Ella felt the strange flutter in her stomach at the thought that Gabriel was in town. It both excited her and terrified her to think she might run into him somewhere.

"He was here in London, briefly. He came to the theater to see me and we dined."

"Well, pardon my frankness, Monsieur, but I'm curious, what is the purpose of your visit today?"

"I know how deeply Gabriel cares for you. And I only wish that you would give him another chance. An opportunity for redemption."

Ella thought about his request. She was not ready to give in. As much as she longed for him, his presence in the flat was at times, overbearing. She hadn't realized how much she relished her freedom until she had kicked him out. But the nights, oh the nights were empty and lonely now. She lifted the cup to her lips while she collected herself. Maybe Gabriel was sorry. He had, after all, given her that lovely topaz necklace.

"Madam?" Berton was waiting for a reply.

"I'm afraid you have caught me off-guard today, Monsieur," Ella said. "I was thinking how fine it would be to attend the opera next week before dining with my brother and his wife at the Savoy Hotel. Perhaps you could join me, and we can discuss this further?"

Berton perked up at the suggestion of opera followed by dinner at the luxurious Savoy Hotel. Ella had calculated correctly; she knew he wouldn't be able to resist.

"That," he responded, "would please me very much." Smiling, he raised his cup in toast and tilted his head a fraction.

Ella was impressed with the depth of her deception. William would never know he was not the Frenchman she had courted this past year. And she had no intention of telling him.

SIXTEEN

England

As they disembarked from the steamer that had carried them across the Atlantic, William was greeted by the smells and sounds he remembered so well from his youth. He inhaled deeply. The bustle and excitement sent his senses surging. He was home.

Janet, who did not enjoy sea travel, looked peaked as he guided her to their waiting cab that would take them to the train headed for London.

"Once we reach the hotel, you will have plenty of time to rest," he assured her. She didn't respond. Her lack of enthusiasm was tedious. She had spent most of the trip in their cabin, while he had socialized with the other passengers. If she wasn't in the cabin she was taking air on the deck, trying to avoid vomiting overboard. Between her lack of sea legs and her constant complaints about missing the children, William wondered how he was going to stay positive about this trip. As it was, he dreaded his inevitable confrontation with Ella over her inheritance. But he'd worry about that next week, when they finally met at dinner. He told her to bring an escort, knowing she would never dare talk about their family finances in front of someone who was a stranger to him and Janet.

Or maybe not. Ella had lost all sense of propriety. Lately she had been clawing information out of anyone she could: cousin Estelle was her latest target. And Estelle, being the dimwit that she was, had told Ella everything. Or at least what little she knew. Estelle could never have known how much the railroad actually sold for or how William had finagled the transfer of the land rights. This he kept to himself. The only others that knew about it were his lawyers, and Huntington. And, as co-conspirators, they would never breathe a word of it to anyone.

A few hours later, they stepped out of their carriage and onto the curb in front of the Savoy.

"It's a remarkable hotel," William said to Janet with wide-eyed excitement. She produced a tepid smile as they entered the grand brass revolving doors. Everywhere around them, ladies wore the latest Paris fashions, hats of all colors and sizes with large plumes of feathers fastened to the brims, floating in the air above their well-coiffed heads. William guessed at least a dozen species of birds from the Florida Everglades were represented on the heads of the women in the lobby. The place was a whirl of activity, and William couldn't wait to dive into it.

"I think I'll take a short nap before we have supper, dear," Janet said.

William took her elbow more firmly than he should have and guided her to the front desk receptionist. "We have to register for our room," he said.

Once he had her snugly in bed, he pecked her cheek and went to enjoy the talk and a cigar in the men's lounge. Approaching the warmly lit room, William was confronted with the reality that he didn't know anyone in it. He found a place to sit in the corner by a window overlooking the street, ordered a drink and found a *Times* cast aside by another. He picked it up to read, not wanting to look as if he was unoccupied while listening in to the conversations around him. He glanced at the yacht racing news. The *Valkyrie* was forced to withdraw from the America's Cup, and the Island Sailing Club in Cowes was admitting ladies. On the society section was the headline that Queen Victoria had, much to everyone's surprise, invited Ellen Terry and Henry Irving to perform *The Merchant of Venice* at Sandringham, and even more shocking, to dine with her afterwards. The actress Lillie Langtry had divorced her husband, and was now racing horses. He put the paper down briefly to light his cigar and revel in the sound of the clipped British accents of the men gossiping nearby.

Two dapper young men were drinking heavily and talking too loudly about the Prince of Wales and his son Eddy. From what he could make out of the conversation between the two prattling fools, Eddy enjoyed the company of both men and women.

While tolerance was expected for the members of the royal family, even as the Prince of Wales grabbed the headlines for his exploits, things had certainly changed in sixteen years. The country was becoming more relaxed and accepting of decadence. William was neither relieved nor surprised. It was to be taken in stride. The key was to adapt.

"Durant, old boy!"

William was jolted from his eavesdropping. Blocking his view was Charlie Arkwright. "My God, you startled me. How are you, old friend?" He stood up to greet his old hunting companion.

The two men shared in the jubilance of being re-acquainted after years apart. They reminisced on old stories from their exploits in Egypt and ordered another round of drinks.

"How's Florence?" William asked.

"Florence?" Arkwright said, confused.

"I imagined you two were married, although I must admit I haven't heard anything from the Napiers about it."

"Thought they were sparing you some grief about the fate of their cousin, did you? Well, old boy, I assure you it was a brief affair. Florence's father didn't approve of my gambling habits. To say nothing of my womanizing." He laughed.

William didn't join in the laughter. He would have been a better match for Florence, given the chance. He didn't want to know where she ended up. It would only stir up old wounds. He changed the subject.

"Still playing cards with your friends at St. James's?"

"Yes. And you should join us. How long are you staying?"

"I have some business to attend to with my sister, and then Janet and I are traveling to Thirlestane to take in some grouse shooting."

"Marvelous! I will be there as well." Arkwright gulped his drink and settled back in his chair.

William studied him. His face had puffed with age and his dark hair now had streaks of gray and was thinning at the top of his head. Arkwright was always a big one for drink, gambling, and women, and it was catching up on him. He also appeared preoccupied by something, glancing around him every now and then and not wanting to look William in the eye. Finally, he got to it.

"William," he said as he leaned in, "I was wondering about Ella. Have you heard from her lately? How is she doing?"

William stiffened and tried to sound nonchalant. "Well, she sounds happy. Her new play on Dante is about to be published, and—"

"I know all of that," Arkwright said, his impatience apparent. "I'm talking about this French fellow. What the devil is she doing with *him*? He trades thoroughbreds."

William shrugged. "You know my sister, she loves excitement. I understand her new passion is horse racing."

"Well, *I* was the one that introduced her to the races," he huffed. "Granted, I haven't heard yet if this Count of hers is involved in any scandals at the tracks. He's never been reported by the Jockey Club. Yet I don't trust him." Arkwright landed his fist on the table between them. "And I know you've come into quite a bit of money. Please, whatever you do, William, be careful about giving it all away to your sister. She needs guidance."

William couldn't help question Charlie's motives: was he bothered that Ella was infatuated with the Count and not him, or was he being protective of an old friend? Charlie had always been a big flirt with the ladies and thrived on the attention.

Instead of questioning Charlie about his motives William said, "Thank you. I'll take that into account. Now, let's change the subject shall we? Conversations about my sister never fail to annoy me."

They didn't stop talking until William had to leave for supper with Janet.

"You wouldn't believe," William said to Janet when they finally sat down to eat in their suite, "what Ella has gotten herself into now."

Ella could understand why William wouldn't like *The Mikado*. It was a cleverly disguised attempt to make fun of British institutions, although the Prince of Wales found it hilarious. That, and the poor Nanki-Poo, fleeing an overbearing father to pursue love, would have been salt in the wounds for William. Still, she loved the whole production.

Ella introduced Monsieur Berton to William and Janet and then they were led to the parlor of William's hotel suite to dine on beef with oyster sauce. William asked Ella about her play, *Dante: a Dramatic Poem*.

"I understand it will be published soon?" he said.

"Yes," she replied.

"That's wonderful. Congratulations," Janet said.

"I believe it has a lot of potential," Monsieur Berton remarked. "Especially for audiences in Italy."

"Really?" William seemed surprised that his sister had the potential to reach the international stage with her writing.

"Yes. Indeed, I thought I might send your manuscript to some of my contacts." Pierre turned his head toward Ella.

"Contacts? In the theater?" William brows flicked up.

"Yes. Your sister didn't tell you? I am a playwright." Pierre Berton chuckled. "Perhaps I am better known to you as an actor. Did you ever chance to see *Camille*, when it played in America?"

"The Bernhardt production?" William asked incredulously.

"Why of course. I was one of the leads with Madam Bernhardt."

Williams face fell as it slowly began to sink in that he was in the company of a theater man from the notorious company of Sarah Bernhardt. His glacial stare at Ella caused Janet to gasp slightly as if waiting for something to strike.

"I see." William stabbed his steak with exaggerated enthusiasm.

Ella's heart sank. Why hadn't she warned Pierre?

"Of course, our French productions, although they make a lot of money in your country, are always met with mixed reviews. Americans are sometimes shocked by our, how shall I say, overt displays of affection?" He smiled at Janet as if she would know what he was talking about and would agree with him if she could.

Janet's cheeks turned crimson and she reached for her wine goblet.

William sat stonily chewing on his meat.

When the meal was finished, through intervals of polite but guarded conversation between Janet and Ella, Pierre stood, and, as planned, excused himself for another engagement. He bowed to Janet and took her hand in his to kiss it. He was about to do the same to Ella when William interrupted. "You will be seeing my sister home as well?"

Pierre waited for Ella to reply.

"I thought I'd stay and discuss family matters with you, William. It has been so long since we've seen each other," Ella said.

"No need tonight. Janet is tired and I'd rather you leave now," William said brusquely.

Ella got up from her seat and went to hug Janet goodbye. With a swish of her petticoats, she whirled toward the entranceway where Pierre was waiting with her cloak in his hand.

"You could have warned me," Pierre said with amusement once they were in the carriage. "I am an actor you know. I would have played my part for you." He grinned.

"I'm so sorry for the embarrassing way my brother treated you," Ella said.

"No harm done." Pierre waved it off. "But," he said over the horse's hooves clopping along the streets, "you owe me a favor for your trickery."

"Whatever I can do for you," Ella said.

"You must be my guest then for my opening performance next week. You may sit in my box. Bring a friend."

"And?" Ella hardly believed this qualified as comeuppance.

"Gabriel will be attending, of course." He smiled slyly.

It was Janet that apologized for William's behavior. She sent a note to Ella the next day. William was to spend the afternoon with Arkwright at one of his clubs, and Janet had nothing to do. *Would Ella join her for tea?*

She shared pictures of the children, and Ella gushed over them. Then Janet became quiet and said, "You know how William can be. He is very," she hesitated, "belligerent at times."

Ella was alarmed by her confession. "He's never hurt you has he?"

"Oh no, no. Nothing like that," Janet assured her. "What I mean is that he can be very stubborn and forceful. And if you don't go along with him, well, you must know how surly he can be."

Ella sat thoughtfully. She and William had fought, that was true, but they had always been loyal to each other, until recently. Now, Ella wasn't sure if she could trust William. "Tell me," she said. "What do you know about the sale of the railroad?"

"I only know that it went through, and that William has been making plans on how to invest it. Possibly, he may buy more land in the Adirondacks. I'm not quite sure. He never divulges any of his business to me. He speaks with John Barbour in hushed tones in the library. I'm never included in the discussions."

"Janet, I must speak to William about my inheritance. Last night did not work as I had planned. Can you invite me to dine with you both this evening?"

"Yes, of course." Janet said, visibly relieved. "I'd enjoy your company. I'm sure William is sorry for the way he treated you and your guest last evening."

"Has William even offered to show you around London?"

Janet stared at her blankly, afraid to admit he hadn't.

"Well then. Let me take you out. He'll be gone most of the afternoon. Let's go shopping together."

When they tumbled back into the hotel room later that afternoon, William was stewing in a chair.

"Where have you been?" he demanded when he saw Ella tagging along behind Janet. All the flush Janet had from spending the day outdoors ran from her cheeks as she stood in the doorway with Ella beside her.

"William, is that any way to greet your wife and sister?" Ella scolded.

"You are not welcome here," he said as he turned on her.

"Nonsense!" Ella retorted. Janet stood frozen in place. "I am your sister and whatever has happened in the past between us must be amended. Janet has asked me to dine with you this evening and I plan to return at seven. Now if you'll excuse me." She took Janet's hand. "Thank you for a lovely day. I will see you later." She left before William could protest.

Dinner was stifling. Janet's eyes were puffy and red, probably from crying. Ella felt sorry for her but was not in a position to tell her how to manage her domestic affairs. Ella had her own interests to take care of during William's short stay in London. He was about to leave for Thirlestane, and Ella needed to get some answers from him before he left.

When they commenced with a strained dinner conversation, and Ella had felt they had skirted the issue long enough, she said, "I understand the railroad has been sold."

William didn't even wince as he replied, "Railroads aren't sold; the interest in them is transferred to the people who hold the stocks and bonds."

"Where is the money from the transfer then? Am I not entitled to one third as you promised me when I signed over the power of attorney?"

William cleared his throat and gazed at her. She could not read him. "You don't understand business, dear sister. Never have. It would be impossible for me to explain."

"Try me," Ella said. When William remained silent, she scoffed: "You don't understand it yourself, do you? That's why you can't explain."

"How dare you insult me!"

Janet kept her eyes downcast, pushing her food around her plate. Ella remained calm and waited for him to regain his composure and then resumed her attack.

"How, then, do you explain where you are getting your money

from? Surely, as you said yourself to me once in your letters, you are not paid very much by the railroad. And this hotel suite," she gestured at their surroundings, "does not come cheaply. And what about mother? How is she able to send me my allowance? Who is giving her money?"

"I will take care of our mother and her inheritance. She's my client."

"That's ludicrous! How absurd to call our mother your client. Estelle has told me everything, William." She dared him with her eyes to deny he knew anything more. Estelle may not have provided her with *all* the details, but it was enough for William to guess how much she knew. The sale of the railroad was practically public knowledge once Estelle heard about it from Howard and spread the news like wildfire amongst the Durant clan.

"I know why you're so eager to talk," William said before she had a chance to continue. "And I am prepared to direct Barbour to deposit twenty-five thousand in your account here in London."

Ella placed her fork down, stunned. It was a lot of money. Was it enough though? And how much did she deserve?

"Thank you, William," she said. He had taken her off guard. She needed more time, and more information about the sale now that she knew it was complete. Maybe Estelle was misinformed about the payout. One look at Janet told her this was not the time to ask. Better to take what she could for now.

Later that evening, Trixie brought Ella her mail before heading to bed. A letter from Anny was at the top of the pile.

> *Congratulations on the sale of the railroad, dear. Don't spend all your inheritance at once, especially on your friends. Can you meet me for tea at the Kensington Hotel on Sunday?*

Anny took the wind out of her sails over tea, telling her, "But dear, only twenty-five thousand?"

What had seemed like a lot of money to Ella suddenly felt meager.

"Didn't you tell me once that combined with the land your father's estate was worth over one million?"

Ella tapped the side of her teacup with her fingernails. Anny was right.

"You must not let him deny you of your inheritance," Anny said indignantly. "You must see him as soon as possible and demand an accounting from him."

"Well, that's impossible now. He's left for Thirlestane and won't be back for another week."

"In a week then. You must promise me that in one week you will march right over to his hotel and demand an audience of him. And this time, find out what happened to your money." She smacked her linen napkin down on the table with bravado.

Ella knew Anny was right. William was evading the truth about her money and it had been going on for too long.

"I will," she said.

SEVENTEEN

Scotland

The beaters shouted and waved flags along the ridge as the men huddled with their rifles in anticipation. The covey of grouse, which had been basking in the sun amidst the heather, took to the air in a straight line. Their perfect symmetry lasted until they realized their mistake at taking to the air and began to dart in angles to avoid the guns. Shots rang out and the setters went wild with excitement.

The men patted each other on their backs in hearty gestures of approval and mounted their horses to ride back to Thirlestane for the breakfast they'd missed.

"How are you making out with the land sales?" Bill Napier asked William.

"The Baedeker Poultney wrote has yet to procure me any new business from England or the Continent," William replied as the servants filled their plates with sausage and potatoes.

"Look old friend, as I told that Bigelow fellow when he last visited, you may be looking for clients in the wrong place, I'm afraid."

"How so?"

"Because the only one with any money to spare is our friend here," Jack Napier said as he whacked Charlie Arkwright on the back so hard he almost collapsed into his food.

William glanced back at the door to make sure the ladies hadn't arrived yet.

"What my brother means is that we, and other landowners like us, are in no position to make investments in land overseas. Many estates are entailed, to prevent them being broken up into smaller and smaller parcels of land. American farmers are flooding the markets with their cheap corn, and our tenants are barely able to make their rent payments," Bill said.

"You can ask any member of the House of Lords and he'll tell you. We need tariff reform," Jack said.

"Yes," Bill agreed. "They may have had good intentions when they lifted the tariffs, but grain is now cheaper to import from America than it is to grow here."

"Yes, well my workers in the factories like their bread reasonably priced," Arkwright quipped.

Bill Napier exchanged a somber look with his brother Jack. "And the crofters are demanding more reform. They're withholding their rents in protest," Jack said.

"It's a good thing I work for Her Majesty's government," Bill said, "or I'd never be able to keep up the estate once I inherit it."

The ladies entered the dining room just as the men were about to indulge in another round of coffee.

"So tell me, William. Now that this railroad business is behind you and you have all of this land at your disposal, what do you plan to do with it?" Arkwright asked.

"Develop it, of course. In due time." He met Janet's curious stare across the table.

"You must keep us all abreast of your ventures," Bill said. "And perhaps now that you are not burdened with the day-to-day activities of the company you could make an effort to visit us during the yacht racing season in Cowes?"

"He'll not only do that! He'll be coming to visit us with his very own yacht!" Jack proclaimed.

"Wouldn't that be a thrill to see," Arkwright said. "Be sure to invite me when you host the Prince of Wales."

Again they all laughed at Arkwright's joke, although William didn't find it quite so amusing. Arkwright came back to the point of their earlier conversation.

"If it's investors you want in these land speculations schemes, William, you must talk to the right people: industrialists with money to spend. Your father always knew that. It was his approach that failed him."

"I'd agree with your summation of my father's negotiating skills." William's mouth set in grim acknowledgement.

"Money attracts money," Arkwright continued, "Seriously, why don't you attend the races in Cowes next summer and show off yours? That's where you'll find people eager to spend some of their own."

William mulled over what Arkwright said. It was true that racing week in Cowes attracted royalty as well as those clamoring to meet them. Arkwright would be able to open doors for William that had been shut on his father during the financial panic of 1873 when his fortunes took a turn for the worse and everyone knew it. If they could see how William had changed the direction of the Durant fortunes, they might be impressed enough to invest in his land development plans in the Adirondacks.

The subdivision his father wanted at Eagle Lake may become a reality. The Durant steamboat lines would take off as more visitors flocked to the region. Game hunters would want a piece of the action once they learned about all of the wild game roaming freely about the woods, just ripe for the taking. Sailing into Cowes was not that far-fetched. William had done so before, on his father's yacht.

Janet was quiet on the train ride home. It was not unusual for her, but William wished she were enjoying the trip as much as him.

"Maybe we should take you shopping for some new gowns in London before we leave?" he suggested.

She took her gaze from the window. "Yes, dear."

"You could show a little more in the way of enthusiasm," he said as he flicked a speck of lint off his trousers and let off an irritated sigh.

Janet's eyes returned to the view of the Scottish countryside. "I'm sorry. I miss the children so."

"I do as well," William lied. He hadn't thought about them once while they were here, but that was because he knew they were in good hands at home with their governess. Wasn't that enough?

"Your sister sent word to me at Thirlestane." Janet lifted a letter out of her purse and handed it to him. "She wants to dine with us once more before we leave."

"I believe I've had enough of my sister for a long while."

"Really, William." Janet's hat bobbed as she swung her head around to face him. "She's your sister. Where's your sense of family loyalty?" She was visibly shaking with anger. William had never seen her this upset since Lawrence had inadvertently let one of the dogs into the dining room while they were eating their supper.

"If it will please you, I'll see my sister once more before we depart," he said.

"It would please me very much," she said.

William returned to his paper.

EIGHTEEN

England

Ella took Anny with her to see Sarah Bernhardt's latest production. No one else was in the box when they arrived, but as soon as the curtain rose, she saw out of the corner of her eye someone slide into a seat behind her. She immediately felt Gabriel's presence. She fidgeted in her seat, feeling his eyes boring holes into the back of her head. It was a relief when the intermission gave her an excuse to scurry from the box in search of the ladies' lounge. Anny went with her.

"Was that your Count sitting behind us in the box?"

Ella rolled her eyes. "Please, let's not acknowledge him," she said to Anny.

"Why, how are we to do that? He'll be waiting for you when we get back."

Anny was right. When they entered the box, he stood up and took Ella's arm to guide her to her seat. She tried to quell the small flutter his touch caused in the pit of her stomach.

"Thank you," she said as she sat down.

When it was over he stood at the exit, waiting for her. She smiled politely at him and a friend of Anny's came up to talk. Anny, sensing that they would never shake Gabriel if Ella didn't finally confront him, said, "Ella dear, I'm going to say hello to some friends, just over there," she nodded her head toward a group of ladies across the room. "You'll be alright with Count de la Salle for a moment?"

Ella strained to appear calm. "Of course."

Anny gave Gabriel a warning look before she left them.

"You haven't responded to my letters," he said when Anny was out of earshot.

"You forget that I never wanted to see you again," Ella said.

"That, I'm afraid would be impossible," Gabriel said languidly as if he thought she would no more deny him than deny her own mother.

"I've reserved a table for us at the Café Royal this evening. It would be my pleasure if Mrs. Ritchie would join us."

"Pffft, as if I would dine with you after what you did to me."

His gray eyes didn't flinch. "The reservation is at nine," he said with utter confidence. "Now if you'll excuse me. I must find my friend Pierre." He bowed slightly and left her standing, dumbfounded, in the hall.

The audacity of that man.

"Let's get a cab, dear. I'm very tired." Anny came up beside her and tugged at her arm.

"Yes," Ella said, tearing her eyes from Gabriel's retreating figure. She accompanied Anny home in the cab and then the driver turned toward Ella's flat. The ride provided just enough time for Ella to debate with herself whether she would dine with Gabriel. If she met him, she could tell him exactly what she thought of him.

"Driver, take me to the Café Royal," she called.

"I've been waiting for you, ma chérie." Gabriel stood up when she entered his private booth at the restaurant. He was smiling with delight. Ella was pleased to think he was unsure if she would show up.

"I can't stay long. I've a dinner engagement with my brother tomorrow evening, and I will need all of my strength for it," she said, trying to sound non-committal. "I only came out of deference to our mutual friend, Monsieur Berton. He insisted I speak with you."

"Of course," he smiled like a cat that had just caught a mouse. He showed her to a chair, sat down himself, and then took a cigarette out of the case on the table. The lighter cast his face in an eerie orange glow as he cupped his hands over the flame. The lids of his eyes lifted slightly and he narrowed them on her as he exhaled the smoke.

"I see you're wearing the topaz I gave you."

Ella fingered the pendant around her neck, feeling naked, exposed, and vulnerable. "I'll have a glass of wine and you can update me on your activities if you wish. Then I must take my leave," she said, trying to remain resolute.

"Oh, but, ma chérie, I'd so much like to hear about you. You've published your play? And how is your brother and his wife?"

Ella put one fist into the other palm to control the shaking in her hands.

He crushed his cigarette into an ashtray and took her trembling hands in his. "Tell me everything," he said.

A flood of warmth mingled with trepidation washed over her when she realized she was still in love with him.

The next morning, she lifted her head off her pillow and was greeted by a bright light that came pouring into the room when Gabriel opened the shade that had been blocking it.

"Please!" she cried, shielding her eyes and trying not to feel the pounding in her temple from all of the wine they drank the night before.

"Wake up!" Gabriel said with exuberance. "The day is young and we must prepare you for the encounter with your brother."

"Oh no," Ella groaned. "Must you remind me?"

"Trixie is bringing us tea and toast. I think we should discuss strategy."

"Whatever do you mean?" Ella said yawning.

"I mean that if you are to obtain what is rightfully yours, you need to learn some humility," he said.

"Oh for goodness sake," Ella laughed.

"I'm serious," Gabriel frowned down at her.

"I know you are," she said and lifted herself out of bed. She was sore from their lovemaking.

"I'm going to have Trixie draw a bath," she said.

He stood up and gazed admiringly at her legs dangling over the side of the bed. Swiftly, he took her ankle into his warm hand and traced his finger along the instep. A tingle ran up her leg and spine. Trixie knocked on the door with their tray.

"Leave it outside," Gabriel called to her. Then, turning his attention back to Ella's other foot, he lifted her legs back onto the bed, lifted her nightgown off over her head and pressed his warm body on top of hers.

They were lying in her bed looking up at the ceiling after love making. Gabriel was smoking a cigarette.

"I have a tip on a colt that will bring in enormous sums of money at the tracks. If we could buy her together, we could become very rich," he said.

Ella was intrigued. No one had ever considered her as a business partner before.

"What we need to do. What you need to do, today, is figure out how much you will receive from your brother. This investment, this colt, will be costly to train and stable."

"If I am to face the wrath of my brother for the sake of a horse, I would like to know, besides money, what is in this for me exactly?" she said.

"What would you like?" he said nonchalantly.

"You and I both know the answer to that," she said.

He flicked his brow in surprise at her assertiveness. "Ma chérie, are you proposing to me?" He laughed and the crow lines at his eyes gave him a softness she rarely witnessed.

"Why of course not," she said, tussling his thick black hair. "That's your job."

He jumped off the bed and onto the floor beside her. Kneeling down, he placed his hands in hers and said, "I've been waiting for this moment. It would be an honor to marry you, my love. However, I'm afraid that along with my title, I've inherited an estate in disrepair. Before my older brother died and left the home to me, he had sold off many of the furnishings and art to pay off his gambling debts. Now it is up to me to bring the house back to the splendor it once was. I've spent the past three years trying to do so. I cannot marry you in good conscious until it is complete, and I can bring you home with me."

Ella could hardly believe it; he wanted *her* to be *his* wife. And he wasn't hiding anything from her, as Poultney had once insinuated. If Gabriel had been hiding anything it was because he was both embarrassed and waiting to make his estate ready—for her. If they had the money to bring his estate back to all of its former glory, she would be a Countess. Gabriel's wife.

"How much do you need for this winning colt?" she asked.

She was late and knew it would infuriate William. Dressed in her finest silk gown made of a deep lavender-colored cloth, she entered their suite with an air of confidence, and graciously thanked him for inviting her to dinner. All through the evening she kept the conversations on topics she knew would interest him: hunting at Thirlestane, the Napiers' children, her delight at seeing the photos of his children. They talked about shopping, and the latest fashions, and even managed to laugh at the gossip that plagued the Prince of Wales. They drank a lot of champagne.

And then, when Ella thought she had him as relaxed as he'd ever be, she said lightly, "Excuse my impertinence, but I do *have* to ask. I thought you told me one time that father's estate was worth more than one million? Where has all of that money gone?"

William coughed and clenched his teeth. Then he slammed his fist down on the table so hard the champagne flutes jumped.

Ella hadn't calculated correctly. She had waited too long, and now he was drunk.

"If you were a man I'd shoot you down!" he spat. "Because you imply I have no integrity."

Janet blanched. "William, dear," she said, placing her hand on his arm as if to calm him.

"You, Janet, should not get involved. You are my wife, not Ella's friend," he said, "your rooms are around the corner." He gestured toward the bedrooms down the hallway. "Go there, now."

Janet gasped and opened her mouth to reply but with one glance at William, thought better of it and clamped her mouth shut. She stood up, gathered her skirts and left the room.

"Shame on you," Ella said to William as she watched Janet retreat.

"I will have you arrested for slander if you so much as imply to anyone that I have shirked my duty toward you in any way," William said.

It frightened Ella to see him this way. She held back a building panic inside and clutched her throat, which failed to produce a sound. She bided her time, trying to think of what to say next that would assuage his anger. This was not working out the way it was supposed to. Her head was clouded from all of the champagne. She tried to recall what Gabriel had coached her to say and do. Humility was the one thing she was not altogether good at. Now here she was, facing down her brother who, for all intents and purposes, had become their father: a tyrant.

William got up from the table and started to pace the floor, another reminder of their father, who would do the same thing whenever he was agitated.

"William," she said, in a soothing voice. "Let's talk reasonably. Shall we? I'm not asking for a king's ransom."

"You have no idea what you need or want, Ella. That has always been your problem. You were supposed to be a companion to Aunt Sylvia. If you had done what you were supposed to, none of this money would matter."

Ella was shocked. So he was behind the plan to have her while away her time with their aunt.

"You know that was never to be. I tried my best, but sitting with her every night reading from one of the old books in her library by the fire while I watched her fall asleep in a chair was so boring! I have friends and literary acquaintances here in London. They were beckoning me to join them, and it is a good thing I did, because now I'm published once again."

"Aunt Sylvia would not have gotten in your way," William scoffed.

"Aunt Sylvia was dragging me to every tea parlor in London to meet up with her old bitty friends. She had a disapproving sigh over every garment I wore, and she reminded me constantly about the costs to board me, as if the guilt would tether me to her forever. It was not my calling to be a companion. You know that. I need my independence. I have yearned for it ever since we moved back to America and I was cloistered away in that dungeon of a town, North Creek."

"Living as a spinster in London is damned expensive, Ella. Why not return to America and find a comfortable place near Mother and settle down? You could write to your heart's content."

"And *you* could watch over my every move. No thank you," Ella said.

"What are you afraid of? That I wouldn't condone you taking up with a Frenchman?"

Ella remained silent.

"Don't try to play coy with me. I know all about him. Arkwright filled me in. He's a horse trader. And for your sake, I hope he's sincere."

"He is." Ella bit her tongue. Gabriel had warned her not to reveal their engagement. He said William would accuse him of being a fortune hunter and never give her any more money. "Who I decide to court is none of your damned business."

"Don't raise your voice to me," William threatened.

"Then neither should you be raising your voice to me," Ella said. "I won't return to America, if that's what you're demanding. I have too many friends here. And my connections have proved worthwhile. If it weren't for Anny, I would never have published my play on Dante. You can't deny me my future. And you cannot dictate with whom I spend my time."

"We're at a standstill then," William stopped pacing.

"We are?"

"Yes. Unless you choose to return to America I will not be giving you any more than the twenty-five thousand I have already promised," he said.

"William, when I gave you power of attorney over me, I did so with the expectations that you had my best interests at heart."

"I do," he said. He would not meet her eyes. "The money you will receive, plus the monthly allowance should be plenty to keep you happy here, cavorting around with your literary and theater set of friends. You can't be trusted with more. Especially when you are courting a man who is most likely a fortune hunter."

He folded his arms across his chest and tapped his foot on the floor a few times, waiting for another onslaught of protests from her. When she could find none, he said, "The subject is closed. I'll ask the porter to find you a cab."

Later that evening, Gabriel met her at the door to the flat with a hopeful smile on his face.

Ella didn't have the heart to admit she had failed. He was only asking for her to invest fifteen thousand dollars to help buy and set up this colt. As long as she could give him this much, and things went as he predicted, they could get married. Besides, he appeared so happy for her, she didn't have the guts to tell him the truth: her brother was holding her inheritance hostage. It might all change if she married a Count. How could her brother deny her then? He'd be overwhelmed with joy when one of his family members was titled.

"I am so happy." Gabriel clapped his hands together and rubbed them vigorously as she took off her gloves. "We shall invest in this colt and it will bring us a fortune. We will set up our home in Paris and live like royalty."

Ella smiled wanly and said, "Yes. It will be wonderful."

PART FIVE

1890-91

NINETEEN

New York

William was on the steamboat with his mother and Margaret, heading to the Stott camp on Bluff Point to meet up with Janet and her family. The Stott women were planning the church bazaar and had invited guests for dinner and a show after their preparations were done.

Francis Stott was fond of entertaining his guests with the ditties he wrote and produced. Arpad and his wife Anna were also invited, and Anna was going to play the piano for them as well.

"What is the entertainment for this evening?" Hannah asked William from her seat on the boat. She was bundled up in a coat with a plaid blanket draped over her shoulders. Margaret was sitting next to her, fixing Hannah's blanket and fussing with her own to protect them from the evening breeze that was skipping across the lake and tickling the back of their necks. William could swear the two of them were starting to look alike. It bothered him that his mother was losing her independence and had to rely more and more on Margaret. Any day now he expected to see Margaret spoon-feeding his once fiercely independent mother. One would never know she was the same woman that picked up her children and took them across the Atlantic to live without their father for more than a decade. They traveled all over England and the

Continent, and she never tired of it. Now, a simple steamboat trip across the lake would tire her out for days.

"As I said, Mother, there will be a mix of entertainment this evening. The Stotts are putting on a production, and then Mrs. Gerster will play a piece on the piano."

"At least she'll lend an air of sophistication to the event," Hannah said. "Well, as long as we don't have to play those awful charades I guess it will be fine." She didn't share the Stotts' proclivity for games. Margaret clucked in agreement.

As they neared the Stott camp, they could see Janet's brother, Louis, in a boat with a guide, in pursuit of a deer swimming in the lake. Louis lifted his rifle in the air and shot at it. His guide pulled up before the deer could drown and yanked a rope around its neck. They were dragging it to shore as the steamboat pulled up to the dock. Curious, William thought, there were no hounds baying on the shoreline.

Louis clambered out of his boat, flush with excitement, and found William. "Did you see that?" he asked.

"Yes. Where are your hounds?"

"We didn't need them. My guide saw the deer swimming over to Indian Point and called me into his boat so we could chase him down. A two-year-old buck. I'd say close to one hundred and fifty pounds. I've met my quota for the season with that one." Louis nodded at the deer that was being dragged on shore by the guide and a few other men that came to help.

"Does it really matter?" William said.

"Actually, yes. It does. The game warden came around just the other day to tell us they may be putting a limit on the season for hounding as well."

"The game warden is making rounds now?"

"Be careful," Louis said with a seriousness that surprised William. "They're starting to enforce the new game laws."

William had never paid attention. In the decade he had been coming up to the Adirondacks, he'd rarely encountered a game warden.

In the main cabin, the Stott women were huddled over a table with papers strewn about, discussing in serious tones the itinerary for the church bazaar. William made sure Margaret and his mother were settled in easy chairs before he approached the ladies, catching the tail end of one of their plans.

"Mrs. Doherty said she would gather the fancy cakes onto the chargers. I suggest we place them in the dining area," Mrs. Stott said to Janet. "I'll be telling fortunes in the garden."

"How many are we expecting?" Janet inquired.

"At least one hundred," her mother replied.

Julia was busy folding paper invitations.

"And I hear Mr. Warren has written a song on the back of a piece of birch bark to auction off," Janet's friend from Saratoga, Cornelia Kirby, chimed in. The ladies all murmured their approval.

"And I have here," Mrs. Stott said as she lifted up a sketch, "a drawing of Alvah Dunning, signed by none other than Dr. Arpad Gerster." They all murmured their approval.

"That will fetch a good price at auction," Julia said.

William leaned over to look at the list, which Janet had protectively tried to hide from his view. "Wouldn't you be better off putting all of those cakes in the parlor? It has better lighting. And if your aim is to sell them, you want people to view them in the best light possible."

The ladies lifted their heads collectively to stare at William. Janet eyed him like she would an errant child who had spoken out of turn at dinner.

"Perhaps, dear," she said as she bit her lower lip and picked up one of the paper invitations to fold. The tension was palpable. William sighed impatiently. Julia rose and left the room.

"I think it was a good suggestion," William persisted, "Look around you, the lighting is excellent here. It will showcase those cakes much better than the lighting in the dining area." He waved his hands about the room and as he was pivoting to gesture toward the light in the windows, Julia was suddenly beside him with a fishing rod in her hands.

She thrust one of them into his and said, "Let's go. The fish are jumping."

The ladies giggled, and William knew he had lost any chance of persuading them. Reluctantly he followed Julia out the door to one of the guideboats waiting for them at the shore.

They dined on venison, onions, turnips and potatoes, after which the guests retreated to the veranda to take their coffee as the sun set. It cast a warm glow on the water as swallows swooped and caught the night insects flitting above the lake.

When the sun had disappeared behind the horizon, they returned to the parlor for the night's entertainment. They assembled in front of the large brick fireplace. *Mollia Tempora*, 'Favourable Times' in Latin, was carved into the wood under the mantel. Francis got up and went to the piano to play a riff.

Julia, Elizabeth, Cornelia, and Janet came in from one of the bedrooms and stood beside the piano. They were dressed elaborately. Janet wore a ridiculous-looking hat in the shape of a bowl with spoons dangling from the brim on pieces of string. Her mother and cousin were wearing the same. Only Cornelia kept her dignity with a simple paper hat constructed to look like a plate. They gathered their song sheets.

"Ladies and gentleman, may I introduce to you the Pudding Sisters," Francis Stott said, twirling his hands in a grand gesture at the ladies.

Louis and his college friend took their place next to the women and lifted their music sheets in the air flamboyantly. They had decided to forego the outfits and stayed dressed in regular attire. However, pinned to their chests were drawings of some sort of fruit.

"And they will be assisted by the Pie Brothers: Apple and Huckleberry," Francis continued with flare. Louis and his friend gave a mock bow. They lifted the music sheets and started to sing a song Francis called the *Brandy Sauce Dance*.

William, Hannah, Margaret, and the Gersters applauded politely. The other neighbors in the audience clapped their hands and whistled loudly.

The show went on for about a half hour. One made up song after the next, most to tunes that everyone knew such as *My Bonnie Lies*

Over the Ocean, and *Dixie*. William suppressed a yawn.

Finally, as the night started to wear on and the skies became dark, Anna Gerster went to the piano and played a composition by Bach. The audience went silent and calm. Hannah nodded off to sleep. The night came to a brilliant ending.

"Are you sure you need all of this?" Arpad was sitting with William the next day on the chalet porch, examining the drawings of Uncas.

"It may look enormous on paper, but I assure you, it will be a gentleman's camp, although no luxury will be spared."

"Hmmm, that's what I presumed." Arpad tapped the end of his pipe on the ashtray to empty it. "I'm afraid all of this money you now have at your disposal has gone to your head. You have a beautiful wife, healthy children, all of Pine Knot at your disposal," he gestured toward the woods, "tell me, what more do you seek?"

William was disappointed his friend wasn't more excited about Uncas, however Arpad could be a curmudgeon. He rolled up the designs.

"And how do you plan to get access to this site to build anything? There are no roads. You can hardly drag all of the timber you will need, much less the stone and hardware, over the waterfalls. I hope you aren't planning to dam the stream. That inlet is too narrow and shallow for a steamboat to get through."

"Of course not." William put the papers safely away in the bag at his feet. He hadn't shown anyone but Arpad his plans yet. "I plan to build a road into the site."

"A road? That will cost you a fortune." Arpad arched his brows in surprise.

"George Vanderbilt is doing the same in the Blue Ridge Mountains. He's built a railroad just to transport his materials and workers."

"Don't even think to compare yourself to that man, William. For one thing, you do not have his vast resources at your disposal. For another, his idea of a country manor is Versailles."

When William didn't respond, Arpad went on, "This is all well and good, but what would your father make of it?"

William turned his attention to the lake. "He'd never approve, of course. Then again, he never approved of anything I did if it didn't turn a profit. I've got the steamboat line, which I'm expanding to other lakes. And I'm making plans to subdivide some property on Eagle Lake as well. As much as I appreciate your concern, you shouldn't worry about my finances."

"Humph." Arpad filled his pipe and lit it, waved his hand around to put out the match and puffed before he spoke again. "You can't continue building these castles in the air without turning a profit somewhere," he said.

William was about to reply when John Callahan showed up on the porch.

"Mr. Doo'Rant. The game warden is here to see you in the trapper's cabin," he said.

"What's this about?" William said.

Callahan shrugged.

William and Arpad walked to the trapper's cabin to find the warden standing in the middle of the room with Ike and Nate. Ike had his arms folded over his chest as if he had to contain the rage that was oozing out of him. He did not take his eyes off the warden as the man surveyed their traps and furs hanging from antler mounts that were nailed into the walls.

The warden was of medium height and build, wearing a State-issued drab green uniform, with well-worn boots to match. A tag on his shirt identified him as Padraic Clancy. His beard was short stubble on his face, as if he hadn't shaved that day, and he wore a red bandana around his neck to ward off biting insects. He was sweating. He must have hiked to Pine Knot—from where, William had no idea.

"Mr. Durant, sir. These all yours?" he asked William as he gestured at the furs.

"Yes," William said protectively.

The warden took a steel jaw trap out of his sack and threw it down on the floor in front of them. "This yours?" He directed his question at Ike.

Nate scooped it up and handed it to his Uncle. "It's mine. See here? My initials are carved into it." Ike pointed to the small scratch marks on the steel.

"I thought so." The warden turned his head and spat a wad of tobacco juice into the spittoon by the door.

"I found it on the lands owned by the Adirondack League Club. They contacted me," he said. "Said there were poachers."

William was as perplexed as Ike.

"I didn't see no signs," Ike said in his own defense.

"Start payin' attention then." The warden stood face to face with Ike and eyed him ominously. "I don't like havin' to answer to irate land owners."

"Since when are property owners posting no trespassing signs?" Arpad said.

The warden turned to him. "Since the game has been scarce. And they started stocking fish in their streams."

Arpad let out a laugh. "That's preposterous! Fish and game have no boundaries. They wander wherever they care to wander."

"Not when they're being fed to stay put." The warden returned his attention to Ike. "I see your traps everywhere, and I know you don't own any of the land you're placing them on."

"I trap in a twenty-mile radius. And when the game runs low I move on," Ike said. "It's always been this way."

"Well, not anymore. If I find one of your traps again where it's not supposed to be, I'll confiscate it and fine you thirty dollars."

He doffed his hat at William and Arpad, and said, "Excuse the intrusion."

"Just a minute." William stopped him as he made his way to the door of the cabin. "I own most of the land where Ike hunts. He is allowed to use his traps on my lands."

"Then post it," the warden said dryly. "That's what everyone else is doing around here if it's not already owned by the state." And he lumbered out of the cabin and into the woods.

"Nate, be a good boy and hang this up for me, will ya?" Ike patted Nate's head and motioned to William and Arpad to follow him outside the cabin.

"That man is a menace," Ike grumbled. "He caught me and my brother Jake crustin' deer last winter and fined us both."

"It's been illegal for a while now Ike. You and your brother need to find other ways to obtain meat for your families in the winter."

"Pardon me for saying so sir, but this isn't Saratoga. There's no grocery stores for miles around here, Mr. Doo'Rant," Ike said with a flicker of contempt.

"Yes. Indeed, you're right. And I know you and your brother have growing families, Ike, but times are changing. Game is becoming scarce, and landowners are becoming greedier. People pay a lot of money to protect what is rightly theirs."

"It never used to be this way," Ike muttered and sulked back into the trapper's cabin.

"I don't like it," Arpad said to William as they walked back to the chalet. "Everyone is getting squeezed out. These friends of yours think if they can own Wall Street, they can own everything."

"So now they're *my* friends?" William smirked with amusement.

"You must admit; you *are* the one inviting them all in; you and your cousin with his big fancy hotel. 'Come to the Adirondacks. Enjoy the wilderness while sipping on champagne and when you're bored, you can always play billiards'," Arpad mimicked.

"Arpad, are you making fun of the Durant enterprises? You are the one that just told me I need to make money if I'm to build my castles in the air."

"Do as you wish," Arpad said as if he knew arguing was no use.

William took Janet to his cousin Frederick's Prospect House Hotel before returning with their family to their home in Saratoga at the end of the season. His cousin Frederick was clearly agitated as he spoke about his finances, and his brother Howard.

"Ever since he took over my father's refinery business he acts like he knows everything about everything. I tell you, he wants to take this place over," Frederick said to William as they sat in his office at the hotel.

"You have asked him for money. I suppose he can lay a claim on the place," William said. "What is the trouble anyway?"

"The trouble? Look around you William. There are hotels going up all over the place. Smaller, and cheaper to stay in than mine. I might claim exclusivity and attract guests such as the Vanderbilts and Astors when they're not in Newport, but they don't stay here long. It's a short season."

"Stretch it out then," William said matter-of-factly.

"Hah," Frederick scoffed. "No one comes up until the black flies are gone in July, and after October it's too cold. I'm at the whims of the Astorbilts."

William smiled at his use of the term coined by one of the New York society columnists for the socially over-competitive families.

"They dictate the season and the amusements, not me. They fill a sandbox with diamonds and rubies and have their guests dig for them with silver spoons. My billiards and bowling alley can't compete with *that* type of entertainment."

"I'll concede that you may never be able to compete with Alva Vanderbilt's flair for entertaining, but the winter season could prove to be quite enchanting for your guests. And what better entertainment than a sleigh ride over the frozen lakes?" William said.

"Not enchanting enough. It would cost me a fortune to heat the rooms."

They left his office and took a tour of the hotel, starting on the wrap-around veranda. William assessed the peeling paint on the verandah and was glad he didn't have to deal with this type of wear and tear at Pine Knot. He used logs instead of milled planks and left the bark intact to protect the exterior walls whenever he could. He didn't have to paint anything but the window frames.

Only a few brave souls were outside, bundled in their coats to keep out the biting wind that was sweeping off the lake and turning the waves into frothy white curls of foam. Blue Mountain, which always appeared as if in a shadow, was a hovering behemoth at the far end of the lake.

They left the verandah and entered the grand parlor. The door hinges, in need of grease, squeaked loudly as they passed through.

People were sitting in the many wicker chairs strewn about the place, reading or talking.

"You seem to have a full house." William tried to coax his cousin out of his foul mood with optimism.

"Yes, for now, but in one more month this place will look like a ghost town," Frederick said. "Maybe it is all for the better if Howard took it over," he sighed. "Clara has been begging me to spend more time with her at Camp Cedars, and this place has become an albatross. I can never enjoy the Adirondacks or my camp while I'm here."

"It's not all lost yet," William said, putting his hand on his cousin's shoulder to assure him. "Howard may have some good ideas that will pull you out from the brink."

"Possibly," Frederick replied. They turned toward the dining room for a seven course supper with their wives.

TWENTY

England

All spring, Gabriel kept Ella apprised of the results of any races their two-year old colt, *Merry Wind*, entered. He was doing well, gaining a reputation.

Gabriel had big expectations for the Brighton Cup. Word had spread, he told Ella, that *Merry Wind* had a high purchase price and came from an excellent blood line. This, coupled with his good showing all spring, ensured that the odds were in his favor.

Ella was enthralled. She was now a part owner of one of the most highly regarded racing horses in this year's season. And if Gabriel's predictions were correct, they would make a fortune off *Merry Wind* and announce their engagement.

She had to keep her enthusiasm to herself, however, never divulging to anyone she had used part of her inheritance to support Gabriel's investment in the racing world. It would be her undoing if William ever found out. Ella had spies all around her: Poultney, Alfred Locock, the Napier brothers, Aunt Sylvia, and Charlie Arkwright. Anny was the only loyal friend she had.

No one except Ella needed to know how she was using her money. Once she was rich, she could claim it was from other investments she managed to secure.

One thing did vex her though. She had made a terrible blunder by not seeking counsel when she gave her money to Gabriel. Women weren't allowed to own horses. Even the famous Lillie Langtry used a male pseudonym for the horses she owned. Because her name could not appear on the documents claiming ownership of the colt, Ella was really no more than one of Gabriel's backers; she had to rely on his sound judgment, and love, to protect her interests.

She had made a leap of faith. It tantalized her and left her feeling vulnerable at the same time: in sum, how she always felt about Gabriel. Their financial commitment to each other mirrored their personal one.

So far, he had given her no reason to doubt his integrity about this colt. He faithfully sent her checks, her stake in the winnings from any races, and he paid all of the bills to the stables and trainer. She didn't have to do anything but wait with him, for the day *Merry Wind* was old enough for one of the bigger races, such as the Epsom Derby, where a winning horse could bring in fifty thousand dollars or more. Ella was confident her investment would pay off handsomely.

She was taking tea in her parlor one day, planning her trip to Brighton, when Anny showed up at her door with papers in her hands.

"Have you seen these yet?" Anny said as she bustled into the parlor.

"What are they?" Ella asked.

"Your reviews." Anny laid one of the papers down.

Ella's hands shook as she opened up the *Times.*

"*An interesting interpretation of Beatrice.* Hmmm, not exactly glowing, but I'll take it," Ella said.

"How about this one?" Anny picked up the paper in front of her and read aloud, "*Miss Durant's play on the life of Dante sheds new light on the poet like no other.*" She set it down and grinned.

Ella beamed as she picked up *The Academy* literary review magazine. The holy grail of critics. She started to read it aloud.

"*Miss Durant has attempted an ambitious task. She has endeavored to turn the life of Dante into a dramatic poem...Now without being champions of the much abused unities, we must raise our voice against this drama to a purpose for which it is obviously unsuited."* Her voice faltered and she stopped reading aloud.

Anny watched her with concern. "What more do they say?"

"Oh Anny, it's awful!" She flung the literary magazine down in dismay. Anny swiftly picked it up and continued reading where Ella left off.

"Miss Durant's blank verse, which is up to an average level, is spoiled by a persistent and irritating elimination of the definitive article." And on and on it went. The worst came at the end: *"she has traduced Dante's memory."*

Anny stopped reading and gave Ella a sympathetic pat on the shoulder. "Don't look so glum," she said to her. "Every legitimate author should expect a thrashing by the critics."

"Oh Anny, what am I to do? How will I show my face at your dinner parties? Everyone will have read this scathing review."

"Oh hush," Anny said. "These old codgers don't know good literature when they see it set down in front of them. They are probably jealous, all of them, due to your connections to Longfellow. Why I bet none of them ever thought to put Dante's life into a play."

Ella pressed her fist to her mouth trying to suppress the tears that were pooling in her eyes.

Anny handed her a handkerchief she produced from her small clutch. "You should read what some critics say about Rhoda Broughton's novels. They say they're 'too fast'. They portray her work as much more scandalous than it really is."

Ella wasn't convinced.

"Now, stop your pouting. I came to bring you good news."

"What is it?" Ella attempted to show interest in what she was about to say next, but her hand reached reflexively for the literary magazine as if she needed to read the condemnation once more.

Anny grabbed it from her. "A colleague has asked me to recommend a speaker for their literary conference in Italy next year. And I was going to recommend you, but not if you are going to act like this," she said.

"Oh Anny. How could I talk in front of a large crowd when they will all have read this?" Ella pointed at the accusatory magazine.

"Hah," Anny scoffed. "This rag will be tomorrow's bird cage liner." She tossed the magazine aside as if it were worthless. "Now tell me you'll go to Italy." Anny wasn't going to take no for an answer.

Gabriel had secured a small cottage for them to stay together, in Brighton. It was discreet, he told her, but Ella demurred, telling him she had to keep up appearances, if for no other reason than the fact that Alfred Locock would relay any news of impropriety to William. There was no way for her to avoid visiting with the Lococks if she wanted to go to Brighton, so she travelled once again with her Aunt Sylvia, this time to stay for three weeks.

Within days of her arrival, Gabriel sent her a note to meet her at the tracks. He arranged for a driver to pick her up and escort her to the box he had secured in the grandstand.

Ella brushed off her disappointment that he wasn't picking her up himself but almost panicked when she got to the box and found it empty. She picked up her spy glass to view the crowds on the lawns and spotted him talking with a man she didn't recognize by the betting posts.

When he finally met her in the box he was as excited as a little boy playing a game of jacks with friends, and winning.

"*Merry Wind* showed well in the trial runs. The odds are in his favor today," Gabriel said.

Ella picked up her glasses again to see if she recognized any ladies or gentlemen promenading about on the lawns. She spotted Arkwright flirting with a young woman on the far side of the track. Typical, she thought. People were sitting in their carriages on the lawn, holding drinks, talking with friends and acquaintances standing nearby, waiting for the races to begin. Roars of encouragement swelled through the crowds as the horses were led to the starting line marked by chalk. The crowd went silent to wait for the Starter to signal the beginning of the race. He dropped his flag and the horses were off.

Ella found herself caught up in the thrall of the race and the swell of the hollering voices around her, calling out the names of the horses they wanted to win. Quite a few were backing *Merry Wind*. Her excitement went sour however, when it became apparent that *Merry Wind* was not keeping pace with the horses in the lead. The spectators began to hiss and jeer at the jockey. "He's not going all out," one cried.

Ella returned to her glasses in time to see a horse named *Dashing Beauty* coming into the straight. *Merry Wind* was lagging behind. The mood of the crowd turned ugly. She thought she heard someone threaten the jockey.

"The horse was nobbled," someone shouted and threw a program in the air with disgust. Others were not so polite. When the race was over, all types of items began to shower down on the track: apples, rocks, and unconsumed fried fish.

"He was pulled," another yelled, referring to *Merry Wind's* reluctance to race full throttle.

"It was fixed," said another.

People on the lawn in front of the tracks were shoving fists in the air, badgering the jockeys as they led their horses off.

Ella sat quietly, wondering what Gabriel planned to do next. He kissed her lightly on the forehead. "I'll be back," he said, seeming unconcerned.

"You *are* jesting? You won't leave me here alone will you?"

"I have to meet up with the jockey. Obviously something went terribly wrong. I'll come back as soon as I have this business settled."

An hour went by. More races were run; none included *Merry Wind*. Ella was filled with apprehension and dread. Gabriel never returned.

"Ella!"

Startled, Ella turned in the direction of her name. Arkwright was standing over her.

"Come with me," he said, holding out his hand to her.

Ella took it with a wave of relief.

"Keep your head down; don't look at anybody. Do as I say," he said urgently.

Ella's body pulsed with alarm. Something had gone terribly wrong.

"What is it, Charlie?"

"Not here," he said leading her out of the racecourse and into a waiting cab.

Once they were securely away from the crowds he explained.

"They think Gabriel nobbled the race at considerable advantage to himself."

When Ella responded with a dumbfounded look he continued. "He fixed the race, Ella. He knew the odds were in *Merry Wind's* favor, but he backed another horse with less favorable odds and told his jockey to lose. Or, if the jockey wasn't involved, then he had someone drug the horse for him."

"Why on earth would he do that?" Ella said.

"Because he could win a lot of money that way. Members of the Jockey Club are investigating him now, asking the bookmakers that took his bet, and examining the horse."

Ella turned away from Arkwright to stare at the endless green hedgerows that bordered the roads.

"He's being called before the Jockey Club. If they discover foul play they will have him and his horse kicked out of any future races."

"I highly doubt Gabriel is capable of foul play."

"Oh, Ella, I'm afraid he doesn't deserve the confidence and loyalty you bestow on him. There are rumors he has not paid his trainer fees, and the stable where he keeps *Merry Wind* is threatening to take ownership because they haven't been paid in months either."

Ella was paralyzed with dread and remorse. Her money was lost. She knew, deep down, she would never see Gabriel again. He would vanish, like he had in the past, but this time he would not return. He would never be able to face her and explain this scandal. She had been taken. It took every ounce of dignity she had left in her not to crumble before Arkwright. But when he took her hand in his and eyed her with a look of compassion, her resolve melted and she broke down, crying.

"Now that your friend the Count is being investigated by the Jockey Club, you won't be seeing much of him around here," Alfred said, folding the newspaper in half and placing it beside his plate the next morning before breakfast was served.

"I'm sure it will all come to nothing." Aunt Sylvia glanced sympathetically at Ella.

"Ella, we need to talk about your future," Alfred said.

"Alfred, dear, not now," Anna said.

"Of course not. After breakfast then. Ella, why don't we meet in my study?"

Ella bit her lower lip and said, "Why yes, of course."

She hardly thought she could withstand the lecture she was expecting from Alfred, but contrary to what she perceived, he ended up giving her an option she had never considered. He had no idea how closely tied she was to Gabriel's antics. Although Alfred knew Gabriel had escorted her to the racetrack the day before, he didn't know the depth of her duplicity in Gabriel's scam. He only knew that Ella's options, as a woman living alone in England, were limited, and that this scandal would create more challenges.

"What are your plans?" he asked.

"I haven't thought them through as yet," she answered. "Anny has told me about a literary conference in Italy she thought I might want to attend next year. I'm waiting for their invitation to be a guest speaker. Other than that, I'm not sure what I will do."

"No new books in the works then?" Alfred said.

"None," Ella admitted. Her muse had left her after the scathing critique in *The Academy*.

"Well then. Let's consider your options: as a spinster there are a few afforded to you that you may not have considered before. Your aunt is moving in with your cousins, I understand, so she will not need you as a companion anymore."

Ella nodded.

"Your writing is hardly enough to keep you fully employed and cover your expenses," he added. "And your brother has not been forthcoming about the rest of your inheritance."

Ella raised no objections with his assessment of her financial state.

"How much have you saved from what he did provide?"

"Only half. The rest I gave to—" She stopped herself before revealing too much. Although Alfred was her champion he would be scandalized if he found out she had invested her money in a thoroughbred owned by Gabriel. "I invested in a company in Germany. I received a tip from a friend and am waiting to receive dividends. Of course, I still have my monthly allowance."

"So now, we must decide what to do while you wait for these, dividends." He rested his hands on his lap and examined her skeptically. "You could study nursing. Our church has set up a nursing school to train nurses to attend to the poor at a nearby hospital."

Ella started, never thinking of this vocation, although she had tended the sick while at the convent in the States.

"Of course it will cost to be trained. It's not much, mind you, only fifty pounds. Once you have finished a year of training as a probationer, you receive a similar salary per year. It is a respectable profession. Only ladies are accepted of course. We want ladies with an education and ability to instill moral principles to their charges, especially the sick children. You may start in the fall. And if that doesn't suit you," Alfred continued, "I have a friend, General Ardaugh, seeking a chaperone for his three daughters. They intend to travel to Germany next spring and need someone such as you, who has a command of languages."

"Thank you Alfred, I'll consider what you have suggested."

That night in bed Ella tossed and turned, mulling over her future. Why did it seem as though she was replaying her past? The last time she had been thrown over by a man it had been Poultney. Afterwards, she was abandoned by her father, and sought refuge in the convent of the Sisters of St. Mary. Now, here she was again, in a similar predicament. How was it all of her efforts to become an independent woman ended with scandal and humiliation, where the only recourse for a woman of her station was to turn to the church for comfort and redemption?

When would she learn that men were not to be trusted? Her own brother was proving untrustworthy, and he had always been her loyal companion.

However, maybe Alfred's suggestion for her to train as a nurse would soothe her tortured state of mind. Not only would it keep her from thinking about Gabriel and his deception, it would provide an outlet for her energies that didn't include socializing with friends who would inevitably throw sympathetic glances her way as if she was incapable of writing, or worse, question her about what happened at the races in Brighton. And, as Alfred suggested, if nursing didn't prove fulfilling enough, she could always travel as a chaperone after attending the literary conference in Italy.

"I'd like to study nursing," she told Alfred the next day.

It was settled in the next few weeks. Ella was to move to a flat owned by the Church, near Queens Gate in London. Her training would begin in the fall.

When she returned home, she immediately wrote to her mother informing her of her decision.

She inventoried her belongings, shipping some items, such as her fine gowns, with Aunt Sylvia for safe storage. She gave notice to her maid Trixie and sent word to Anny about her plans. Anny was not only surprised but incredulous. She came knocking on the front door one afternoon while Ella was packing away her things, demanding an explanation.

"How can you become a recluse when you just published? What will everyone think? Now is the time for you to be out giving talks and presentations about your work."

"I've promised Alfred, and I will not go back on my word to him," Ella said. She lifted another dress in the air to spread it out on her bed before packing.

"But why not? What are you running from? If it's Count de la

Salle, well then, don't worry," Anny said. "Everyone knows you two were in a tempestuous affair. No one would blame you for leaving him. You don't need an escort for every event. You have me."

Ella rested her eyes on Anny and smiled. "You make a good escort and friend, but I hardly need a companion. I am only taking this reprieve at the suggestion of Alfred Locock. He asked for my help at the clinic for the poor, and I am training to become a nurse."

"Really, dear. You think I believe that? And *you* in nursing school?" Anny arched her brows.

Ella stopped flailing her dresses in the air and planted her hands on her hips to confront Anny. "So maybe this is an escape for me. Just for a while. Until I can make peace with the fact that Gabriel has betrayed my trust, and I am almost bankrupt as a result."

"What are you talking about?"

"Oh Anny," Ella plunked down on the side of her bed, "I gave half my money to him to invest in a horse."

"You *didn't*?"

Ella nodded her head in shame.

"Well I hardly believe what they are saying about him." Anny waved her gloves dismissively in the air. "He's from a titled family. There must be some explanation for what happened at the races in Brighton."

"I'm afraid I'll never know. I don't understand these games men play."

"Obviously, dear," Anny said.

Ella sighed. "I know what a fool I've been. He promised me he'd marry me once the racing was over. And then poof, he just left me, as if the proposal meant nothing to him."

Anny stared at her in disbelief.

"I fell in love with his mystique," Ella continued. "The more elusive he was with me, the more I wanted, then needed him. I was in love with the challenge. How, I kept wondering, could I make him fall in love with me? And then, when he told me about this horse business, I thought my money would tie him to me. But I was wrong, so wrong. And now I am ruined because of it."

"You've always been searching for recognition," Anny said. "Perhaps you thought Count de la Salle would provide it for you. You were wrong, yes, but you're not ruined. Far from it. You still have friends and maybe you are right about this nursing vocation. As you said, if it is not to your pleasing, you can do other things. All of your options are respectable, and understandable given your situation. However, you must promise me, Ella, that you will not give up on your writing."

"I will Anny. And if I can fit it in, I will attend that conference in Italy as you suggest."

"That's my girl, then." Anny said, hugging Ella.

Ella closed the lid to her trunk, having chosen the most practical gowns she owned to take with her to the mission house. There would be no need to flaunt her wealth with the type of clientele she would be assisting.

TWENTY-ONE

New York

"Have you seen this yet?" John Barbour slid a map across the desk in front of William.

William picked it up to examine. It was a map of the Adirondacks, made by the New York State Forest Commission. There was a blue line circling a large area.

"What is this?" William pointed to the line.

"That, my friend, encompasses all of the land area the state would like to own. They want it all to be part of the new park, kept forever wild, and untamed. No more cutting the forests, no more mining the land, no more free-will to men that might make a claim to the land for their own uses," Barbour said grimly.

"Is this a joke?" William said.

Barbour shook his head.

"But I own a lot of land within this circle." William remained fixated on the map and the line.

"So you do," Barbour said matter-of-factly. "So you do."

"All the better for you," Huntington said when William showed him the map over drinks at the Union Club later that week.

William shook his head. "I'm not sure you understand the implications of this."

"Of course I do," Huntington bellowed and picked up his tumbler. "Don't you see? You now own what the state wants. They sold it to your father for a pittance, and now you can make a fortune selling it back to them." He lit a cigar, took a large drag, sat back in his chair and let out a billow of smoke. "Idiots. All of them," he said.

"I hadn't planned to sell my land to *them*," William said.

"To the highest bidder then." Huntington gesticulated. "Whoever that might be."

He smiled mischievously. "You are in control now William." He swiped William's leg with his free hand. "Don't you see that? Everyone will be clamoring to buy up parcels for speculation, and the State Forest Commission will never be able to keep up with it. They think they want to own all that land? Let them have it. At a price." He let out a hearty laugh at the thought of William putting one over on the bureaucrats.

"Your father would be greatly amused, let me tell you," he said. "Hang on to it William, for as long as you can. The longer you wait, the more it will be worth."

William sipped his sherry. If only his father were alive to witness this comeback of the Durant family fortune, he thought.

Huntington's predictions proved correct. A few nights later William was invited to a meeting of a group of prominent businessmen calling themselves the Committee of 100, formed to protect the Adirondack forests from destruction. The meeting was held at Delmonico's. He entered the private smoke-filled room they had reserved in time to see Verplanck Colvin, the state surveyor, showing slides of various streams in the Adirondacks, before and after a timber cut.

"And as you can see, gentleman," Verplanck said, while drawing the audience's attention to the picture projected onto a screen, "this stream, only a few years after a clear cut, is down to a trickle of what it once was." He turned to his rapt audience.

"These Adirondack streams are the sources of the principal rivers running through the agricultural valleys: the Hudson, the Mohawk. And each year the water supply is lessened due to the destruction of the forests surrounding them, to the detriment of commerce."

There was a general mumbling of agreement amongst the audience. Morris Jessup, the financier, stood up. "Gentleman," he said. "The time to act is now! Before our rivers and canals dry up and we witness the ruin of agriculture and industry in the Hudson Valley."

Now people were becoming agitated. Shouts of encouragement and indignation at the State were echoed throughout the meeting room. Verplanck looked pleased with himself.

"We must insist that the state take action!" Verplanck said. "The Forest Commission must continue with its efforts to purchase lands to protect them from lumber interests."

He scanned the crowd and spotted William sitting in the back. William tried to hide from his view, but it was too late, Verplanck pointed him out to the rest of the crowd.

"I see we have amongst us one of the largest land owners in the Adirondacks," he said. "The man who has lured tourists to the region, proclaiming the benefits of the vast wilderness with abundant game." Heads turned and eyes darted around the room as the men tried to discover who Verplanck was addressing.

"Mr. Durant. Perhaps you could enlighten us as to your plans for protecting the land you now own?"

William cringed. Verplanck was putting him in a spot about the Adirondack Railroad Company promotional brochures, which did just as he said: promoted the abundance of wild land in the Adirondacks. He had no choice but to stand up and make some type of statement. It was the price for attending. If he didn't, he would appear to be a spy, eavesdropping on the enemy as if worried that his own interests would be hindered by their actions. He stood up and the men swiveled around to face him. William cleared his throat.

"As you all know, the Durants have opened up this great wilderness to people like yourselves, to enjoy and appreciate the natural wonders the region has to offer."

There was a general murmur of agreement and William began to relax.

"While I encourage the State to protect and preserve the land it now owns; I don't think the answer is to put everything in the hands of the State. But rather, in the hands of those men with adequate resources to preserve the timber, game, and water for the future."

Not everyone agreed. William could hear men talking amongst themselves, debating the merits of state versus private land ownership. Someone was waving the map John Barbour had showed him, with the blue line outlining the land the state planned to own one day. Verplanck waited for his turn to speak.

"Gentlemen, if what Mr. Durant says is correct, then we would not be seeing the mass destruction of the forests that we see now. Not all men are as altruistic as Mr. Durant," he said with a touch of sarcasm that did not escape William's attention.

"If what you say is true, Colvin, then why hasn't the State done more to save our forests? Maybe Durant is right. Private preserves may be the answer," someone from the middle of the room yelled out.

The conversation became chaotic as men debated and shouted their opinions on the matter, until Jessup stood up again and called the meeting back to order. Realizing they would not be able to come to a definitive conclusion, he asked for the subcommittees to report, and then called for another meeting the following month. William slipped out through the pocket doors unnoticed. As he was leaving he overheard someone remark, "Durant can't have it both ways, you know."

A few days later William came home to Saratoga to find Janet waiting for him in his study.

"Why didn't you tell me about this?" Janet was holding

William's plans for Uncas.

"How on earth did you find those?" William said as he took them from her.

"Your son found them. He was playing in your study and started rifling through your things before the nanny was able to stop him. How could you William? How could you plan such a thing and not tell me?"

"I don't understand why you're so upset. It's not as if I'm building a family home. This is a private hunting cabin. Here, let me show you. It's very close to the one I now share with Arpad. Only this will be bigger and have more amenities." He opened the map of the area and placed it on his desk to show her the lake.

"But, William," she said while leaning over the map, "why not build a family home we could all enjoy? Why not build a new home for us, here." Janet planted her finger over one of the lakes on the map. "We're outgrowing Pine Knot. And I wouldn't mind a camp that allowed us to all be in one building. I'm tired of walking from our cabin to the children's cabin, and then again to the dining hall. If you can build this fancy hunting cabin of yours, then why not build a camp for your wife and children that will allow us more luxury and modern conveniences?" She stood up straight and looked down at him.

Her boldness momentarily shook him. This was a turn of events. She rarely asked anything of him.

"I didn't know you were tired of Pine Knot," he said.

"I'm not tired of it. I'm only asking that you extend the same courtesy toward your family as you would toward your friend Arpad and other guests you might entertain at this camp Uncas." She tossed her hands in the air in exasperation.

"All right," he said.

"All right?" Her jaw dropped in surprise.

"Yes. I'll build you a fine home on this lake, here." William pointed to the map again. "I'm meeting with an architect soon about the building plans for Uncas and will ask him what he thinks. It's a fine little lake, and I'm sure we could build a wonderful home on it for our family."

Janet clamped her mouth shut and lifted her lips slightly in triumph.

"Now," William said. "There is something else I must discuss with you." And he proceeded to tell her about the yacht he had commissioned.

On his way to the Adirondacks William stopped to visit his mother. It was evening when he arrived. Gore Mountain stood majestic and foreboding, framed by the picture window in the family's parlor. Dusk was descending, and it lent an air of heaviness to the household. He noticed the parlor furniture was dusty and worn. The air in the house was stifling, as if the windows hadn't been opened all day to let fresh air in. He started up the stairs toward his mother's bed chambers. As he reached the top, Margaret came out of the shadows and clutched his arm. William jumped at the sight of her.

"Christ, Margaret, you startled me."

"Your mother is resting," she croaked. Her breath smelled like stale wine. "She's not been feeling well."

"Where is everyone? Where's Daisy?" he asked.

"Your mother insisted she only come once a week. We don't use most of the house anyway."

"Who does the cooking now?"

"I do," Margaret said. "I do most of the work around here for your mother while your sister is having a fine time in London. Did you know she claims to be doing God's work?" Margaret laughed in the shadow of the hallway and it echoed down the stairwell.

"I know everything," William said, as he disentangled himself from Margaret's grasp. "I'm here to speak to my mother about Ella. Now if you'll excuse me."

"I'll leave you two alone," Margaret said, and tottered down the hall to her own room.

"Mother, what the devil is going on here?" William said as he sat down beside his mother's bed.

She lifted her head off her pillow and said faintly, "William, dear. So nice to see you. I wasn't expecting a visit."

He picked up a medicine bottle and examined its contents. It was laudanum, and the bottle was half empty.

"Mother, how much of this are you taking?"

"Margaret gives me my dosage."

"It's only four p.m. and you are both half crocked," he said. He handed her a glass of water that was sitting on the nightstand.

"I've been ill." Hannah's head wobbled as William helped her take a sip of the water.

"I've come to talk to you about Ella," William said.

"Oh, my poor, dear girl." Hannah sighed.

"Poor, yes, that would about sum up her predicament."

"William," Hannah clutched his hand, "you must speak with her. Someone must speak to her about coming home."

"She won't come home. I've already tried that tack. You know how stubborn she can be. She has already written to me and told me she intends to work at Alfred Locock's church clinic for children and become a nurse."

"You know about her then? You know she lost half her money to some investment scheme?"

"Of course I do, Mother; I was the one that told you all about it remember?" He had received word from Alfred about Ella and her plans. Included in the letter was a warning that she had given half her money away to a 'friend' for some kind of foolish investment.

"I thought it was Margaret," Hannah sighed.

William didn't like the way his mother looked, nor how she was acting: weepy and delirious. Her face was gaunt and she was breathing heavily. Her lids drifted between open and closed with effort. He knew she was getting on in age, sixty-five years now, but he had never seen her this weak.

"Mother, are you reading Ella's letters?"

"No, dear, Margaret said they would only upset me. She reads them and responds for me." She spoke with her eyes closed and her head resting on the pillow.

"I will talk to Margaret then," he said. "Don't worry about Ella. I'll take care of everything."

William kissed her lightly on her forehead and left the room highly disturbed. His mother needed better care. And Margaret was not proving to be trustworthy. It may be time, he thought, to sell this house and move them somewhere closer to his home.

Before he left he went to his father's study to look through his mother's mail. Stacked in one corner of the desk were square envelopes, opened: letters of correspondence from friends and family. In the other corner were the long envelopes, sealed: unpaid bills. William scooped these up and rifled through them quickly, noting the addresses. There were bills from Tiffany's jewelry store, a medical doctor, a dressmaker in New York City, a florist in North Creek and a letter from the bank. William put the stack of envelopes in the pocket of his waistcoat and sighed thinking about the rope of pearls strung around his mother's neck while she was deliriously sleeping off the laudanum. *Given these bills, one would never guess she was practically a recluse.*

Winter was closing in on the mountains, and William didn't have a lot of time. He instructed his work crew to finish the road before the first snowfall, although when that would occur was always unpredictable in the Adirondacks; it could be as early as October or as late as December.

Twenty men went to work clearing the path of trees. They cut with large saws, set dynamite to the stumps, and dragged them away with horse and sled. Then they had to level the ground as best they could, using a roller led by a horse. Some soft spots in the road required a corduroy of wood laid down so that a wagon with supplies could travel without getting stuck in the mud. They worked from dawn until it was too dark to see by torchlight and tented out so they wouldn't have to go home. Jerome Wood came to help, along with Ike Lawrence, John Callahan, and his nephew Maurice. Even Nate came and assisted by bringing water to the workers when they got tired. William hired Jerome's wife to cook for the men.

Two weeks went by, and then the day came when William

watched as one of the last White pines standing in the pathway was felled by two lumbermen and a double saw. It creaked and swayed in the stiff afternoon breeze and then fell with a large crash to the ground, revealing a glimmer of Mohegan Lake in the background. They had finally reached the site where William would build Camp Uncas.

He had a few days before he had to leave for Saratoga and he spent them at Pine Knot making sure the cabins were closed up and prepared for the winter months ahead. While surveying one with John Callahan, Ike ran up to them. "Mr. Doo'Rant," he said panting.

"What is it, Ike, a fire somewhere?" William said.

"No, sir. Worse. They've gone and scuttled your steamship, *Buttercup,* on Forked Lake." He held his hands on his knees for support as he doubled over to catch his breath and waited for William to respond.

"What? Calm down, Ike. Explain this to me again? Who's done this?" William led Ike over to a bench and sat down next to him.

"The guides, sir."

"The guides on Forked Lake?"

Ike nodded his head.

John Callahan gave off a low whistle. "Dear Lord," he said. "Now they've done it."

"But I don't understand." William said.

"They's mad as hell that you're thinking of opening up Forked Lake for tourists," Callahan explained. "And they don't want that dam flooding the stream neither."

William hated to think his cousin Howard's prediction was right. The guides on Forked Lake had scuttled his boat in defiance.

"My father and I planned that dam years ago. I only just got started on it. It's needed for navigation. How do they expect to get anyone to visit the lake if they can't get there by steamboat?"

"The old-fashioned way I suppose, Mr. Doo'Rant. By guideboats. *Their* guideboats. The ones they've been carrying in and out on their backs and taking passengers upriver with for years now."

William scowled at Callahan, although he knew he was only

telling him the truth. "Take me there, Ike," he said.

Ike caught his breath and nodded at William in agreement.

The two took off in the morning. A heavy fog was settled over the lake, making it hard to navigate. William's private steamboat took them as far as the Raquette River outlet, where they got into one of Ike's boats to paddle the rest of the way to Forked Lake. Huge granite boulders rose out of the inky black water like the backs of giant turtles. Twice, they had to get out and portage around small rapids. They stopped overnight and put up a tent. It was getting cold and damp and they had to hurry before the lake iced over.

They found the dam at the outlet intact, but someone had started tearing away at the foundation with an ax. It was only a matter of time before it collapsed. "I'm surprised they haven't used dynamite yet," Ike said.

They found the launch site where the small steamship, *Buttercup*, equipped to carry at least a dozen people, was once moored.

"They took it off the mooring in the middle of the night," Ike said. "And scuttled it out there." He pointed to the middle of the lake.

Although they circled the area where it might be found, there was no sign of the boat.

"Are you sure it sank?" William said.

"That's what I heard," Ike said. They both tried to find a clue to the boat's whereabouts in the dark water.

William's mood turned grim when he realized Ike was right; the steamboat was gone.

"Ahoy there." Someone came upon them in a canoe.

"You boys looking for something?" He was an older man, most likely a guide. He was wearing heavy clothing, fit for the weather and what was to come, his boat filled with packs loaded with supplies. He watched as they eyed his belongings and said, "I'm on my way south. Heading out of here for the winter months. It will take me a while to get to where I'm going."

"I can see that," William said. "But what's the hurry?"

"Hurry? Do you know how fast the weather changes this time

of year? I don't want to be stuck in the ice."

They sat there on the water as the waves lapped against the gunnels of the boat, and a flock of Canada geese flew overhead, honking in unison, warning them that winter was coming.

"We're trying to find the *Buttercup*," Ike said.

"Oh, you'll never find her," the stranger said with such force they had to believe he was right. "She's been scuttled alright, in the deepest part of the lake. Where no one will find her." His eyes betrayed he knew more than he should about the event.

"And how do you know this?" William asked.

The man shrugged and dipped his paddle back in the water. "Word travels around the lake. Just like the geese." He let go of one of the paddles briefly to doff his cap, and chuckled. They watched as his small canoe skimmed effortlessly away from them on the water.

"Damn it," William swore at the air as he lifted his oar.

TWENTY-TWO

England

Ella began her nursing career at a Children's Hospital. Sister Beatrice, the head matron, was a righteous elder who believed nursing was the highest calling from God. When Ella first reported to the hospital ward she made an attempt at cordiality which was wasted on the Sister.

"I'm so very pleased to meet you, Sister," she had said. "Alfred, I mean Reverend Locock, has told me many good things about this school and your ward at the hospital."

Sister Beatrice eyed her up and down in a manner that betrayed her distrust. She wore a tight-fitting blue dress with a starched white apron and a cambric cap like the ones Ella saw the fishmongers wear in the streets.

"We have over one hundred applicants each year for forty probationer positions," she said through tight lips. "It is not lost on me that you managed to obtain a spot based solely on your family connection with Reverend Locock. Please don't expect, however, that such friendship extends to me."

With a wave of her hand she motioned toward a closet. "You will find your uniform in there."

Ella quickly went to find her uniform. There were two types hanging in the closet.

"The probationer's uniform is black and white checked, the nurses are blue and white. Everyone must wear the cap," Sister informed her.

Ella found a dress that would fit her and lifted it out of the closet before turning her attention back to the Sister.

"What we do here, tending to the poor children who would otherwise have no care, requires patience, humility and attention to details. God will notice your good deeds and be pleased." She lifted the reading glasses that were hanging from her neck on a sterling silver lorgnette. "And what God doesn't notice, I do." With that she placed a check mark in a small book she had retrieved from deep within the folds of her dress. "You may change and start by cleaning out the urine bottles with chlorinated soda. The supplies may be found in the second room down the hall."

With that command, Ella was dismissed to begin her duties as a nurse in training.

The pace of nursing school was grueling. After prayers each morning Ella washed and cleaned the furniture, medicinal bottles and jugs. Afterwards she went to class for an hour. She was back on duty by the afternoon, preparing beef tea for the patients. Her work also involved bathing the children on rotations, dressing their wounds, and giving them medicine as prescribed by the doctors. She repeated her tasks until she was finally discharged from duty at eight p.m. Her twelve-hour days continued like this for six days of the week.

Sister Beatrice was omnipresent. She inspected the ward every day to make sure they were doing things according to instruction and she always had her small book in hand to tick off any slight infraction or good deed of the probationer in case God wasn't paying attention.

One morning while cleaning the Sister's office, Ella happened to glance down at a ledger sitting open on the desk. It was a chart of the 1889 probationers' records. It listed their names and ages. Only a handful were under the age of thirty. Next to their ages was their status—either widowed or spinster. On the far right-hand column was the results of their tenure while probationers. Many were dismissed with notations indicating why: insobriety, insubordination, or incompetence. Some married and left of their own will, some resigned with no reason given, others died while on duty. One dismissal in particular caught Ella's attention—*Moral Character Defective.*

"Are you finding what you are looking for?"

Ella jumped when she heard Sister Beatrice's voice from the doorway. She moved the ledger aside and vigorously rubbed away the non-existent dust from the desk, stammering, "Just dusting in here, Sister."

"You may leave, at once," Sister said sharply.

As she scurried from the room Ella noticed out of the corner of her eye Sister retrieving the dreaded book out of her dress to record Ella's indiscretion. Ella wondered how often she appeared in that book and whether God was keeping track as well.

Although nursing was hard work, Ella found purpose, and was somewhat fulfilled. She never wrote home for money, since her room and board were paid for, and she didn't have anything to spend it on anyway.

One day, while she was examining the wound of one of the patients—an orphan girl lifted off the streets by a good Samaritan and deposited at the clinic door—a doctor came up to assist.

"This looks as if it has festered," he said. The deep gash was oozing slimy, white pus, mixed with blood, all of it spilling out onto the bed sheets. "I'd guess she cut herself on something filthy."

He held up the girl's arm as Ella placed a clean cloth under it to stop it from staining any more of the sheets. The girl let out a painful groan and tried to wrest her arm away. Ella gripped her shoulder to hold her down.

"I've got her," the man said. "Get me a bowl of water. Make sure it's warm. We'll clean this together."

Ella did as she was told and watched as he carefully lifted the child's arm and placed it into a bowl of water. The clear liquid quickly turned into a cloud of blood and dirt. "Infected," he said.

"Yes, doctor," Ella said.

His face betrayed a hint of embarrassment as he said, "You don't have to call me that. I haven't obtained my degree yet."

When they had finished their business with the girl, he wiped his hands on his smock and bowed slightly in front of Ella.

"My name is Arthur Frethey."

He was dressed in a white medical gown. He had slight wrinkles at the corners of his eyes and streaks of gray hair at his temples, which told her he was about her age if not older.

"Miss Ella Durant. Pleased to make your acquaintance."

"Yes. I've been watching you with the patients. You seem to have a knack for this," he said.

Ella blushed at the compliment. "Are you in medical school?" she asked.

"No, no. Not yet, anyway. I'm just trying to learn as much as I can while I conduct God's work."

Sister Beatrice's ability to be everywhere and know everything was made known to them almost the minute their conversation became friendly.

"Are you done with the patient, Miss Durant?"

Ella swung around to face the Sister's pinched face glaring at her. It was too much: *this woman is the devil herself.*

"I'm assisting the doctor today. He requested that I do so." She knew it was a lie but somehow felt that this kind man, Mr. Frethey, would not let her down.

The sister glanced at Arthur, then back at Ella.

"Yes indeed, Sister. I am very appreciative of Miss Durant's assistance."

"I am sure you are, Mr. Frethey," Sister said, and to Ella's horror, penciled in her little book: *indiscreet conduct toward doctor in training,* before telling them, "Go about your work then. I expect you both to maintain your distance." With that final dictum, she swept from the room to find her next victim.

Ella and Arthur stifled themselves lest they laugh out loud. Ella didn't care what that curmudgeon thought of her, she spent the day with Arthur attending the sick. She was so tired by the time she arrived at her flat that evening she could barely hold herself up to take her tea and toast.

On one of her days off, she was standing at her stoop, locking the door behind her when she heard, "Good day, Miss Durant," and turned around to see Arthur Frethey standing in the street with his hat doffed.

"Good day, Mr. Frethey," she replied.

"It would be even better if you allowed me to walk with you," he said.

Ella let out a small laugh. "How bold of you, Mr. Frethey."

"I suppose now that I have shared the vagaries of the clinic with you, I am allowed to take liberties," he said.

"How did you find me?" she asked.

He lifted his shoulders and hands in the air, feigning innocence. "I asked around. The other ladies told me where you live."

As they walked, he revealed more about himself, telling her he was studying homeopathy.

"I've sat in on some classes at the London Homeopathic Hospital, and I've read books about it," he said.

"And how did you find your way to working at the clinic?" Ella asked.

"A friend of mine was sick. He had no money, poor chap, and ended up at the clinic. I promised when he died I'd devote some of my time to the cause."

Before Ella realized what was happening, she seamlessly entered into another relationship, spending any free time away from the clinic exploring the city of London with Arthur. He was the most unpretentious man she had ever known. Both of his parents died when he was young, and he was left in the care of his Aunt Caroline. He became attracted to homeopathy when he learned how his mother had died at the hands of a doctor whose treatments proved useless.

"Why in heavens name would anyone extract blood with leeches from a dying woman?" he asked Ella one day.

She never thought about it before. His own explanation of how homeopathy worked was confusing. She picked up on a few of its tenets: treating the patient with the same agent that caused the symptoms, diluting the agent with water or alcohol to create tinctures. But his enthusiasm for his vocation won her over and she found herself wondering if this is what first attracted her mother to her father. When Hannah met Thomas Durant, he too was on his way to becoming a doctor. It was a profession that had more value, Ella thought, than bringing railroads into the wilderness.

TWENTY-THREE

Philadelphia

It was a crisp day in March when William inspected the *Utowana* one last time before the big event. The cameras and newsmen would be at the docks in an hour and he wanted to relish this time alone. The *Utowana* was one hundred and eighty-six feet in length, she had three masts for sailing, and an auxiliary steam engine. Only Vanderbilt, the richest man in America, could claim to have a mightier vessel.

No luxury was unaccounted, no small detail overlooked on the *Utowana*. The oak paneled rooms were designed with the same attention to detail William demanded for his cabins in the Adirondacks. Nooks and cubbies were built to store items and keep the ship tidy at all times. The dining area was ensconced in glass mirrors, chandeliers hung from the ceilings. The dining table was mahogany, the couches wrapped in soft Italian leather. The master bedroom had all the necessities that Janet and William enjoyed at home in Saratoga. The children had a play area. The endeavor cost him a fortune, two hundred thousand when it was all over, from design to finish.

He walked around the stateroom and sat down in one of the

leather chairs. A porter knocked. "Sir, is there anything you desire?"

"Yes. I'd like a glass of champagne."

William reached for the humidor and lit a cigar. He heard a gull cry from out the portside window, which made him think about his trip to Egypt when he was nineteen. He and Arkwright had spent the night on a boat on the Nile listening to the caterwauling of a large cat outside the window of their cabin. When they opened the window they saw a lioness prowling the shoreline. Arkwright tried to take a shot at her but missed.

William imagined himself traveling to Egypt, this time with his own yacht. Maybe he'd host the Prince of Wales on the *Utowana*. It wasn't that far-fetched. He had met the Prince before on the same trip to Egypt with Arkwright.

They were docked on the Island of Elephantine and William's chaperone had used a ruse for wanting to visit with a colleague—the Prince's doctor—to get onboard the Prince's dahabeeh, a shallow-hulled boat especially suited for travel along the Nile. Once they were allowed on deck they managed a short introduction to the Prince and Princess who were engaged in a conversation with Lady Gordon. Not wanting to appear too forward, they bowed and excused themselves as soon as possible to find the doctor below deck.

William was jolted from his reminiscing by the porter who brought his champagne in a crystal flute and set it down on the table in front of him. William lifted it to his lips and thought of Florence. What would she think when she saw the *Utowana* sailing into port during Cowes week on the Isle of Wight? He relished the thought, the look of envy, maybe even regret, that would wash over her when they were reunited at one of the galas. William knew he'd be invited now that he had this yacht. Arkwright all but assured him of his place on the guest lists. Yes, William had his connections, his yacht, and now his chance to show everyone who had doubted his ability to bring back the family's fortune that they were mistaken.

Janet and her father arrived before the newsmen.

"Do I look all right, dear?" Janet asked him as she nervously looked in the mirror to check and reposition the hat pinned on top her head.

He knew she was never one to appreciate the attention of the camera. He also knew she never approved of the yacht. He wasn't sure if it was because she hated sea voyages or because of the expense. But it was Janet's duty to christen the ship with a bottle of champagne and she would do it for his sake.

Janet's father was agog at the size of the ship.

"William. You've outdone yourself now! This more than rivals your father's yacht, *Idler*."

William just smiled.

The newsmen came in droves and pressed William for answers: How much did you pay for it? How long did it take to build? Where did the wood come from? Who designed it?

When the time came, Janet stepped up and smashed the bottle against the hull. It shattered into bits and everyone applauded. The photographers caught it all on film.

The ship was launched and with a wave Janet, William, their friends and family were off, heading toward the docks of the New York Yacht Club. Sitting on deck the next day William read the article about the launch of the *Utowana* in the *New York Herald*. He couldn't help but notice Janet's forced smile as she held the jagged bottle in her hands while the *Utowana* slid from its slip and into the Schuylkill River.

TWENTY-FOUR

England and the Continent

Arthur surprised Ella with a proposal to get married.

It was a Sunday afternoon, a clear day in April when he made his request with the same enthusiasm he showed for everything. They were walking in Battersea Park, talking about the recent cases of typhoid that were plaguing the hospital, when he abruptly changed the subject.

"With so much death and misfortune around us, I often wondered whether I would find any joy in life. And then you came along." He stopped, picked up her hand and said, "Ella would you consider marrying me?"

Ella's heart skipped a beat and just as suddenly sank. "You aren't serious?" she said.

"Of course I am." His eyes were clear. "Ella Durant, would you do me the honor of marrying me?"

Ella didn't respond right away. He knew nothing about her or her past. If he did, he would not be asking for her hand.

"I'll have to think about your proposal," Ella said finally.

Seeing how crestfallen he was she continued, if only to encourage him to see the folly of the idea.

"There are many things to consider," she said. "How would we support ourselves?" After losing half her fortune to Gabriel, Ella was not prepared to reveal she had any money, even an allowance. "We can't survive on the charity of others," she said.

"Of course not," he said. "I plan to take my degree in a school of medicine and become a practicing doctor."

"But I thought you disdained traditional medicine?"

"I do, but the best homeopathic doctors have first trained themselves in the old system. This will give me the opportunity to test them both. It will allow me to compare the two," he said.

"But where would we live?" Ella pressed him.

"We can stay with my aunt while I attend school. She has always encouraged me to pursue my dreams."

Ella bit her tongue, afraid to ask where his aunt lived and whether it would suit her.

"I will need some time to think on it," she said.

"It will have to do then. At least you haven't denied me." He held her hand up to his lips and kissed it.

That night Ella took tea to her room and sat in front of the hearth to contemplate whether there was a future with Arthur. She had never met a man quite like him. Her experience of men had been nothing but negative. First there was Poultney, who, after pressing himself upon her with his boyish charm, backed off when he realized her father would never approve of their union in marriage. She wondered what Papa would think about Arthur. He'd be impressed with his ambition to be a doctor, but cynical about his prospects as a husband. "He's an intellectual," he'd say, "intellectuals don't know how to make money."

And then, there was Gabriel. Their relationship was based entirely on lust, Ella now knew. He filled a void left by her unrequited relationship with Poultney.

Ella still had no clue where Gabriel was hiding. Her letters to Gabriel's friend, Monsieur Berton, were returned, unopened. She would have been in utter despair if it weren't for her blossoming courtship with Arthur.

At thirty-six years of age, she was well beyond what other men would deem suitable for marriage unless it was a second one, and Arthur's offer might be her last chance. He knew nothing about her inheritance, which meant he was sincere, and perhaps even in love with her. Did she love him? She wasn't sure yet, but his good nature was endearing.

Arthur's proposal brought another revelation. She examined herself in the mirror, fingering the lines of crow's feet radiating from her eyes. The nursing profession was taking its toll on her once youthful appearance. It was utterly exhausting and there was no end in sight. Once she finished the training she'd be expected to keep the same hours at the same pace, with very little pay. Was it her calling? No. What she wanted to do was write a novel. The lifestyle of a nurse would never allow that. She barely had time to sleep.

Ella sighed and picked up her mail. A letter from Estelle caught her eye, inside was a newspaper clipping. She quickly read Estelle's gossip and then glanced at the news article with disbelief. There on the page was a picture of William's new yacht, with a heading that claimed no one had ever before seen the likes of it at the New York Yacht Club. *Utowana*, Ella realized, was the name of the lake they traversed on the way to Raquette every summer. The natives said it meant 'Big Waves' in Mohawk.

Yes, William was making big waves—with *her* money. How was it fair, she wondered, that he could afford such a luxury while she toiled with scrub brushes and chloride in a hospital ward?

She rubbed her hands, red and raw from too much exposure to water and the caustic cleaners the Sisters insisted they use every day.

"Bahhh!" She tossed Estelle's letter away from her, looked through her stack of mail for something better and found it in Anny's letter: an official invitation to the literary conference in Italy. Ella was invited to speak about her play on Dante. Her mind was made up.

"I believe I'm not suited for the nursing profession," she told Arthur the following day. "I've been invited to speak at a literary conference in Italy and afterwards I plan to chaperone some young ladies to Germany. If, when I get back, you still feel the same about me, I'll consider your proposal more seriously."

His eyes lit up like a firecracker. "You will?" Then he realized she was leaving him and his face fell. "You're leaving? You don't want to become a nurse?"

"I know my calling is elsewhere," Ella said. "I'm just not sure yet how to proceed. Marriage right now would complicate matters. I feel I need time to think over your proposal."

"I'm overjoyed you are even considering it," he said.

Sister Beatrice was not at all surprised when Ella gave her resignation.

"I'd expected as much," she said, shaking her head and tssking as she scribbled something Ella imagined was derogatory down in the wretched notebook she carried around like a bible.

Ella was confident her turbulent tenure with the ward would not go unrecorded. She just hoped Alfred Locock would be spared any incriminating details. In the end Ella really didn't care what the Sister thought of her; she wanted to attend the literary conference in Rome and time was running out. After the conference she was to act as companion to General Ardaugh's three daughters in Munich.

In both cases the hosts were paying her way, and the trip to the Continent would allow her to visit places she hadn't seen since her childhood. Perhaps she would take a refresher course in Italian while in Rome. Leaving the confines of the hospital ward would be like taking a breath of fresh air after sitting in a smoke-filled room with no window. She would regain her strength and be able to rest.

She had been in Rome less than a week when Arthur showed up at the door of her pension.

"Arthur, what in heavens are you doing here? I thought you were attending medical school?"

Arthur stood dejectedly on the doorstep of her apartment. He was coughing and his skin was tinged slightly gray. "I had to see you," he said.

"Come in, foolish man." She led him into her apartment and made him tea.

"Ella, I have a confession to make. I'm lost without you. I have been in love with you since the first time I saw you working at the clinic." He took a sip of his tea and began another coughing fit.

"You've gotten yourself sick," she said, putting her hand over his forehead.

"It's nothing," he said waving her away. "I caught a cold from one of the patients. I needed the rest anyway. I thought if I came here I could stay and rest for a while before I start medical school. I've rented a place down the street."

It would have been lovely to share the glorious, old city of Rome with Arthur, but he was too sick. She gave her speech to the literary society and signed up for a language course. In between her activities, she spent her time nursing him back to health. It went on like this for weeks until he finally found his strength and suggested they travel to Spain.

"The air might be better for my lungs," he said.

They rented a villa with two rooms looking out over an olive grove. They spent their days reading and nights playing cards together. Spain was much better for Arthur's lungs.

"Amongst these olive groves I can feel my lungs expanding," he said one evening. "We should stay longer if we can."

"Yes, dear, but what about your medical school?" she reminded him.

He took her hand in his and kissed it again. "I cannot leave you just yet."

Their courtship was a curious one. He never made any other advances toward her beside a light kiss on the lips, a brush on her cheeks. If he was caressing her, his hands never wandered any further than her waist, shoulders, or neck, although she wouldn't have minded if they did. He, however, remained the perfect gentleman, and still he didn't know anything about her inheritance.

Finally, Ella had to tell him to go home. "I'm going to Munich to accompany some young ladies to see the *Passion Play* in Oberammergau," she said. "I'll meet you in London this summer."

"The *Passion Play*? I'd love to see it as well," he said.

Ella wondered more than once, where he got his money. They had both paid their half of their bills at the villa in Spain, and he was always generous with her when it came to dining out or buying small gifts or flowers. But she couldn't understand how he could be spending so much time with her and not feel the need to finish school and get a job.

When he booked a train to Munich with her she finally gave in to his proposal for marriage. If this man was going to follow her around the Continent she felt it was the least she could do. That evening, under the oil lamp in her room at her small flat in Munich, she penned a letter to William and her mother informing them of her decision to marry. When she sealed the envelope with wax and placed it into the silver dish for the post she felt relief mixed with regret that it was Arthur, not Gabriel, she was writing home about.

Ella should have been happy about her impending marriage, but the cold days and damp evenings in Munich made Arthur's coughing fits grow worse. Ella had to relinquish her responsibilities as an escort for General Ardaugh's family and hire a doctor; his illness becoming more than she could handle alone. Arthur insisted on being attended to by someone trained in homeopathic remedies.

The doctor brought tinctures, diluted substances she had never heard of, and instructed her how and when to administer them for Arthur's cough, and the fevers that inevitably followed. It was during one of these awful spells, a bitterly cold winter day in Munich that he brought up their future plans and asked if she had reconsidered his proposal.

"Of course not, dear," she assured him.

"Then let's marry soon," he said.

His body was weakened from days and nights of racking coughs, and her pity for him caused her to lose her sensibility. "Yes," she said, tucking the blankets up to his chin and kissing him lightly on the forehead.

As Arthur regained his strength, Ella became ill herself. It was bound to happen, Arthur told her. She had been running herself ragged taking care of him, and not looking after her own welfare.

For a few days, Ella was in and out of delirium. Afterward, she was too weak to leave her apartment. Arthur hired the same doctor to look after her.

Ella was never sure if his tinctures cured her or if it was her own determination to get better. She never enjoyed being idle, and the days when she was feverish and had no energy to even lift her head off her pillow were the worst. It was on those days, when the sun was bleak in the sky, and the wind was whistling through the windows, she willed herself to get better so she could begin planning their wedding. She worried if they waited too long she would have increasing doubts about her decision to marry Arthur.

Arthur must have felt it too, because one day when she woke he was sitting at the side of her bed waiting, staring at her with a face full of concern.

"Who is Gabriel?" he asked as she sat up in bed and took a glass of water from his hand.

Ella gulped before answering. "Is the window opened? I feel a draft," she said as she wrapped her shawl around her shoulders.

"No. It's not."

Ella avoided his stare. "I'm not sure what you're talking about."

"You were dreaming, tossing and turning in your sleep today and saying something about Gabriel. You were begging him not to leave you," Arthur said.

Ella couldn't avoid looking at him anymore. "He was once my friend. A very close friend. He has a home in Paris, and I haven't seen him in months." It was, she felt, close enough to the truth to not be considered a lie.

Arthur's face relaxed and then he said, "You were very upset by it, I can tell. You were crying."

Ella's hand went reflexively to her face and felt the telltale signs of puffiness and moisture.

"It's nothing, I assure you." The bile started to rise in her stomach. She hadn't eaten in days, and the tinctures the doctors had prescribed were both acidic and disturbingly vile tasting.

"Arthur, please—" she put her hands over her mouth but was too late. A white foam and spittle slithered through her fingers and landed on her shawl.

"Oh, my dear," Arthur rose to get some linens to clean it up. "I'm so sorry I've upset you." He never brought up Gabriel again.

TWENTY-FIVE

New York

It was spring and Arpad and William were sitting on the porch of the chalet listening to the songbirds flitting about the trees. Every once in a while Arpad would motion to one and identify it for William by its song.

"Can you come with us tomorrow to see the progress on Uncas? It will be my last chance for a while. Janet and I are leaving on our voyage at the end of August and we need to prepare."

"Oh yes, that new yacht of yours. You still have not invited me onto it," Arpad said with a mock scowl.

"You'd never come," William said. "It would be too luxurious for you. I'd hate to subject you to it."

They both laughed. There was more than a grain of truth to what William said. If he knew the amount, Arpad would never approve of how much William spent on *Utowana*. He'd keep his opinions to himself, out of courtesy to William, but trying to impress Arpad with ostentatious displays of wealth such as a yacht was always a waste of time.

A steamboat picked them up after breakfast in the dining hall. Julia Stott and Janet came with them. The boat took them to the landing on the other side of the lake. From there, a horse and carriage took them down the six-mile road to where Uncas was under construction.

"You've put in a foundation," Arpad said.

Before them was a stone foundation made from native rock. Rising from that were large timbers framing the main house. As they entered their eyes went up reflexively to the ceiling, eight feet above, held up with massive logs, the bark peeled off, and each at least two feet in diameter.

Masons were working on the stone fireplace when they walked through the entrance. William immediately went over to check on their progress while the others stood with their mouths open, not knowing what to say, the size of the place overwhelming them.

"What's this?" William said to one of the masons as he pointed at the façade around the fireplace.

"Sir?"

"This stone, the cut side is facing outward." William pointed accusingly at one of the large stones that had been plastered into the facade.

The mason stared at the stone and scratched his scruffy beard. "Dunno how it happened," he said.

"Well, you'll have to get it out and put it in correctly, with the natural side facing outward," William said.

The mason gave him a curious stare, wondering if he was serious. "But, Mr. Doo'Rant, sir, if we do that, we'd have to undo all of this." He waved his arms at the fireplace, already rising five feet in the air. "We're almost done with it," he added.

"I don't care," William retorted.

Janet approached and rested her hand on William's arm. William shook her off. "It has to be done right, or there's no use in doing it at all," William said. "I insist you start over."

"I think I'll go and view the grounds," Arpad said.

"I'll join you." Julia followed him and stood in the doorway waiting for Janet.

She hesitated for a moment before leaving William's side to join her cousin and Arpad.

He told them to leave without him, planning to stay at Uncas for the rest of the day, telling Janet, "They obviously need me here to oversee the construction."

William spent the rest of the day monitoring his workmen. If he saw something he didn't like, he'd say so, but he was also willing to listen to reason if one of his craftsmen had a good idea. Which was often. The fireplace was a minor setback, but once the masons took it apart and started over they saw the value in doing it right. William was always amazed at the immigrant labor that found their way to these backwoods. These men brought trades they had learned from their fathers and managed their skills with pride.

It was dusk by the time the buckboard coach brought William back to meet the steamboat at the dock on Raquette. As he was about to board it he saw Alvah Dunning, dragging his bark canoe into the woods to conceal it.

"Alvah," William called to him.

Alvah stopped what he was doing and eyed William suspiciously, as if William cared where Alvah hid his boat and would actually try to steal it.

This made William chuckle to himself. Ever since Ella had taken off in Alvah's canoe for a joy ride on the lake years before, without telling anyone, Alvah was overly protective of it.

"Whadya want?" Alvah said.

William reached into his coat pocket.

"I've been carrying this around thinking I may run into you one day." He handed Alvah a pocket watch with a gold chain.

Alvah took it from him and his eyes lit up. "For me?"

"Yes, Alvah, for you."

"But why?"

"You don't remember? You lost your watch in the lake while guiding Arpad. He told me about it that day and I went back and found it."

Alvah clucked with surprise and examined the watch. Then he lifted his head and shot William another suspicious look. "This ain't the watch I lost in the lake."

"Of course it is, Alvah. Your eyesight is getting worse, that's all. I took it to Benedicts in New York City and had it cleaned and asked the jeweler there to put a new chain on it for you."

"Thank you, Mr. Doo'Rant. What do I owe ya?"

William laughed. "Nothing, Alvah. Nothing at all," he said and climbed aboard the steamboat that was waiting at the dock.

The next morning William woke early, planning to meet Arpad for fishing. He approached the dining hall, expecting it to be empty, but stopped short when he overheard Julia say to Janet, "I don't understand why he's building this manor house so far off in the woods."

They were sitting with their backs toward him watching a pair of loons bob up and down in the water; otherwise, they would have seen him coming.

"It has always been a dream of his, I suppose," Janet replied.

"Yes, but he already has his hunting cabin with Arpad on Sumner Lake, and you told me yourself there is a small hunting cabin only a mile down the path from here," Julia said.

As much as William admired Julia's assertiveness, he didn't take to her aiming it at him. He was about to enter to break up the conversation and stop her further inquiries about the hunting cabin—the cabin he once shared with Louise—when what Janet said next stopped him.

"Cornelia has asked me to approach William about purchasing the land and what's left of that cabin. She wants him to renovate it for her so she can stay there in the summer," Janet said. "I haven't told him yet, although I think he won't mind. He no longer uses it and it's falling apart."

"Between this Uncas and his yacht, *Utowana*, I doubt he has had a moment to think about anything else," Julia said.

One of the loons let out a strong wail and the ladies quieted down. William hesitated at the entrance, experiencing a moment of apprehension. At first, he was angry that Janet had already made plans for him to sell the land and the cabin he had once shared with Louise. She knew it held fond memories for him, although she may not have known the extent of it. He was sure her mother and sister had kept quiet about his affair with Louise, but he also knew how people around the lake liked to gossip.

However, this new development, and the new home she was making him build for the family, were a huge distraction.

"Well, I suppose you can't really call Uncas a hunting cabin anyway," Julia continued. "It's more like the manor house of an English country squire."

"Well, if we ever go broke we can always take in boarders," Janet said. They laughed at her joke just as William entered the room.

He sat down at the end of the dining table as the ladies busied themselves with their cups of coffee and cleared their throats.

"Hello dear," Janet said, her embarrassment evident. "I didn't know you were here."

"Obviously." William snapped open the newspaper and pretended to be interested in the news.

The dining hall stood by the waterfront and provided splendid views of the lake and forests. A covered walkway led between the kitchen and the hall so that the servants and the food were protected from the weather. Its walls were framed windows of leaded glass. A small potbelly stove stood in the corner to keep the room warm. The table had ten leaves and could accommodate up to twenty-four people. It was usually William's favorite place to take breakfast.

Julia broke the silence. "Janet and I were up early to watch the sunrise this morning."

When William failed to respond she continued, "I threw out a line and caught a trout."

"Hmmm," William said.

"You made the paper, William. It's a glowing review of Pine Knot. On page five," Janet said.

William turned to page five to find an article about New York State's plans to protect the Adirondack forests. His name was mentioned in a brief description of the tourist attractions:

Mr. Durant has brought much attention to the beauty of the area with his magnificent creation. One could hardly call his dwelling a 'camp' it is more like a work of art. Many in New York and elsewhere are clamoring to the mountains trying to emulate his example.

William was glowing inside from the compliment. It was about time the newsmen gave credit where credit was due. He wondered what his father would think if he were alive to read this. Dr. Durant never approved of all the time and effort William put into Pine Knot. But William knew what he was creating here was more than just a dwelling to entice and entertain the wealthy businessmen his father wanted so desperately to invest in his Adirondack Railroad Company. No, what William created at Pine Knot and would create at Uncas, was a lasting legacy that no one, not even his father could sully. They were, as the newspaper stated, works of art and William was the artist. People would remember that about him. It was a far better reputation to have than the one his father had left behind.

A servant walked in with a silver egg stand filled with four soft-boiled eggs and interrupted his thoughts. He put the paper down as she brought one to William and set it down on his plate then walked over to the ladies to serve them as well.

"Are the children up yet?" William asked.

"No, dear. I told Minnie to allow them to sleep in this morning. They were up late last night."

"How is Minnie working out for you?" Julia turned her attention to Janet.

"Just fine. I'm so glad Cornelia recommended her."

The ladies watched William as he ate.

"Speaking of Cornelia," Julia said as she set down her toast and removed her napkin to dab at the sides of her mouth.

Janet shook her head as if it would quiet her cousin.

"I understand she would like to buy that small piece of land near Golden Beach and renovate the cabin." Julia waited for William to lift his head from his plate.

William's eyes strafed Janet's and then he answered Julia. "I might consider it, although the cabin is in disrepair. I can't imagine why anyone would think I have time to deal with that project right now."

Julia opened her mouth to speak, and Janet motioned for her to shush.

"Of course, dear. It was just a thought," Janet said.

"I'm sure Cornelia has the necessary resources to take care of that cabin. Unless there is some reason you think no one should inhabit it?" Julia said.

Not willing to take the bait Julia was casting, William stood up and dropped his napkin on his seat. "If you'll excuse me ladies. I have to meet Arpad."

Janet caught up to him on the path back to their cabin.

"Dear, I'm sorry if we upset you." She walked with him until they reached the cabin steps.

A servant walked past them with a bundle of wood in his arms. "Good morning, Mr. and Mrs. Doo'Rant."

They nodded and retreated to their cabin but were foiled in their attempt at privacy by a servant who was cleaning out the hearth, and another who was making the beds.

William took Janet by the arm and led her back out of the cabin and down a path.

"You didn't. It's time I got rid of that cabin anyway. If Cornelia wants it, it's hers," he said.

Janet face lit up. "She'll be so happy to hear that."

"There's no need to worry either, darling. I won't let us become so destitute we need to take in boarders."

Janet blushed. "I was joking, of course."

"Of course."

"It's just that I hadn't realized how splendid Uncas would be," she said. "I don't understand it all sometimes. How you are able to build something like it and this yacht."

Now William understood why she was so anxious. William forgave her lack of confidence in him. He stopped walking and gently lifted her chin up with his fist, then kissed her on her forehead.

"No need to worry. I have it all figured out. My steamboat line is doing well. I'm selling some of our land. I have a development planned for Eagle Lake. You'll see. It will all be fine."

"Yes, dear," Janet said with relief.

"Now come with me, I want to show you something," he said.

He brought her to the end of the point where they kept the Durant houseboat–the *Barque of the Pine* – beached. It had been built years before as a refuge for his mother. They launched it out on the water on nights when the biting insects were too much to bear, before they had screens and glass windows on all of the cabins.

"What have you done with it?" Janet said, astonished.

"You like it?" William said. He took her hand and led her inside.

"You've changed it completely! It's so modern," Janet said.

"Yes, I knew you'd like it."

He toured her around inside. All spring, he had directed his workmen to add additional rooms to the houseboat. There were now two bedrooms with bunks bolted to the walls. There was a reading area, deck and a small bathroom with a toilet and sink.

Janet stood in amazement, unsure what to say.

"It's for the children, a houseboat to play on and pretend it's their own yacht."

She laughed. "Oh, William. You've outdone yourself!"

He was delighted she was pleased, and they soon forgot about their quarrel.

TWENTY-SIX

Munich

Once spring arrived in Munich Ella began to feel better.

"I think we should go home now," she said to Arthur. "I'm feeling strong enough to travel."

Arthur was sitting in one of the chairs in the parlor of her flat, reading a book on homeopathy.

"I've been thinking, Ella, why don't we get married here?"

"In Munich? Whatever for?"

"If we wait until we get back to London, we have to find an apartment, then plan a wedding, and guests. It will all be too much for you, especially after your sickness."

"But what about all of our friends?"

"Well that is the brilliant part really. We will save ourselves a lot of money this way. The British Consulate here in Munich only allows a few witnesses to attend so we won't be responsible for a big event."

Ella hadn't thought about economizing on their wedding plans. She wondered too, how much of his eagerness to marry was due to his concern about her commitment. What if, when they got back to London, she saw Gabriel? Would she regret her decision to marry

Arthur? Maybe, if she had no choice, she would not question whether she made the right one.

"I'll agree to it if it makes you happy," she said.

When it came time to discuss where they would live, Arthur suggested his Aunt Caroline's house in Sussex.

"Her home is too big for one person anyway since my uncle died. And I'm sure you would appreciate companionship while I'm studying," he said. "And we will need to economize once I'm in medical school. My aunt has been very generous with her allowance to me, but I must use it now to pay for school."

The idea of living as a newlywed under the roof of a widow so far from London would not do. How could she explain this to Arthur?

She finally confessed her family history, the inheritance she still had, and her expectations of more to come eventually.

"I have needed time to think on it, and I know that William is still holding out on me. Now that we are getting married, I will write to him asking for more money so we can live in our own place."

Arthur sat tongue-tied, watching her steadily as if she were not the same person he had planned to marry.

"Are you angry with me for keeping this from you?"

"No, dear," he said. "Just, just surprised, that's all. I knew you were a lady with good upbringing, but I hardly knew the extent of it."

"I had my reasons for keeping this from you," she said. "But I've been living alone for so long now. I just can't stand the idea of having your aunt worry about my comings and goings," she explained to Arthur.

"Nonsense, Aunt Caroline wouldn't do that and think of the money we would save," he said. "We have a lot of medical bills we need to pay."

"Arthur, I already told you; I have money we can use to start our life together. And what is left you can use for your schooling and to pay off our bills until you find a position."

"If you say so," he said. "But what if something were to happen to me? What then?"

"As I said before, I can manage for myself."

"Would it help if I intervened for you?" he said.

"With my brother? How would you do that?"

"I can write to him."

"And what would you say exactly?"

Arthur rubbed his chin and thought for a moment. "I'd tell him I'm sick and I would be more distressed if I thought you were not taken care of," he said.

Ella wondered if William would ever be distressed over her well-being, as he used to be when they were young. His response to her letter announcing the engagement was gracious, yet he had added that he hoped Arthur could provide for her as she was used to—an under-handed attempt to say he doubted Arthur could. But his letter also hinted he was now somehow relieved of any duty toward her. This made her worry he would cut off her allowance once she was married.

"Go ahead," she said. "But I question whether it will make any difference. Send word to my mother instead."

TWENTY-SEVEN

New York

It was early evening and Arpad had sailed his small skiff to Pine Knot for a visit with William. He was smoking his customary pipe on the porch of the chalet as he read the letter William had handed him. It was from Ella's fiancé, Arthur Frethey, and addressed to William's mother, Hannah.

"It's not that I don't have an opinion on the subject, William," Arpad said after he read it and handed it back. "I just wonder whether you want to know what I think about homeopathy and your future brother-in-law's prospects, or whether you want me to confirm that your sister's future husband is a charlatan and after her money."

William took the letter and read again. In it, Arthur stated his intentions to attend medical school and pursue a career in homeopathic medicine.

He also asked William's mother if she would continue to send the monthly allowance once they are married, something William thought presumptuous.

> *Of course, we shall both regret if after our marriage you find it*
> *necessary to reduce Ella's income; but even on very small means*
> *I think we can manage to be happy...*

He went on to pursue the real reason for his letter:

> *There is one thing I feel is my duty to mention before our*
> *marriage, which is that, whatever money may be coming to Ella,*
> *you will settle exclusively as soon as you can on her, so that*
> *during the next few years, if anything happens to me before my*
> *assured income, I should know Ella will be provided for. We are*
> *to be married in June.*

"Both," William replied, putting the letter aside. "Do you think he's sincere or just another rogue?"

"I know very little about homeopathy except that it appears to depart from the current scientific views on disease," Arpad said.

"But can he support my sister or is he gold mining for a rich American heiress? I daresay my sister seems to be vulnerable to the whimsy of these types of men."

"There are many proponents and followers of homeopathic remedies. It has attracted quite a lot of attention amongst the well-to-do that are in a position to choose their doctors. He may make out alright in the end," Arpad said.

William wasn't convinced. He wasn't planning to attend the wedding either. It all appeared very rushed and Ella's life was in constant turmoil. When she had written in December she was training to be a nurse, then less than six months later she sends word she is engaged to be married. He had written her back with his half-hearted congratulations and questioned her as to whether her fiancé would be able to support them.

And now this letter from her soon-to-be husband appears in their mother's mail. Thankfully, Hannah was coherent enough to read it and give it to William without Margaret intervening, but not before she had sent off another check for a thousand dollars as a wedding present to Ella. God knows if she really was to be married or if it was a guise to squeeze more money out of their mother.

William was beginning to worry about the state of his mother's health and mental capacities. One small cold left her bedridden for weeks. He had sent her and Margaret off to Florida for the winter, and when they returned he informed her that he had placed the house in North Creek on sale. It was too big to keep up, and since his mother never entertained anymore they did not need so much space. He planned to move them into an apartment near his home in Saratoga.

"Are we fishing while you're here?" Arpad said, bringing William back to the present.

Later that day, the guides rowed William and Arpad to Stillman Bay. As they approached the open waters of the bay they spotted two boys in a rowboat, hauling away a net of trout.

"Where did you boys get those trout?" Arpad asked as they swung up beside them in their boats.

"The spring in Stillman. We's dropped a deer head and they came at it like a cat to cream."

"What in heaven's name do you need all of those fish for?" William said.

"We's sellin' 'em to the hotels," one of the boys answered.

"Well then," Arpad scoffed, "there goes our lunch."

They had to travel further than they expected, ending up in North Bay. There, they found another spring where the fish were pooling in deep waters and caught enough to satisfy their appetites. They climbed onto the sandy beach and made makeshift seats for themselves while their guides gutted and cleaned the fish. They then made a fire out of the driftwood scattered along the beach, and, as usually happened when the two men were together, they ate their fish in silence, listening to the sounds of the woods and lake. Exchanging small talk was never their style.

The next day, William got on his horse and followed the trail he once knew so well to the Lawrence family compound on Eighth Lake. He hadn't been there in years, not since Louise died in 1882. But when Ike didn't show up with his load of spring furs for William to deliver to the furrier in New York City, he became worried something had happened to him or someone else in the Lawrence household.

What he saw as he approached the home site, made him despair.

The longhouse had long since buckled to the ground. The few cabins that were built around it were still intact, but the chickens scratching out an existence in the yards were scrawny, and a few young children, probably Ike's latest offspring, were running after them half-naked.

They stopped when they saw him coming. Their big moon eyes were transfixed on his large horse and fine clothing. They said nothing as he dismounted, but one of the boys ran into the cabin.

Ike came out with his pregnant wife, a slender, red-headed young woman whose bleached skin was spattered with freckles. Her appearance and skin tone contrasted sharply with Ike's dark brown hair and copper-colored skin. She stood close to Ike and, like her children, said nothing.

"Mr. Doo'Rant. What a surprise," Ike said. A warm smile came over his face as he held out his hand to shake William's. He turned to his wife. "Becca, will ya fetch Mr. Doo'Rant something to drink?"

"No need to, thank you," William said. "Ike, I was concerned when you didn't come to Pine Knot."

"I meant to send word, sir." Ike patted the head of one of the girls that came up to his waist and flung her arms around his legs.

"I don't have any furs for you this year. What few animals I was able to trap I traded for supplies. It was a lean year again, and the winter was harsh. We're jus' thankful the maple sugaring season was bountiful this spring. The children went without sugar all winter."

William looked down at the young girl clinging to Ike's legs. "Where's Nate?"

"He's workin' with my brother Jake while they're runnin' logs," Ike said. He exchanged a guilty look with his wife. "He'll be back."

William's lips tightened. He closed his fingers firmly round Ike's arm and led him out of earshot of his wife.

"Nate's too young to be working at a lumber camp," he said to Ike.

"I know what you's thinking, Mr. Doo'Rant. Nate's only a few years older than your son. But we don't have no choice. We need the money. Jake's gotta family to feed as well."

"Were you able to find a job for the summer while we're gone?"

Ike shook his head. "Charlie Bennett agreed to let me guide at his hotel."

William frowned. "His pay is paltry."

"Yes, but he pays. We don't have much choice since you'll be gone and I don't have any other clients to guide."

William tried not to show his frustration with the turn of fortune for the Lawrence family household.

Ike noticed him looking over at the decrepit longhouse. "My father's longhouse was never made for this climate. The snows are too heavy. But Isaac kept his old ways. He'd be heartbroken to learn that my trapping days may be over too."

"How so?" William asked.

"It's like what happened to him. As he was chased outta Canada for trapping, I'm being chased outta the Adirondacks. There're too many places where I once could trap without anybody botherin' me. Now they're off limits."

"I'll need someone over the winter months, to help John Callahan keep up with the care of Pine Knot. Would you be willing? You can bring your family to stay."

Ike was shocked by the generous offer. When he realized his good fortune, he spoke rapidly. "Yes, Mr. Doo'Rant, sir."

His wife came up beside him, took his hand and squeezed it to make sure everything was all right. "I'd be very happy to help you out when winter comes around, sir." Ike grinned.

William halted construction on Uncas. They'd be gone for a year on their voyage, and he would finish what they started when he returned. He and Janet returned to their home in Saratoga so they could plan their trip.

He entered Janet's bedchamber to inquire about the housekeeping arrangements when he found her at her writing desk, the checkbook resting next to her stationery.

"Are you leaving instructions for the maid?" he said, glancing at the checkbook and wondering why she had it out.

She lifted her head from the stationery and said, "No, dear. I'm writing to Ella."

"Whatever for?"

"I'm sending her a wedding gift."

"Money?" William said.

"Yes."

"That's the last thing you should do." He crossed the room and stood over her.

Janet set her pen down and gazed up at him. "We are missing her wedding and I feel terrible about it. I believe it's the least I can do. She wrote to me and told me that her fiancé, Arthur, has been sick, and so has she. As a result, she has numerous doctor bills along with the expense of the wedding."

"She has plenty of money to get established. And besides, this Arthur fellow sounds like a man with ambition. I'm sure Ella will be well taken care of, and he can pay the doctor bills when he is feeling better."

Janet remained silent.

Sensing she wasn't going to agree with him, William said, "We'll see her in London this October, we can buy something for her there."

Janet's eyes narrowed. "I don't think that will be adequate."

"What do you mean?" he said.

"She has written to me. Both she and her future husband were stricken. I'm sure they contracted it from the poor people they tended to at the hospital. She has doctors' bills, and she has to pay them now in addition to trying to set up her new home. We owe it to them to offer our assistance."

"For Christ's sake. Ella always has one sob story or another to try and draw sympathy and attention to herself," William said.

Janet stood up. "You should be ashamed of yourself. The way you and your family treat Ella is a disgrace."

William was shocked. When he stayed silent, she continued.

"Margaret berates her constantly, intercepts her mail, and lies to your mother about Ella's true state of affairs."

As William was about to say something in protest, Janet raised her hand in the air to shush him. "I've heard her speak of it; she told me she felt it her duty *to spare your poor mother the sordid details of Ella's life*," she mimicked Margaret. Janet's lips started quivering. "Your poor mother, yes. She has no idea the extent of Ella's happiness or misfortune. Your sister's life is scrutinized and deciphered by that crusty old woman you trust as Hannah's companion."

"Margaret has served my family well for many years. You have no idea what you are talking about when you speak of her this way," William said.

Janet placed her hands on the desk and lowered herself into her chair. Her right hand was trembling as it picked up the pen. When she saw him eyeing it, she set the pen down.

"And you never stand up for her. I understand your frustration over Ella's lack of convention, but it should hardly matter to you. You used to be her loyal brother and friend. Why, if my brother Louis turned on me the way you have turned on her, I'd be heartbroken."

William felt his pulse throbbing in his chest and temples as he tried to suppress his rage. "How dare you speak to me this way."

Her eyes deadened. Turning away from him, she retrieved the pen, dipped it into the inkwell and began writing her letter to Ella.

William left the room before he said or did something he would later regret.

His final preparations for leaving were to visit his mother's home in North Creek and make sure everything was packed for her impending move after spending the winter in Florida.

"I had a visitor recently. He was inquiring about your father's affairs at the Union Pacific," she said to William while they went over her household accounts.

William put the papers he was reading down and waited for her to continue.

"Mr. Huntington," she said and leveled her eyes on him.

"Collis came to see you? Here?"

"Yes. He said he was on his way to the Adirondacks to visit friends and thought to pay me a visit. He was quite gracious."

"What did he want to know about father and his business with the Union Pacific?"

"He asked me if I knew where your father had kept some old records, having to do with Credit Mobilier." She put her pointer finger to her lips and knitted her brows in concentration, as if remembering was a task. "Hmmmm. I think that's what he wanted. Yes, that's it," she recovered, "it was the Credit Mobilier."

William felt a strange twist in his gut. "What about the Credit Mobilier?"

"He asked me if we had a safe with documents in it. He said his lawyer asked him for some records dating back to that time and he thought your father had kept them." She flicked her hand in the air dismissively. "Or something like that. It is getting harder and harder for me to remember everything. Maybe Margaret can recall. She was there."

"Mother. Think back. What did you tell him?"

"Of course he believes that your father has some type of damaging information about the politicians that are going to decide his fate with all of this railroad business," Hannah went on, ignoring his last question. "Why else do you think he has taken a sudden interest in your business with the Adirondacks?"

William had entertained that thought as well but didn't want to believe it was true. He liked Collis Huntington and saw him as a mentor, but his mother was probably right. Why else? The Adirondacks Railroad Company was not profitable, even William knew that when he inherited it. And there was no future likelihood of developing the line further to Canada, so Collis had nothing to gain financially by being on the Board.

William had thought, perhaps naively, that maybe Huntington was after his Adirondack land. But did he really need William in order to purchase a property in the Adirondacks? Even if he was one of the largest land owners, he didn't believe this would be reason for Huntington to take such an interest in him and the company. No, it had to be as his mother said: if his father had proof hidden somewhere that implicated any political leaders in the Credit Mobilier scandal, Huntington would have the upper hand in the Railway Commission hearings. He wouldn't have to pay back to the government the hundreds of thousands—or possibly millions—his company, the Central Pacific, owed for their fraud while building the transcontinental line, because he could use his father's documentation as blackmail.

"So what did you tell him? Do you know where father put these documents?"

Hannah's expression was unreadable. "No dear. I told him I was not aware of any such documents having to do with your father's business or the Credit Mobilier company. If I've learned anything from being married to your father, it's that he always held on to the card in his hand that would prove most valuable at the end of the game."

TWENTY-EIGHT

Munich

At Arthur's insistence, they decided to marry in June at the British Consulate in Munich. Ella had to agree he was right. Since they were only allowed a few friends it would alleviate the costs of a large wedding celebration, which was a relief, given that their combined doctor bills were still unpaid.

Arthur gave her a ring made of rubies and diamonds that once belonged to his mother. Ella invited Anny, her husband Richmond, and Aunt Caroline. She also invited William and Janet, but her brother had declined on the grounds that he was unable to change his plans at such short notice. They ordered flowers and rented a small room at a restaurant for the dinner celebration.

Everything appeared to be going smoothly until the day they were to be married. When they went to pick up their marriage certificate the lawyer appointed to sign off on the documents suddenly refused.

"You don't have a baptismal certificate," he said to Ella in a thick German accent.

The man repeated himself in German, just in case Ella didn't understand his English.

"I didn't know it would be needed," she said back to him in German. "Surely you can find a way to allow us to marry today? We have guests that have travelled from England to witness our marriage. We have hired florists and caterers. Our guests are waiting for us at the British Consulate as we speak."

He shook his head. "You must have a baptismal certificate; it is our law." He sat entrenched behind his desk glowering at the couple.

"You could have told us this before our wedding day. Who made up this rule?" Ella continued in English so Arthur would understand.

He shrugged and said with complete indifference to their plight, "Everyone here knows this. Everyone but you Americans."

Ella was stricken. The room began to spin, her head became dizzy and she clutched Arthur to keep from fainting in front of the lawyer who was doing everything in his power to keep them apart.

Arthur led her over to a small chair in the cavernous office and confronted the surly German who was standing in his way of marriage. "Come now, sir. You can see what state my poor fiancée is in. You've caused her great stress. There must be some recourse, some loophole in the law that would allow us to marry today as planned?" Arthur said.

He crossed his large arms over his stout chest and stared at Arthur defiantly, not saying a word. They gave up and left. Ella started to cry.

"What are we going to do now?" she said.

Arthur took out his handkerchief and handed it to her. "I'm so sorry. And you look so lovely in your new dress." He tried to console her by taking her hand in his and rubbing it gently. "But we have everything we need to celebrate don't we? Our friends are here, we have a sumptuous dinner planned, and we remain in love. Who cares if we have to postpone the wedding for another couple of weeks? We can return to England and be married in the church in my town St. Leonards-on-Sea. It's a lovely place to be married."

"But how will I ever explain this to my friends? My family?" Ella sniffed into the handkerchief.

Arthur shrugged in the good-natured way that Ella found so disarming. "We'll tell them the truth. That's all there is to it. Our wedding plans might be delayed, but they are not over."

She stood on the street with him, ignoring the passing carriages, the clomping hooves, the sounds of horns, people passing, speaking in their foreign tongue, going about their bloody business as if everything was all right in the world. But it wasn't. She was speechless, defeated. Yet here was Arthur, her future husband, with his enduring optimism, talking her out of a sulk. She had no choice but to stop feeling sorry for herself. It suddenly occurred to her that this husband-to-be of hers was someone special, in a very different way to the other men in her life. Something in her expression must have conveyed her thoughts to him, for his eyes lit up, causing her to smile. Ella was convinced that everything would turn out for the best.

"Maybe it was meant to be this way. Maybe now my brother and his wife will be able to attend the wedding," she said.

"That's the spirit then." Arthur hugged her. He held her in his arms as he hailed a cab.

TWENTY-NINE

New York

They took off on their voyage the second day of September. The children were giddy, Janet was nervous, and William was ecstatic to be on the *Utowana*. As they set sail, William stood on the deck bracing against the wind and watched as the island of Manhattan faded into the distance.

"I've done it now," he said to himself.

ACKNOWLEDGEMENTS

I am grateful to the libraries and museums that hold the collections of the Durant family, staff and colleagues. Sources may be found on my website: wwdurantstory.com. Thank you to my editors: Mary Beth Hinton, Theresa Mendez, and Alex Beldon. And to my public relations expert at Highland Words, and all of my beta readers.

AUTHOR'S NOTE

This is a work of fiction. Although I have tried to stay true to the timeline of events, I invented many elements of the story.

Many of the famous characters mentioned during Ella's time in London were acquaintances or friends of Anny Thackeray Ritchie. I discovered her connection to Ella in a group photo showing Anny Ritchie standing with Ella and William Durant and William Napier sometime in the early 1870s. I also found letters from Anny addressed to Ella in the papers of Heloise (Ella) Durant Rose at the Syracuse University Library. Although there is scant primary source material on Ella Durant, I was able to piece together a biography and timeline on her by studying her writing, her correspondence, and from newspaper articles of the time period. All my sources may be found on my website.

Much of the correspondence found in the novel is word for word from evidence presented at the trial of Heloise D. Rose against William West Durant (1903).

A timeline of events can be found on my author website: wwdurantstory.com

If you enjoyed this story please consider writing a review for Amazon, Goodreads, or Barnes and Noble websites or anywhere the book is sold online. I appreciate any and all feedback. This novel is book two of a trilogy. Book one: *Imaginary Brightness*, was published in May 2015. Stay tuned for book three by subscribing to my website. I post blogs frequently to document my research journey and only send out email notices quarterly.

Proof

Made in the USA
Charleston, SC
02 April 2016